THE PATCHED SEA

LOODIE

outskirts
press

Outskirts Press, Inc.
http://www.outskirtspress.com

ISBN: 978-1-9772-4169-6

Outskirts Press and the "OP" logo are trademarks belonging to Outskirts Press, Inc.

PRINTED IN THE UNITED STATES OF AMERICA

Dedication

To one of God's precious little angels, TTW-I wish time could've permitted us to see each other, but I understand God's will for him to keep you. Love you!

To a humble, loving angel, Uncle J.J.S.-May you rest in divine peace. Love you always!

WATER RUNS DRY

As I sit and stare out at the vast sea ahead,
perplexity strikes in my head.
So, I ask it, "What should I consider you to be? A murderer or a romancer?"

It responds, "If you're looking for a black or white, I can't give you an answer,
I provide replenishment gracefully than a dancer.
The grayish area is where I lie; I work only as a freelancer."
I respond, "Your hue is fickle. This is what I can't understand.
You make young kids giggle but devour bodies like you're an innocent ripple. When I think of happy blue, I think of you, but there's another mood to you that I don't find true. It's not elating but hating when others feel down and gated. I guess when it comes to you, there's never any clue.

It responds, "I'm not a green light shining on the brown grass; the sun is my pass.
Don't look at me as a perpetrator; I was created by my creator.
For many years, men used me to cruise, explorers wanted to pursue, and environmentalists wanted to reuse.
I didn't sink the Titanic; I didn't call for natural disasters in the Atlantic."

I respond, "I'm drawn by your spell, which you would say 'allure.'
But I can't help but to think how you feel separation can be so pure?
A broken heart buried deeply in sub-zero temperature,
Could never again see hope as a mere pleasure."

It responds, "That's enough! No more blaming me,
If you studied your history, you would find my victory.
In my savior's days, spiritual cleansing was divinity. Don't forget about the captives who decided to die on their own terms than to face humility.
Yes, many did not have choices, with so many excessive forces, but my waves paid in full the serenity of their voices.

After hearing the sea make a liar out of me, I couldn't help but close my eyes and listen to its energy. What I thought was an enemy was just an ugly side of my enmity.
How can I pass judgment on my father's creation?
Through his will...through his work...there's a common relation.
The syncopation of my heart clashes with the rushing waters,
Coming to the shores, like sons coming home to fathers.
It comes a time when everything must die,
It comes at a time when water runs dry.

Prologue:

FLOODGATES (2018)

*T*he clouds were crying an abundance amount of rain as the thunder and lightning were chastising the skies. The effect of it led to a traffic jam on Interstate-20 to Columbia, South Carolina. The weather wasn't letting up; neither were the drivers who were racing to get to their destination. They were waiting impatiently as the highway patrolmen were trying to clear the highway after what appeared to be a one-man accident where a driver ran off the road and hit the railings right off the shoulder. Luckily for the driver involved in the accident, he had on his seatbelt, and his airbag worked. If he was speeding any faster, he could've knocked down the railings and ended up falling into the nearby river.

Summer Holidae was one of those people who was anxiously waiting for the road to clear. She was coming from a business meeting in Florence, South Carolina and was already late for her twelve-year-old daughter's school swim meet. She knew it meant the world to her daughter to be present, but this accident had still had her at least thirty minutes away. It was just her luck to be caught up in a crossfire on a busy Saturday afternoon in the summertime. She knew she had a lot of explaining to do, so she connected her iPhone 8 to her car stereo and dialed her phone. It rang a couple of times before a soft but disappointed voice was on the other end.

"You're not coming, are you?" a child's voice answered.

"I am on my way. Don't worry, honey," Summer reassured with a regretful look on her face.

"Where are you? You're running late. Dad is already here. How far are you?"

"Season, I will be there. I'm just getting out of this traffic jam, and the weather is pretty bad."

"A traffic jam? Mom, why can't you be early for once in my pre-teen life?" Season joked then laughed.

After hearing Season laughing at her current situation, she couldn't help but laugh too. "I know, I'm a real 'Johnny Come Lately.' I'm sorry, dear. I will try to do better next time."

"It's cool, just be careful and make sure to bring my good luck charm!"

Summer looked over to the right of her to find her daughter's old swimming goggles lying on the passenger seat. Those were her first pair of spectacles when she began her first practice at the age of five. Summer would always make jokes to her daughter about throwing the old "shades" away. Season would just tell her that it serves as a milestone in her swimming career, and when she gets into the Olympics, her mom would be glad to hold on to something so priceless. Summer smiled at the memory playing in her head as she picked up the goggles to look at it.

"Ma, you have it, right?"

Season's voice brought Summer's attention back to her as well as the road, which was clearing up already, "Uh-huh, yes I do… It's not like you need them anyhow, because you can't wear them," she laughed at her joke.

"Ha, funny ma…. really funny."

"Guess what? The road is clearing up, so now I can pick up some speed to get to the performance!"

"Well, it's about darn time!"

"Watch it…." Summer warned with a stern tone.

"What? I didn't cuss."

"You should know by now, young lady…anything that…"

"Alludes to it is just as bad. I know, ma," Season interrupted with a groan.

"Thank you! Glad to know you listen to your mother sometimes," joked Summer.

"Yeah, well, I can't help but listen when all you do is repeat things over and over."

Summer laughed. "Well, you better go. You know Coach Vie does not like phone calls during meets. You'll get both of us in trouble."

"Yeah, you're right. It's about to begin. Take care, ma, and please be careful."

"I will, honey. Love you to pieces. See you soon."

"Love you whole! See ya."

Summer felt satisfied after talking with her daughter. Ordinarily, Season could be quite a brat at times when things didn't go her way. After being tardy at many events, she concluded that her mom's body was synchronized to CPT (Colored People Time). Summer thought she was hitting the gas pedal to the metal at 75 mph as the rain continued pouring at a reasonably fast pace.

As she passed and cut cars left to right, she thought about how much of a strong bond she had with her daughter. They were thick as thieves; not anyone or anything could tear them asunder. They had done everything together. Shopping, exercising, and traveling were habitual leisure for these two. They laughed and cried at movies or pretended to be Motown singers by playing dress-up just to reenact a singing performance. The best night was family night when Season, Xavier (her husband), and she would play board games. Their favorite was Monopoly. Season would play the banker and let her mother steal money from the bank without her dad noticing. Once he caught wind of it, he would pretend to get upset and quit the game just to watch his reruns of football games. Season and Summer would get a kick out of it and laugh.

As the rain began to pick up more, the wind started to

blow harder, causing Summer to concentrate more on the road after swerving a little to the right. She held onto the steering wheel with both hands and reached for a button to turn on her radio so it could keep her focused. When a familiar song from the rock band *Queen* came on, it struck a chord in her mind. She thought about hitting the dial on her steering wheel, but something in her just couldn't do it. The song took full control, to a past she had to escape from. At first, the memories were pleasant, reflecting on the big oak tree she used to climb with her friends, running through the meadows and laying on a bed of perennial plants. The serenity of it all put her at ease for a moment, but a dark cloud shifted all those thoughts away immediately. She couldn't explain why these bad memories were rushing like a floodgate coming for her. Unknowingly, she began speeding up to 90 mph. She couldn't explain why she was using her steering wheel as a therapeutic tool, gripping it to the point of making small swerves all over the road. She couldn't explain the tears that shielded her eyes from the highway, and she couldn't explain how her SUV flipped over three times, killing her instantly.

Chapter 1:

THE CLOSENESS OF FAMILIARITY

(ONE YEAR LATER, 2019)

O utside of the Holidae's residence, nature was blowing its horn to announce the first day of summer. The marigolds were the first to open its golden flakes to emulate the sun's hue. A sparrow was perched on its nest, watching over its newborns while singing good morning to the other creatures stirring. It was a beautiful day in the neighborhood. A couple of men woke up early to manicure their yards, while a few women were beautifying their gardens. Inside most residences, families were either waking up, showering, or eating a full breakfast spread. Children were at the dinner tables, thanking God for schools being out or planning what their next adventure may be.

Inside the Holidae's residence was a different story. There was no life inside of the once happy home. The drapes blocked the sunshine from coming in, leaving only a small spray of rays to let the broken family know that it was daytime again. To Season, it wasn't a brand-new day but the same old one. The same day it was yesterday and the day before that. Another year did not bring any joy or jubilance to the home. From June 5, 2018 to June 5, 2019, the anniversary of her mother's death weighed heavily on her. No days were able to bring Season happiness because it couldn't bring back her mother. She felt numb and spiritless to anything the world had to offer her. It was not only a terrible time for Season, but it was a terrible time for Xavier as well. He lost his soulmate and his best friend. The pain was so unbearable that he would work nights at the hospital instead of being at home. Being at home meant coming home to his wife and child, having a good home-cooked meal at the dinner table, talking about each other's days, or having his best friend in the bed with him, promising a better tomorrow. He couldn't face his own daughter because her sadness reminded him of what he lost. He just couldn't do it anymore.

"Good morning, Season," greeted Xavier as he passed by the den area, heading straight to the kitchen.

"Morning, dad," Season responded in a lousy tone while binge-watching her favorite dance show on the television.

"You're up early," he called out from the kitchen.

"Yeah, well … there's a first for everything."

"Had breakfast?"

"Nope. Wasn't hungry."

"Baby, you need to eat something. I just bought some cereal and milk yesterday."

"Dad, I'm not hungry. I'm good," retorted Season as she turned up the volume.

Xavier came out of the kitchen with a huge bowl of cereal, crunching loudly as he flopped down on the leather couch next to his daughter. "You sure you don't want any Captain Munchies? It's banging!"

"Dad, no one says banging anymore. Besides, I am watching my weight. Captain Munchies have too much sugar in it," she explained with her eyes glued to the television.

"What weight? Gal, you're nothing but skin and bones! We'd talked about this before with your doctor. She specifically gave you the go-ahead to eat whatever you want, considering how underweight you're looking these days."

Season looked down at her size one frame and did not see any flaws. She was a typical size of any fit swimmer: five feet and four inches. That did not take away from her creamy, dark hazelnut complexion nor her long, frizzy brown hair that she kept in a secure bun on the top of her head. Summer and Season shared the same hair type with the same honey brown eye color, only Summer's complexion was a light, smooth caramel. The only features she shared with her father was his cute, sunk-in dimples and high cheekbones.

"My doctor doesn't know squat. She gets paid to tell people what to do and prescribe medicine that requires you to see her at least once a month, leaving out the long-term effects that will eventually disintegrate your body or your mind."

"Wow, pretty morbid today, are we?"

She looked at her father in a senseless way, "It's getting better by the minute."

"Oh, really? Because I can't tell. Did you give advice to our neighbor, Mrs. West, on the perfect contraception yesterday?"

Season couldn't do anything but smirk.

"Oh yeah, I heard about that. You thought that wouldn't get back to me? She was so frustrated because of what you told her that she took it out on me last night."

Season shrugged her shoulders as she played with the remote control in her hands. "What can I say? The lady has about seven kids. She has enough to start her own tribe."

"Okay, first, the Wests have five, not seven kids. Second, who are you to tell this woman what to do with her body?"

"Dad, you're an OBGYN for crying out loud! You mean to tell me that at her age, she should be having twins?"

"TWINS?!"

"Yes, twins. That explains my count. You know she's too old to be having more kids. Not only is it dangerous, but it's downright rude to have the other children knocking over trash cans or feeding the neighborhood dogs their leftovers out the window. That's so repulsive!"

"Why couldn't you just tell her that, instead of giving her your personal opinion?"

"Well, my point again, if she can't handle those five, she needs to give procreation a rest."

"That's cruel, honey."

"It's the truth!"

"Okay, stop this! I'm not going to do this with you today."

"Do what?"

"Have arguments every single day because you choose to be heartless,"

"Oh, really? How am I heartless? I hardly see you for most of the day. You're either away at the office or the hospital and leaving me to take care of a babysitter. On another note, I am thirteen; I don't need a babysitter!"

"Season, you know I have to work to take care of this family."

"What family?! Where's the family? Ma is dead, Dad. D-E-A-D. There's no point of return for her. After she left, the word 'family' left with her!" Season slammed the remote control on the floor and began crying.

Xavier, who was careful not to let her see the same hurt as well, didn't respond back to Season's outcry. Instead, he got up and headed to the kitchen. "You know, you're not the only one who lost someone. I thought counseling

because she would always raise her hand and correct everyone's responses, especially in math. Suki thought Season was arrogant because she would walk past her with her nose stuck up to the air, and lips would not move when Suki greeted her hello. It wasn't until that fateful day when Season and Suki were paired together to do a science project on habitats. Science wasn't Season's favorite subject, but it was Suki's. After spending time working on the project at Season's home, Summer's hospitality toward Suki turned into more of a family embrace. Season finally decided to give Suki a chance. They found out they had more in common than they realized, where one thing was dancing. The only difference was that Suki was more interested in hip-hop, where Season was more into classical ballet.

After elementary school, Suki began to delve more into hip-hop culture. Some girls were jealous because she was much prettier than they were, and some were critical because they thought she wanted to be Black. Maybe it was Suki's yellowish-brown tan, or the silk six-millimeter eyelashes painted with glitter-smokey eyeshadow she glued on her slanted eyes. After watching a season of Disney's *Andi Mack*, Suki started her seventh-grade year by cutting off her lengthy, black hair to rock an asymmetrical pixie cut. Suki, who was then standing at five feet and four inches, became the most popular student at school by being rated as the most fashionable girl. This really caused a lot of tension and jealousy among the girls. Season observed their motives and thought it was just insane for them to criticize her friend without getting to know her first. They didn't realize that Suki's mother was half-black and half-Japanese, and her father was full Japanese. Suki took pride in understanding and adapting to her mother's culture, which Season thought was cool.

"Well, if it makes you feel bad, then I'm sorry, Pooh."

"Pooh? So, what are we now? Ghetto?" Season laughed.

"Pooh is not a ghetto term, Season. It's whats happening now."

"I wish you could stop subscribing to the Ghetto Black Teen Vernacular Language of Today, Suk. It's unbecoming of you."

"Excuse me? If I didn't know any better, I would say you're jealous Season."

"Ha! Jealous? Of what, Suk?"

"Jealous of me, of course! I am more in tune with my culture than you are."

"What are you talking about, Suki? I'm black and have been black for thirteen years! There's no changing that."

"Yep, physically, you are black, but based on the mental chemical imbalance, you're Blike - a white girl in a black body."

Season shook her head as she laughed at her friend for sharing her psychoanalysis. Suki always joked about her being blacker than she was from how she walked, dressed, and even talked. Suki always knew how to get Season in a good mood.

"Maybe you're right."

"That I am, so give me my black card."

"I can't because I'm wearing it."

They laughed as they walked their mile around the track. Suddenly, the girls spotted a young Spanish teenage male walking on the other side of the field. Suki, being as bold as she was, whistled so loudly that he stopped to see where it was coming from.

"Whew, honey. You are lookin' good, Micah!"

Season tapped Suki on the hand and whispered, "Stop it! What's wrong with you?!"

"What?!"

"You are something else, Suk!"

"You can't tell me that Latino is not muy caliente," Suki said while snapping her fingers with emphasis.

"Yeah, but do you have to make a spectacle of yourself?"

"Only when I see potential arm candy, Seas. C'mon, let's holla at him."

"No! We're not going to 'holla' at anyone. You're supposed to be walking with me."

"Girl, please. You're already in shape, and I'm already in love. So let's go!" Suki yanked Season's arms, trying to pull her to Micah's direction.

"Noooo, Suk!"

"Too late."

"Too late for what?"

"Too late because shawty's comin' over."

"Who-" before Season could get a sentence out of her mouth, Micah approached them with the most handsome smile. Season couldn't help but blush at him. He reminded her so much of a young Adam Rodriquez, an actor from one of her favorite Tyler Perry's movies *I Can Do Bad All by Myself.*

"How are you ladies doing?"

"Fine." Season and Suki responded in a synchronized manner.

Micah laughed at how the girls responded to him. "I'm glad to hear it." Then, he looked at Season, "Hey Season, how are things holding up? I'm sorry for never sending my condolences when your mom passed. As a matter of fact, wasn't it around this time of the year?"

"Actually, today marks the first year."

"Man, I'm really sorry to hear that! I can't even imagine how hard this must be for you," Micah stated apologetically.

"Yea, it's really hard, but thanks. I appreciate it," Season replied as she lowered her eyes to conceal the incoming pain written in them.

"If there's anything I could do-"

"As a matter of fact, there is," Suki interrupted. "What you got going on later?"

"Suki!" Season snapped.

"What? I want to know…"

"Well, some guys and I are going to a house party out on Bull Street."

"Oooh, that sounds lovely. What time?" Suki inquired.

"Suki, no!" Season whispered.

"Aren't you both a little too young to hang out?" Micah asked with a confused look.

"How young is too young?" Suki asked offensively

"Young as in a nine pm curfew."

"How old are you, then?"

"I just turned sixteen, so my curfew got moved up to twelve."

"Well, that's our cue. Thanks for talking with us." Season grabbed hold of Suki's hand as she moved past Micah to leave off the track.

"Hey! Why did you do that? I was going to lie, Season!"

"Suk, we're thirteen, and he's sixteen. Micah knows we are not of age to go to some house party. Heck, he even knows we are in middle school! Besides, my dad would kill me if he found out that we sneak off to a high schoolers' house party."

"Wait, wait, and wait. Who is this new Season? Is this the same Season from last week who paid a twenty-one-year-old to buy vodka from the liquor store last Saturday? Or what about the same Season who was smoking weed with two stoners from our school? Outside of the back alley of a grocery store like three days ago?

She could not respond quickly because Suki was right. She was dreading this day of her mother's passing, and she thought her actions would help her face up to it, but it only made matters worse.

"Not to mention that you're a hypocrite," Suki stated, continuing with her point.

"How am I a hypocrite?"

"Well, how are you trying to keep up this clean, spiritual body image when you're drinking and smoking poison, Seas? Nowadays, I just don't get you."

"You're right, you don't. I don't even understand myself. I'm trying to adjust to this new normal, but I can't. It's hard, and sometimes I feel like throwing in the towel!" snapped Season as she wiped her tears.

Suki felt terrible for calling Season out. She understood the dynamics of Season's relationship with her mother. It made her even question how Season was going to live something like this down. "Sis, I'm sorry. I didn't mean to call you a hypocrite. I was just a little pissed about not going to the party. I guess I wanted to see if the rebellious Season would be down. I'm sorry, okay? And you should know, you're not going through this alone. You have your dad, and you have me. I got you!" She gave Season a long hug and wiped her tears away. "It won't be easy, I know. But we will get through this together."

Season gave Suki a small, sincere smile and held her hand. "Thank you! And no, we are not going to that party."

Suki chuckled a little, "How do you know I was about to ask that?"

"Because I know my Sis Suki."

Suki let out a huge sigh and draped her arms around Season's neck as they walked. "Well, it was worth a shot."

"You know…. I have a better idea if you still want to be a rebel."

"What's that?" Suki stopped walking.

"Let's do a klepto at the mall. I heard Chapman has this new lipstick that maintains its glossiness and color. I need to get a plum."

Suki looked at Season sideways. "I don't know about that, Sis. Usually, I'm down for dirty deeds, but stealing isn't one of them, especially not for something as simple as lipstick."

"It's not just any lipstick; it's like $25 for a tube."

"Especially for expensive lipstick to put on these chapped lips," stated Suki while pointing at her lips and licking them.

"Girl, please! Stop whining! Let's do it. It would make me feel better," begged Season.

"But why can't you just buy it? I know you got the money. You never leave the house without any cash."

"True, but how do I look about spending $25 on a single tube of lipstick?" Season asked as she cracked a smile.

"Girl, you're a mess," Suki laughed. "Okay…Okay, but if we get caught, I'm going to blame it all on you!"

"Deal!" exclaimed Season.

Xavier sat in his den, drinking Hennessy out of a double-wide shot glass with his eyes closed, listening to some old Motown songs on his Vinyl record player. About a couple of hours ago, he received a call from one of his good ole' police buddies down at the precinct, telling him his daughter and her friend were caught stealing in the mall. Xavier told the officer to discreetly arrest the girls, hold them at the precinct for an hour or so, and drive them safely back home. First, he made sure to call Suki's parents, who were totally on board with his plan. He was tired of Season's shenanigans. Today was hard for the both of them, but it didn't give Season the right to jump out of character. He knew he had to do something, and it had to be done fast. He looked over to the left and gazed at the beautiful extended set of Louis Vuitton luggage, which was all packed with Season's clothes and toiletries.

"She's in for a big surprise," he said to himself as he gulped down the last bit of Henny left in the glass. Like clockwork, he heard a key turning in the lock and looked over to see Season coming in from the side door.

"Hey Pop, what's going on?" she asked timidly.

"Hey, Pop? You haven't called me that in years. I should ask what's going on with you."

"Ummm…nothing, just went shopping with Suk. You know, girl stuff."

"Hm, sounds like you went shoplifting," he claimed with a stern tone while giving her the stare to let her know that he knew what was going on.

"Dad, let's not start this…"

"Let's not start what, Season? Let's not start how I am raising a juvenile delinquent in training? Let's not start with how you're trying to embarrass both of us in public?

What are you trying to prove, little girl?"

"I'm not trying to prove anything, Dad. I...we were just having fun."

"FUN?!? YOUR IDEA OF FUN IS COMMITTING A FELONY? THAT'S FUN?" yelled Xavier as he banged his glass on the table. Season jumped at the sound of it and began to realize how she really pushed her father to the brink of madness. She had never witnessed him act this way before.

"YOU KNOW, MAYBE I SHOULD JUST BUY YOU AN ORANGE JUMPSUIT SO YOU CAN HAVE ALL THE FUN IN THE WORLD. TOO BAD YOUR SPACE WILL BE LIMITED TO A JAIL CELL!"

"Dad, please, I'm sorry..." Season cried, pressing her hands to the top of her head.

"No. Sorry doesn't cut it. I have been accepting your apologies for too long, and now this 'sorry' is void. I let this go on for so long. I gave you too many breaks, considering what this family has gone through. Nope, sorry, won't do. There are consequences to every action, and your punishment starts now!"

"What do you mean...?" Season responded weakly as she looked over to the other side of the room at the luggage set. "What is the meaning of this? What are you doing?"

"You're going away for a while to live with your Aunt Autumn in Hollins."

"Excuse me, what?!" Season asked surprisingly.

"You heard me, young lady. You're staying with your

Aunt Autumn for a while."

"What is a while?"

"The entire summer!" Xavier snapped.

"You can't do this!"

"Says who? You clearly forgot who's the boss. I brought you into this world, and before the world eats you up, by golly, I will take you out myself."

Season knew her father meant business, but she couldn't imagine how a sweet and gentle person she knew since birth would give her up to some estranged family member she hardly even knows. Sure, Aunt Autumn visited a couple of times over the years, but Summer insisted on Autumn to stay in a hotel and not be around the family so much. Summer would tell Season that her Aunt Autumn was a recluse who preferred not to be around people or family. So why would her dad finally agree to something like this? Didn't he know that Aunt Autumn wasn't a family person?

"But Dad," Season said calmly, careful not to cause any more eruptions. "I don't know Aunt Autumn at all. She's almost a perfect stranger to me."

"Season, she's your aunt. She's the closest to familiarity you have. I'll never understand why your mother shielded her from us, but it ends tonight. I'm taking you to her tomorrow morning—no ifs, ands, or buts about it. If you are thinking about leaving this house or running away in the middle of the night, I'll tell Officer Lowe to lock you back up again. Maybe I'll make it a longer stay!"

She looked at her father surprisingly. She realized that her own father had a hand in her and Suki's arrest and detention.

"Yep, I was the one who made that call. You needed to stay there for a while until you came to your senses."

Season's eyes turned a deep red of fury. She could not believe her father would go that far as to punish her. *Who is this man that's standing in front of me?* She thought. "I hate you, and if Mom was living, she would hate you too!" She stomped out of the room and up the stairs to go to her bedroom.

Xavier called out to her, "You can hate me all you want, but if I hear a slamming door and a lock, I'm taking the hinges and the door off!"

Season was careful to not slam the door or lock it because she didn't want to see or hear from him anymore. One thing she was sure of was that she wasn't going anywhere to see an Aunt Autumn or to some small town called Hollins.

Chapter 2:

WELCOME TO HOLLINS, JAIL TOWN

"C'mon, Season. We have to burn two and a half hours of rubber on the road to get to where we're going," Xavier called out to his daughter, who was standing with Suki near the car.

Xavier just loaded the last baggage into his SUV and was on his way to the driver's side of the car. As soon as Season made it to her room that night, she made sure to call Suki to tell her what happened. Suki, who wasn't supposed to be on her cellphone, was devastated and chastised Season for talking them into stealing the lipstick. When Suki's father overheard her talking on her phone, he immediately came into her room, snatched it out of her hand, tapped the end call button, and left with the phone in his hand. This morning, Suki explained to her parents how she needed to see Season before she leaves for the entire summer. Mrs. Aiko, Suki's mom, was reluctant at first but decided to let Suki go, considering how close the two girls were. Mr. Aiko was totally against the idea. He didn't see Season's farewell as a permanent goodbye, so why make a big fuss over it? It took Mrs. Aiko some time to get through to her husband, and she won. He wasn't happy about it, but he drove Suki over to the Holidae's residence to see Season before they left.

"Wow, girl, so this is happening for real? This isn't a punishment. This is torture!"

"Tell me about it, cruel and unusual, to say the least. I don't even know this lady."

"That's another strange thing. Why would your own dad send you off to a place you haven't heard of or a lady you hardly ever been around? Weird, dude…really weird."

"I know! How long will your father have your contraband?" Season joked.

"Girl, you know my phone is like my life! He said he's not going to give it up until I work it off, so he got me working at the family restaurant."

"Yikes! You hate that place."

"I know, right? That's not even the worst part."

"What's the worst?"

"He told me that I will have to work until I make about the same amount that lipstick cost."

Season shrugged her shoulders. "Well, that's not bad. It was only about $25."

Suki gave her a stern look with her mouth pouted out.

"Making only twenty-five cents an hour?"

"Oh, wow! Man, he's really harsh!"

"Yes, he is! I have never heard that man yell so many words in Japanese before in my life. It was to the point where I had needed my phone for a translator app. It was insane."

Season wanted to laugh but decided against it. It was her fault Suki was in the plight she was in. "Suk, I'm sorry, I shouldn't have made you come with me to do such a foolish thing."

"Naw, I am responsible for my own actions, not you. Besides, at least we're living to tell the story."

"Yeah, you're right."

They looked at each other for a minute and began to cry and hug each other when they heard Xavier starting up the car.

"I am really going to miss you! What am I supposed to do without my ace?" asked Suki.

"I know, Suk. When your father finally gets to calm down, maybe you can ask him for your phone back."

"Yeah, I will most definitely try that. Maybe persuade my mom to talk to him. It's bad enough to work as an employee under him."

Beep Beep

"Let's go! We have to get a move on to beat the I-95 traffic," called out Xavier.

"Okay, Dad, geez! Look Suk, I'm coming back one way or another. There's no way in hell I'm going to stay the entire summer in a place called 'Hollins.' Dad thinks this will work but watch!"

"Wanna bet?!" shouted out Xavier with a stern look on his face.

"Ugh, I can't deal with him! He listens in on everything!"

"I'll tell you what, just pony express me once you get there. In that way, I have your address, and I can send you a letter back," said Suki.

"Good idea! Let's shake on it."

The girls did their secret home girl handshake and hugged each other once more before Season got into the car.

"BYE! DON'T FORGET TO WRITE!" Suki yelled as she waved them goodbye.

"Cheer up, Season. It's not the end of the world. I am trying to teach you self-worth and accountability. You can't just do whatever you want and think it won't affect others, especially if they love and care about you," explained Xavier as he was getting off I-95.

Season didn't talk during the whole car ride, for she did not want to entertain her father and his reasons for sending her away. Instead, she found comfort in browsing through other's social media pages on her phone. Xavier knew she was going to sulk for a long while just to get under his skin, but he was not going to give in.

"I know you hear me when I'm talking to you. That

phone doesn't have all your attention."

She continued playing on her phone, pretending as if she was in the car by herself. Xavier snatched the phone out of her hands and threw it over his shoulders into the backseat.

"Hey, why did you do that?!" snapped Season.

"Because you were absolutely rude is why. You're making this hard on yourself, young lady."

"Dad, I don't want to go. I'll be good, I promise. If you turn this car around right now, I'll be that sweet, enthuse child who you knew once before. Please," begged Season.

"Season, I don't think you fully understand how much you are pushing your luck with me. You think your promises have any credibility now? I'm at my wits end with you. I don't know what to do. Hopefully, being in Hollins with your Aunt Autumn will help you because I'm clearly out of options."

Season crossed her arms as her eyes became watery. She knew she got on her father's last nerve, and a simple apology would not turn the car back around to Columbia.

As her father stopped at a toll bridge, Season pressed an automatic button to wind her window down to take in the low country environment. The skies appeared to be more serene and secluded. The marshes covered most of the land with water, tall needled grasses, and cattails. The subtropical heat greeted Season's face as she used one hand to shade the sun and the other to swat away a few gnats.

"Beautiful, isn't it?" asked her father, driving away

from the toll to cross the bridge.

Season continued to look out her window but replied, "It's different."

"Well, it's not home, but it was home to your mother. Man, she loved this area. She loved its stillness and culture. The city life was too noisy for her at times."

Season squinted her eyes out of confusion as she looked over to her dad. "That's funny... if mom loved this area so much, why hadn't she visited here before?"

Xavier cleared his throat as he sat up in his seat. At that moment, Season knew her father was trying to think of a good explanation.

"We've been to Charleston plenty of times before, Honey. Remember?"

"Yes, we have, but we are miles away from Charleston. We haven't been down this way before. We're almost near Beaufort and Hilton Head," explained Season.

"Well, I guess your mother had her reasons. She loved the low-country environment, just not Hollins."

"Why not?"

"It's hard to explain, baby. I know she was estranged from the Hollins locals. Hollins is a tiny, self-reliant town. I guess Summer outgrew the place. She was always an adventurer."

Season thought about what her father was telling her and couldn't disagree. Her mother had a great mind with big dreams. That's why she went into education sales. She worked as a middle school math teacher for about seven years in a low socioeconomic community and witnessed much illiteracy in students. After years of researching, she received her Doctorate in Education. She then decided to push herself even further and designed her own curriculum program and learning management system called *Educating Children Collectively*—or ECC, which led to significant sales throughout the United States and five other countries. Xavier and Season were proud of how she changed her dream to reality. She never understood her mom's motivation for pushing young minds to greatness, but Summer would always tell Season or the students she taught to never lock their minds inside of a box but open it up to the world. Maybe that would explain why she left such a place like Hollins behind. Before her untimely death, she was presenting at a professional development meeting in Florence, South Carolina. That same fateful day Season wished her mom was there with her.

"A penny for your thoughts?" asked Xavier, looking over to see his daughter wondering in her own train of thoughts.

"Yes, why would you send me to a place where mom obviously tried to leave behind? It just doesn't make sense."

"Well, it does to me. I think a good exposure to something new will help you to find yourself again and to get to know your mom's side of the family a little more."

"But, I thought mom's parents weren't alive."

"No, but you do have your Aunt Autumn and some cousins living there. It will be good for you. There's a nice secluded beach out there for you to swim all day, wouldn't that be nice?"

Season shrugged her shoulders, trying so hard not to give in to the mention of any beaches. Besides dancing, swimming was her next thing. She was one of the top swimmers on her swim team at the country club's youth recreation and school. When she wasn't practicing or walking the track with Suki, she would practice her backstrokes at the recreational pool.

"Man, I remembered my time at Hollins shore. It was like my refuge," recollected Xavier as if he was talking more to himself.

Season had a puzzled look on her face as she listened to her dad talked about the beach. "I thought you were from Charleston?" asked Season.

"I, uh. I am. Sometimes I would go with my parents down to Hollins to visit some of their friends," stammered Xavier with a hesitant look on his face.

"But didn't you meet mom in Columbia?"

"Well, yes. We met in Columbia, but never in Hollins. That's one of those things both your mom and I had in common."

"Well, that's weird."

"What?"

"For you to go on about how small Hollins is, you've never met Mom there."

"Well, it's one of those situations where you can't find that good thing in small places until you go out to big places…it happens."

Season looked skeptically at her father and knew something wasn't right. She was about to ask him another question until his phone rang in his pocket. As if he knew what she was thinking, he took his phone out of his pocket and answered it immediately.

"Hello?" He responded with a concerned look on his face. "Yes… We're like five minutes away. Yep, uh-huh…. Okay, so you're near the bridge? No, that's not what we discussed, Autumn."

Season was trying to make sense of the conversation her father was having on the phone. They were getting closer to Hollins from what she could hear, but what did a bridge have to do with it? What did they discuss? Season pretended to perch her elbow on the armrest separating her from her father to lean in on the conversation. Xavier, who appeared conscious of his daughter's actions, shifted his phone to the other ear.

"Okay, well …hurry. Make sure no one takes notice. Bye," retorted Xavier as he quickly hit his end call button. He looked over to see the perplexity on his daughter's face.

"Why should no one take notice? What's going on?" asked Season.

"Children should never listen in on grown folks' conversation. You know that."

Season shrugged her shoulders to feign her pretentious state of not caring one way or another. On the inside, she was desperate to find out what was going on between her father and her aunt. He was talking to her on the phone as if he was really acquainted with her. From that discussion, Season realized that she needed to be more cognizant as to what was going on.

When they finally reached the beginning of a small bridge, Xavier parked near the grass, turned off the ignition, and got out of the car. Season, who was oblivious as to why they stopped near a bridge, decided to follow suit.

"What are we waiting on, Dad?"

"We're waiting on your Aunt Autumn. She said she would be here. I guess she's running a little late," he responded without looking at her. His eyes appeared to be looking down toward something over the bridge.

Season followed his eyes and saw where the bridge stopped at a steep grassy knoll. As she walked further away from the car, she noticed below the hill sat a small community. It occurred to be secluded from everywhere else in society with every establishment, roads, and homes being close together like Mickey's Toon town in Disneyland. The only difference was that the town lacked vibrant colors and adventures. From Season's hawk-eyed view, the environment was uniformed with dystopian colors. Only a few cars were moving up and down the one-lane highway.

Season shook her head as she looked on at the mundane scene. She turned around and asked, "Where are we?"

Xavier, taking in the same aurora, cleared his throat before he responded, "Welcome to Hollins, Season."

"No. Welcome to Hollins, Jail town," muttered Season, heading back to the car.

Xavier was about to respond to Season's comment before a vehicle approaching the bridge distracted him. Season followed her father's eyes and saw a shabby, black 2000 Toyota Camry coming towards them. As the driver parked on the opposite side of the road, Season took a step closer to see a woman on the driver's side. Xavier went over to the vehicle as the woman wound her window down.

"Well, aren't you going to get out? You haven't seen Season in a while," asked Xavier.

Reluctantly, she opened the car door, took one leg out first, and then got out of the car. Season sized her aunt up and down as if she was picking her out of a lineup. *Homely…. Very homely,* she thought. The lady known to Season as Aunt Autumn was not as beautiful as her late sister, Summer. In fact, her name gave essence to how she looked, indicating that the fun was over, and school was in session. Her long, dark brown maxi dress appeared to bring no fashionista of 2000 styles or patterns. In fact, she looked as if she could play a part of a teacher teaching in a one-room school on the old television sitcom *Little House on the Prairie*. The huge part in the middle separating the two cornrow braids tied in a ball at the back of her head was too cliché. Not to mention the brown thick-heeled Oxford shoes she wore that made vintage not cool anymore.

"Hello… Season," replied Autumn.

Season sensed Autumn's nervousness in her voice. She held her hands together as she rapidly twirled her two thumbs in a circle. *Maybe she's nervous about seeing me for the first time in years. She didn't even come to her own sister's funeral, which was rude and out of the ordinary, but I'll give it a chance,* she thought.

"Hey, Aunt Autumn," answered Season as she mustered up a smile. "It's been a long time, wouldn't you say? I didn't see you at the funeral.

Aunt Autumn's face grew tighter as she was too appalled to comment after Season's remarks. She and Xavier exchanged a weird glance before she turned back to face Season.

"I… uh…I didn't hear about it until the last minute, but I was devastated when I heard about it and couldn't go."

"Mmh…Father?" Season firmly stated as she crossed her arms and looked to Xavier. "You were so much in a rush calling Aunt Autumn to send me to this hell-hole that you forgot to call her about her own sister's death last year?."

Xavier shot Season a deadly eye as he placed his hands on his hips. Season, knowing that look and that stance from anywhere, knew she struck out. She uncrossed her arms and looked down so she wouldn't have to face her father's wrath. "Sorry," she responded meekly.

Surprisingly, Autumn gave a slight chuckle. "Wow, Summer is definitely in this child," she joked.

"Yep, but one more sly comment like that, she would have to eat those words," threatened Xavier as he continued eyeing her.

"Well, where's her bags?" Autumn inquired, trying to change the mood.

"Here, let me get them out of the car, and pack them into your trunk," requested Xavier, rushing with his keys to unlock his trunk.

Season could not help but observe how her father was behaving when he was rushing toward his car. As if he could not wait to get her off his hands. Yes, she was acting a bit unruly, but was it to the extent of him discarding her to this woman? She wanted so badly to cry or to create a scene, but she knew her aunt was watching her every move. Season couldn't let her think she was predictable or a wimp, so she feigned an apathetic look as she shook her head at her father.

"I heard you enjoy swimming, the best on your swim team?" asked Aunt Autumn, trying to strike up a friendly conversation.

Season, pretending not to hear her aunt, continued looking toward her father.

Aunt Autumn continued her one-sided conversation. "Well, we don't have a swim team in these parts. I don't like to toot my own horn, but I'm a pretty good swimmer myself. Maybe we can go out to the beach sometimes and swim a little."

Season finally looked at her aunt and responded, "I'm

sorry, but swimming isn't my thing anymore."

Xavier, who finished loading the bags in Autumn's trunk, turned abruptly and asked, "Since when?"

"Since you decided to take my privilege of being at the country club this summer to drive me all the way here," Season pointed out.

"Excuse me, Autumn, let me have a talk with my daughter," he asked apologetically.

"Sure. If you need me, I'll be in the car."

"Thanks!"

Xavier stormed toward Season's way and grasped her arms to lead her to the other side of his car. "Look, young lady. That's enough! You complained, moaned, and groaned throughout this whole ride. As you can see, it didn't work! You still ended up here in Hollins. Keep it up; you'll be enrolled in school down here, do I make myself clear?"

Season appeared stunned and panicky at the mention of "enrolled" and "school" until she finally calmed down. Xavier sighed after realizing he probably went a bit overboard, but his daughter's ridiculous behavior was getting out of hand.

"Look, I'm sorry," Xavier apologized. "I'm not asking you to love this place, but I need you to respect your aunt and to have a great time. I know you're taking your mom's death hard, but so am I. We're not going to get anywhere near healing if we keep attacking each other, okay?"

Season couldn't respond, but Xavier could see the

silent tears racing from her eyes to her cheeks. "I'm not trying to rid myself of you; you're my daughter. I love you too much to lose you. I would rather send you someplace where you can receive more love from your Aunt Autumn than to see you destroying yourself back home."

"When are you coming back to get me?" Season croaked, wiping tears from her eyes.

"As soon as the summer ends. I will be right back in this same spot with lots of hugs and kisses," Xavier assured, pulling Season in to give her the biggest hug a father could ever give his daughter. "I promise, okay?"

Season nodded her head as she buried her face in her father's shirt. She knew she had tear stains all over it, but she didn't care. She wanted to breathe in the familiar scent of his masculine cologne, hoping to not forget about him.

"I will give you back your phone only if you promised to make the best of this situation," bargained Xavier, pulling his daughter away so he could stare into her eyes.

"I'll try…"

"Here's another deal. Whenever I get back home, I will see if I can convince the Aikos to give Suki her phone back so you can reach out to her. I don't want to take everything from you," he explained while giving Season a warm smile.

For the first time since the long car ride, Season felt relieved and gave her father a prize-winning smile. "Oh, please do so! I need someone to talk to while I'm down here doing nothing."

"Ah, only if you promise to give this place a try. Try

meeting some kids around your age and do KID stuff," he emphasized softly.

"I'll try, I promise," agreed Season as she turned around to open the back-car door to get her phone.

"Come here and give me a great big hug and kiss," stated Xavier as he reached for his daughter once more.

"Oh, dad, I'm going to miss you so much!"

"I'm going to miss you the most baby. Don't worry, summer will be over before you know it. You will have a great time getting to know your Aunt Autumn."

I really hope so…, she thought as she gave her dad a big bear hug.

Chapter 3:

FINDING A COMMON BALANCE

For Season, waking up to a bright Sunday morning in Hollins wasn't all that bad. She woke up and hoisted her window to take in the sunshine. Last night rain showers left a petrichor in the morning air, stimulating Season to have an open mind about the place. As she looked to her right, she noticed a small clock on the nightstand reading seven-thirty am, an hour earlier than her usual wake up time. Maybe she didn't feel comfortable sleeping in a strange house, a strange room, or a strange bed.

She sat down on the mattress and rocked her body back and forth to get a fair assessment of its quality. It wasn't her firm memory foam mattress from back home, but it would do. She noticed the licorice pink and cream color schemes as she looked around the room, a young girl's dream for room decorum. There was a small closet door with magazine posters covering every inch, from the classic rock bands and hip-hop groups such as *Queen, Aerosmith, Kiss, Run DMC, Public Enemy,* and *NWA* to single music legends like *Prince, Michael Jackson,* and *George Michaels.* She couldn't help but shake her head and laugh at how archaic her aunt's taste in music was. Sure, she respected the legends that came before her generational piece of modern hip-hop, pop, and rock, but the closet door was decorated as a hall of fame for some of the departed and the departed music where today's sounds lost its way.

She looked around the room and saw a small brown vanity dresser and stool in the far right corner. It looked to be well-kept and polished, but there were no feminine products or anything placed on top of the vanity. Above it hung a wide cork board that was coated with pictures. She got up from the bed to look at the mosaic. As she walked barefooted on the cold, wooden floorboard to the vanity dresser, she couldn't help but to be surprised who was in the photos. As if seeing herself for the first time, she saw pictures of her mom ranging from toddler ages to what looked to be her teenage years in a timeline order.

From her observation, Season realized that this room didn't belong to her aunt but to her mother instead. She looked at the last picture, which Summer looked to be in her late teen years. Season began laughing at what her mother had on in the image: baggy blue jeans and a pink glittering boob top, which was too short for her to cover up the Joe Boxer undergarment. Her long, frizzy brown hair was cut into a concise style, accompanied with but-terfly clips holding together a few twists in the front. She was standing beside a younger girl who shared almost the same face and complexion as Season, her Aunt Autumn. It seemed her style of fashion didn't change from the picture at all. She wore a plain white shirt under a long olive-green dress. Her hair was brushed back into a more conservative ponytail to convey no hint of fashion or style. The two looked different from night and day, with Summer ap-pearing to be the rebellious sister and Autumn being the conventional one. It's funny how siblings can grow up in the same household and share almost the same nurturance but can still go on different pathways. *Maybe that explains why mom was so tenacious and successful. She was always taking chances in life. The same could not be said about my aunt, who never left her hometown. It must be miserable be-ing her,* Season thought to herself.

As she began looking at the other pictures of her mom and her aunt, she couldn't help but notice the same ex-pression on both sisters' faces. It wasn't a typical candid photo where a picture was snapped of someone caught off guard, but a staged one, with a lack of trying to grace the camera with a smile. The toddler years seemed to be full of life and fun, but it was distinctively apparent that something wasn't right around their preteen years. The ex-pressions on their faces conveyed a countenance of oppres-sion and overall darkness. Even the celebratory pictures of what seemed to be birthdays were a bit off. Knowing her mother, she loved celebrations, especially birthday parties. There was something different; no exertion of happiness. Season traced her fingers over her mom's face in each photo as if she was trying to read them but couldn't get any answers. She couldn't get this feeling out of her head that something troubling went on back then.

"That was Summer's thirteenth birthday. Man, I remember that day like it was yesterday. My parents made a big deal over that party," chimed in Autumn, leaning at the doorway. "Sorry, I thought you would still be asleep. I was going to wake you up to join me for breakfast, if you like."

Season looked at her aunt for a moment like it was the first time seeing her again. She didn't know what to say to her. It was only yesterday when her father left her in her aunt's care. She didn't put up a fight or said anything belligerent to her. She got into Autumn's car and didn't say anything at all.

"Sure," Season responded.

Breakfast was nothing short of amazing. Aunt Autumn's remarkable cooking skills left a huge impression on Season. Creamy shrimp and grits with caramelized onions accompanied with homemade butter biscuits and strawberry jam was hands down satisfying to her soul. Of course, she didn't want her aunt to think that she was getting too comfortable. Although she wanted a second and third helping, she refused to give in to her aunt's witchcraft.

"I was going to tell you to make yourself a bowl of cereal since that seems to be all you kids would eat, but I thought it would be considerate of me to welcome you with a sweet southern home breakfast. If you want any more, I could fix you another plate," offered Autumn with a small smile.

Season thought about the offer and the mouthwatering meal she just had. Clearly, she was a better cook than her mother, but she would never give her the satisfaction of knowing that. She wanted so badly to say yes and ask what she was going to cook for lunch. "Um, no thanks. I'm good," she said as she wiped the corners of her mouth.

"Suit yourself. Well, I'm going outside in the garden. You're going to clean up the kitchen."

Season looked at her aunt as if she had three heads. How dare she give her chores on the first day of her summer vacation? This wasn't her home to do any kind of house labor.

Autumn, spotting Season's face, didn't let it bother her one bit. She got up to straighten up her dress as she continued, "I need you to put some water in the grits pot, save the shrimp gravy in a Tupperware bowl to put in the refrigerator, wash the remaining pots and silverware, and sweep the floors, please.

Season continued looking at her aunt as if she was joking. She didn't even think to give her aunt's tasks any consideration as she moved her chair away from the table and crossed her arms.

"Is there a problem?" Autumn asked nonchalantly.

"Yes, there is. I was under the impression that my stay here was for therapeutic reasons, which didn't involve me cleaning anyone's kitchen. A guest should have accommodations given to them, not chores.

It was now Autumn's turn to look at Season as if she had three heads. The look of condemnation came across her face as if she was a disgruntled church mother who was about to rebuke anything that was not godly in her sight. To say she was about the same complexion as Season, her face dropped to a darker shade.

At that moment, Season regretted the pink tornado that resided inside her mouth. She was raised to have a voice and stand for something or fall for anything. She was notoriously known in school for her deep compassion for expressing what she felt. It was like her gift. Right then, she realized maybe her gift was a blessing and a curse or possibly her fatal flaw.

Slowly, Autumn walked up to her niece. Her approach was scary yet cordial, which was sort of befuddling considering what Season was thinking.

"I understand you've been raised with a silver spoon in ya mouth," her aunt stated pleasantly in a weird dialect. "Ya were coddled, protected, and invested in acquiring only the best. But lemme tell ya something," she pointed her finger in Season's face. "No one...and I do mean, no one, could ever acquire the best if all their lives they have been granted luxuries by someone's hard work. 'Cause baby, God bless the child who gots its own. We all start from scratch somewhere. It's better when you're young and able, but when you're old and senseless, it tends to be a foolish thing. Ya haven't been taught that, and that silver spoon is still in ya mouth, which tells me no one around you wanted to snatch it out. But starting today, I'm going to do so. I'm not ya maid, and this here is no hotel for your accommodations. I'm ya aunt, and ya staying here for a while. While ya here, ya gonna learn some responsibility and reverence to those who put forth da effort to see ya make something outta ya self. Now, let's start wit these dishes, because it can't wash itself. If ya know what I know, ya do dem dishes and everything else I 'quire you to do. There will be some changes' round here, and it starts with you. Now, I ain't Summer, and I'm not tryna be her. I'm me, and if ya stayin' in this here house, we both have to find a common balance. If ya can't, ya can go back to whence ya came and continue workin' on ya accommodated plans for the jailhouse!"

Surprisingly, Season looked at her aunt when she mentioned "jailhouse." What could she have known about her? Did her father tell her about the recent incident she'd been in?

"Yea, I heard about all the trouble you've been getting into, and I don't like it one bit! Lemme tell you something else, I never had to hide any of my personal belongings in this house because it's my home and solace, and I'll be damned if I start doing so because of a thirteen-year-old bandit. If a thought cross ya mind to do so, ya wouldn't have to wait all summer for ya dad to come get ya. Ya be stuck down here under Hollins jail, where no one could find you. Do I make myself clear?" asked Autumn, who seemed to be calming down after her last remark.

For the first time in a long time, Season was stone cold still. No one ever spoke to her this way, and she felt stripped of her opinions. Autumn put the fear of God in her, and she was too insulted and terrified to respond back. She wanted to call her dad and tell him to get her immediately, or she would have to run away. Season was too caught up in her own feelings to see that she wasn't being respectful to her aunt, but she knew her aunt meant business from reflecting on the sudden sound in her vernacular.

"Ye-Yes Ma'am," Season responded quickly.

"Good," her aunt replied while giving Season a warm smile. "That's what I like to hear. If you keep this up, we will get 'long just fine."

Autumn walked away and replied, "Clean the kitchen up, and you can join me in the garden. Today is a good day for building foundation; we're planting not only seeds but some common sense."

As she walked out of the kitchen, Season grabbed for her phone in her back pocket. She quickly unlocked it, pulled up the calendar app, and counted how many days that she would have to remain in this hellhole.

Chapter 4:

SERENE AND YUSEF

*A*fter cleaning up the plates, dirty utensils, cups, and greasy pots and pans, Season felt a bit over-whelmed. Sure, she washed dishes before, but she would assist her mother when doing so. After Summer's death, her father hired a maid for the house chores such as clean-ing the kitchen and the rest of the house. Season had no experience in cleaning a house unless someone counted her room, which she kept spotless. In a way, she felt guilty because cleaning was not her specialty and for someone to call her out on it depicted her parents' poor choice of parenting.

She decided to do what her aunt requested and join her in the garden. The capacious garden was beautiful with each of the same vegetables in two rows: tomatoes, cucumbers, peppers, squash, beans, peas, sweet potatoes, and high yielding corn to embellish the garden's scenery.

Season stood in awe because she never saw something so unique and breathtaking before. She decided to walk between the rows of cucumbers and spotted her aunt tending to the tomato plants. Autumn, noticing how Season was taking a liking to her vegetable garden, began to smile.

"I guess you're finished with the kitchen?" she asked while polishing a juicy, plumb tomato she plucked from a vine.

"Uh-yes. I mean, yes, ma'am. I have," startled Season as she stopped walking.

"That's good. Cleaning up makes you feel better about yourself and your home. My mom always told me, besides family, your home should be your next priority, from where you eat and sleep. A house tells a lot about people and their lives, ya know?"

Season didn't reply. She was still a little irritated by her aunt's speech earlier and didn't want to agree with anything she had to say. Instead, she observed her aunt's garden-wear: a wide straw hat, a white shirt, and overalls that were dirty from the knee down from bending on the ground for so long. She looked as if she was one with nature, and the idea of getting dirty didn't faze her one bit.

"To be honest, I didn't 'spect ya to come out here with me. I figure a child-like ya would rather be inside on ya phone, playing on ya Face-chat or Insta-book or whateva ya call it."

Season feigned a smile, trying to appease her aunt's ignorance of social media. "Well, you told me to join you, and I took it as an obligation, not an invitation," she retorted in a friendly, sarcastic tone.

Autumn took the same tomato, placed it inside a sweetgrass basket, and plucked another to shine it clean with a white wash towel. "If I remembered correctly, I used just the term 'join' without a threatening word behind it. I can't make someone do something that they don't want to do."

Season decided not to respond back to her aunt's explanation of her "request," so she continued walking down the rows. "Did you plant all this?"

"Yep," Autumn replied as she went to the next row of tomatoes to see what she could pluck. "Gardening is a good hobby of mine. Can't seem to get into anything else these days."

Season looked at her aunt with confusion. Although she dressed like an old hobbit, she couldn't be any more than in her thirties. Her mom would have been thirty-four this coming August if she was still alive, so her aunt couldn't be that far along.

"Were you younger than my mom? I'm asking because of the picture."

"Yep, I am the baby and three years her senior. Man, she was the best big sister ever. She always had my back and made sure I was taking care of, because if it wasn't for her…" Autumn reflected as if she was in a trance but finally snapped back to reality. Season waited for her to finish her statement, but she didn't continue. Instead, she had a strange, sad look on her face and continued tending to her tomatoes.

"So, why gardening? Aren't you a little too young to be doing old women's leisure?" asked Season, who spotted a hoe on the ground behind her. She reached to pick it up so she could lean on it.

"Ha! What are you trying to say? That I'm old?!"

"Nope, just saying that a young lady in her early thirties should be experiencing more out of life than gardening in her own backyard is what I'm saying," explained Season.

Autumn grunted at Season's remark. "Mmh, trust me, tending to the Earth is the safest and most practical experience that I would get myself into. I have other hobbies, but gardening is therapeutic for me. Helps me to reflect on matters and take my mind away from stress. I guess it's the idea of sowing things and watching them grow up to its full potential of loveliness. So many things people can take away from you, but they can't take away the talents God has instilled in ya. I can truly say that this is something that could not be brought, stolen, or taken away."

Season was mystified as to why her aunt was so transfixed on someone taking anything away from her. She looked out toward the long rows that covered an acre of the land and agreed that the garden did hold an enchantment to the beholder's eyes, enough to want to claim it herself.

"You okay, child?" asked Autumn, walking toward

Season with her basket in one arm.

"Uh, yes, I'm fine. Just thinking is all. This place is so quiet. How close are the neighbors?"

"Well, let's see, the closest house will be Mrs. Bee; she's about a half a mile down the road," responded Autumn, while pointing.

Season looked to where she was pointing as if she could see that far. Her aunt's house was in a small cul-de-sac with no homes around it, only the huge garden in the backyard to enlighten the private landscape. It was an old, beautiful, small red-brick single-family home with tan shutters on each of the front two windows. The front yard looked as if it could be entered into the *Home and Garden Magazine* with a medium-sized bird bath fountain in the middle, sculptured azalea bushes, and yellowish-brown marigolds. Different decorum of plants was not only inhabiting the front yard, but also the front porch. The mailbox was even ornamented in Amethyst plants at its wooden foot. When they first arrived, Season was awe from the start. This lady should have been the DIY florist in Pinterest.

"So, what's fun in Hollins? Do you have a cinema, rec center, arcade, a country club, or something?"

Autumn gave Season a strange look. "A country club? Wow, you are privileged!"

Season shrugged her shoulders as if what she mentioned was no big deal. "Um, no. My dad has a family membership at the country club back home. I go almost every day to swim."

"Why go to a normal swimming pool to swim when we have the coast near? It doesn't cost you anything. As far as a cinema, we have the 99 cent cinema in town, but it shows only the classic movies. If you're looking for a movie theatre that plays the most recent movies, that's about twenty-five miles away from us in the next city."

"So great! How am I supposed to spend my summer break? Where do the young go to enjoy themselves or blow off some steam?

"Ya have some steam to blow off?"

"Maybe I do."

"Then work 'round the house. There's plenty of things to do around the house to keep ya calm."

Season let out a long sigh as she clasped her hands to the top of her head. She had never liked being subjected to one place. She needed space to explore her surroundings, and being held in captivity was not in her best interest. "Are you going to town anytime soon? Perhaps I can ride along."

"Well, come to think of it, church service starts in about an hour. I was going to Sunday school, but I figured after making breakfast, I could work in my garden for a while. I've been putting it off for a minute, so it needed my attention."

"Church?" questioned Season.

"Yes, church. That's where we are going."

"Um, do I have a choice?"

"Put it this way, Season. Joshua 24:25, 'But as for

me and my household, we will serve the Lord,' which brings me to my next rule. We go to church on Mondays, Wednesdays, and Sundays around here, so that's noonday prayer, bible study, and Sunday services. There's no exception to the rule. You're not about to stay in my house and not go to church. If you miss any of these services, you will be prohibited from leisure time until the required time is compensated by reading the bible and writing a one page summary on what you read."

Season's eyes widened by the consequences of missing services. She couldn't believe what her aunt was forcing her to commit to. She didn't even attend church services that many times in Columbia. Sure, her parents were into church but were too busy in the week to participate in any other services other than Sunday service. She felt as if the weight of staying in Hollins with her aunt was getting too much for her to bear, and she was one second away from calling her father to let him know that she gave up. There was no way she could not make it to the end of summer.

"What's wrong? You said you need to blow off some steam, right?" asked Autumn with a smug look on her face. "The church doors are always opened, come and leave your burdens at the altar, gal!" She laughed as she turned to walk back to the house. "Oh, by the way. Be ready by 9:45am because service starts at 10am," she announced from behind her shoulders and began singing the hymn, "*Amazing Grace*" while walking away from Season, taking victory in knowing that she had the upper hand.

Season's mouth was open but was too revolted to say anything. This was going to be a long summer.

"I'm *gonna lay down my burdens down by…* "
"*Down by the riverside.*"
("Oh, down by…")
"*Down by the riverside.*"
("Oh, down by…")
"*Down by the riverside.*"

Hollins New Deliverance Holiness was packed from pew to choir stand. The lead singer, who looked and sounded analogous to the late gospel singer Mahalia Jackson, raised the roof off the church with a large choir dressed in white robes with the initials HNDH embroidered in a deep red color on both sides of their collars. Their harmony down to their swaying movements were synchronized to the rhythm of the organ and drums. When the lead singer's contralto voice stressed an octave, the choir blended the same words into their respected vocal ranges. Season, who was in no mood for church, could feel the spirit of the choir's aesthetic tribute to the Lord. She caught herself a couple of times swaying to the music and singing the refrain part of the song. Her legs wanted her to rise from the wooden pew she was sitting on and join in on devotional service, but after spotting her superior on the choir stand, she thought against it. She was not going to give her aunt any satisfaction of seeing herself enjoying church service. Autumn, who noticed Season's reluctance from the choir stand, gave Season a deliberate smile as she continued to stay in rhythm with the rest of the choir.

Apart from the choir, Season didn't care too much for the place of worship. The church and parishioners reminded her so much of a stereotypical Southern black church she saw in movies and display in artwork, extensive and uncomfortable! The air reeked of peppermint, old women perfume, and perspiration. Not to mention the temperature of the place! The cooling unit wasn't any match for the overpopulated space. It also didn't help when people were standing up and joining in with the choir. She felt as if she was a single Pez candy fitting tightly into a dispenser. She had to sit up for others to have space in the pew. People were continually fanning themselves with either Dr. Martin Luther King or Former President Barack Obama fans. She couldn't get a good view of the church's front because of the older women's flamboyant church hats decorated in pastel-colored tulle. When the choir finally finished their selection, Season was able to peer across one lady's hat to assess the rest of the church.

The left section in front of the church was occupied by the deacons, who were at least seven old men dressed in their full suits. The building's fluorescent lights shined on top of their bald heads. They were cheering on the lead singer with "C'mon, Dorsey…," and, "Yass sir!" and "Aight 'nah," as they were stomping their feet to the music.

The right section was occupied by the deaconesses, which looked to be the old men's wives. Each of these ladies either wore a broach or a corsage pinned to the lapel of their dress. They appeared formidable, wearing only conservative clothes with nothing out of place; no-slip hanging, no breast showing, no tight-fitting clothing, or no dresses above their knees: the "no naked legs" section. Each lady wore either grey or sheer colored stockings with closed-toe shoes. They sat in the area with white-laced towels placed on their laps like scarves. They appeared dignified but haughty to Season as they looked out at the congregation, taking fashion police's role, ready to stop any young person from violating the church dress code. Earlier, she was greeted by one of those women. The woman stopped to welcome both Autumn and Season but stopped mid-sentence after looking Season up and down.

"And who's this child?" asked the arrogant lady with her nose already stuck up in the air.

"Oh yes, Sis. Applegate, this is my niece, Season. She will be staying the summer with me. She came all the way from Columbia."

Sis. Applegate continued looking at Season with a small look of disgust, "Mmh, Columbia? I guess the church attire has gotten away from the city folks? Gal, where's your stockings?"

Season looked down proudly at her attire, wearing a yellow sundress with matching yellow open-toe sandals.

She thought she looked cute and was personally showing her aunt up when it came down to fashion. She didn't know she would be bombarded with other people who dressed like her aunt.

"Well, since it is a nice and humid day, I thought that I was dressed for the occasion. It's too hot to wear stockings, ma'am," stated Season with a shrewd, plastered smile on her face.

"Autumn! You should know better. Why would you let this child out of the house like that?"

Autumn, too embarrassed to say anything, didn't make any comments.

"And don't tell me that's Summer's child."

"Yes ma'am, it is," Autumn answered, barely a whisper.

"Mmh, well, that explains it."

"What's that supposed to mean?" asked Season, giving the old lady a nasty glare.

Autumn cleared her throat to remind Season to not be disrespectful. It was a cheap shot for Sis. Applegate to take, but Autumn refused to give the woman any satisfaction that her niece was incapable of being handled.

"It means that Summer should've told you better!" vilified Mrs. Applegate, surprised at the young girl's demeanor.

"Excuse me? Lady, my mother is dead, and I would appreciate it if you don't speak about her in that manner. Or, are you so full of yourself to show any compassion?" yelled Season as tears came to her eyes.

Autumn, realizing trouble was about to brew, grasped Season by the arm and gave an apologetic look to a stunned Sis. Applegate. "I apologize, Mrs. Applegate. She's going through a lot right now. Let me talk to her."

Before Sis. Applegate could apologize to Season, Autumn whisked her away to one of the bathrooms located at the back of the church to calm her down. Reflecting on what happened before church, Season couldn't help but to stay mad at Sis. Applegate.

Season was about to look away from the section until she noticed how the women's eyes were directed to the front pew. *Clearly, they had their sights set on victim #2,* she thought as she moved around in her seat to see who the poor prey was. She was about to give up until she saw a young girl at least a year or so older than she was sitting in the front pew. In addition to the few women sitting in the pews far left, the poor girl was sitting at the far right with her head hanging down. From where Season sat, she could only see the back of the child's head. The snooty deaconess section were vipers, ready to attack the girl if need be. Season did not understand the look of disdain on their face or why the young girl decided to sit in that spot. Undoubtedly, someone had to make her sit there as a form of punishment. But for what?

After the choir selection, it was the preacher's turn to deliver his sermon. As he approached the podium, Season couldn't help but think how large he was. His black clerical robe was so tight on him that he was choking in the neck department. His face was covered with beads of sweat as if he preached five sermons this morning.

"Let the church say, 'Amen,' C'mon church, amen!" his voice rolled throughout the sanctuary.

"Amen," voices rang back.

"Now, before I get into the word of today, let me first recognize the beautiful and wise mother of our church, Mother Winnie. Rise up, Mama Winnie, and show the congregation the nice dress you have on!"

Everyone clapped as two women ushers helped an elderly lady sitting in the first pew with the young adolescent girl. Soon as she was up to her feet, one of the deacons gave her a cordless mic to speak in. She turned around to provide the congregation with a wave and held the mic to her mouth.

"Tink ye, Tink ye. First, me tink me savior Gawd fa 'llowin me ta see one mo' day. His grace 'n mercy es da reason me here now. Passa Hollis, deacons, deaconess, and everybody in their respected place, me 'preciate da warm 'knowledgement from me church. Me haf a testimony ta give tis mornin', Passa, If ya don't mind me ta do so,"

"Go ahead, Mama Winnie! Take your time!" yelled Pastor Hollis from the pulpit.

Season, getting agitated from the extensive service anyway, dropped her head in her palms. How long would this testimony be? They began service with a long testimony service, so why didn't she speak then?

"Me been gawin' ta dis church since me was a youngin'.

I got baptized, saved, and married here. Dis place is me roots. Gawd blessed me ta see 93 years on dis Earth, and me neva had ta worry 'bout nothing. Me raised six kids with me husband until he left me ta be with da Lord. Oh gosh, me wonder how I got ova then!"

"By the Lord, Mama, by the Lord!" yelled someone in the congregation.

"Yes....Yes, Gawd favored me well through me life, yall. Me had ta raise dem chullen' at 2, 4, 6, 8, 10, and 12."

Sounds of wonders and sympathy filled the place as the church mother called out her children's ages as if she was reciting her numbers in twos.

"Naw, it wasn't easy, but me kept workin' at dat school-house day in and day out til me got the tree youngest ones in college, HALLELUJAH!"

The congregation and pastor hollered back a hallelujah praise.

"HALLELUJAH! Ya see, them otha ones thought they were grown and decided to up and find them a career out-side of South Carolina, but me taught them my Lawd's ways befo they left. Ya know me had some trouble wit me third youngin'; she was on that stuff and was in da streets. Me was worried and tired, but me membered wat me mama use ta tell me. She would say, 'Winnie, if ya worry, don't tink 'bout prayin'. So, me left it in me Lawd's hands, and she left me with tree youngin' ta raise! Me thought me child raisin' days were gone! Wat an old ooman wit a fixed income doin raisin' tree more kids?"

"Mmmh mmh," hummed some ladies in the deaconess section while shaking their heads.

Oh Lord, when will this ever end? Thought Season as she took in a deep breath.

"But lemme tell ya something, Me thought 'bout what Jesus tole his disciple Peta, and me could tink wat da Lawd would say ta me. Me tell ya. Da Lawd tole me, "Winnie… oh Winnie, da enemy desired for ya ta be sifted as wheat!'

"My Lord," mumbled someone from the back of the church.

"Magine being decomposed less than a grain of salt. So fragile that ya turn into a substance dat can conform to any solution. So fragile that a single blow could dismiss you from da grace of Gawd."

"Speak," chimed in Pastor Hollis, hitting the podium with his fist.

"But Lawd! My Lawd says, 'Mercy says no!' Da enemy already got ta my granddaughter, Serene," she pointed out as she turned to the young girl who was sitting on the other end of the same pew she was sitting in. "Got in them streets and play round till she got some trouble in her stomach. I had ta drag her to church dis mornin' and sat her on the front pew. We gotta pray dat evil spirit out of her, Passa. Da sin is not in dat child's stomach, but her devilish actions got to go!"

Season's mouth dropped as she looked at the young girl who was affectionately known as Serene. How could any adult bring it upon themselves to sit a young child to the church's front because of teen pregnancy? Of course, it was an issue, but it was not a rare issue. Back home, Season witnessed a lot of girls who were pregnant between the ages of fourteen and seventeen, but to drag the child to church to expose her sins to a crowd was absurd.

"Ya know what we haf ta do, Passa!" yelled Winnie as she gave Pastor Hollis a hard stare as if they shared some secret between them.

"Yes, we do. But for now, let's pray for her," suggested Pastor Hollis while reaching underneath his podium to pull out something. His hands came back up with a small bottle of virgin oil. "Dis will have ta do for now. Members, come up and circle around the child as I pray for her."

"This is insane," responded Season quietly to herself. She looked around as the members rushed to the front to get close to the young girl. Season could see the pitiful girl looking around with tears of horror in her eyes. She expected Serene to be at least humiliated by her grandmother's actions, but to witness the expression on Serene's face was far more intense than just a mere shame. It was something frightening and bizarre that Season could not put her fingers on. As Season noticed the large crowd circling Serene, she spotted her aunt still on the choir stand. Autumn appeared to be staring at Season with tears rolling down her face. It wasn't a sense of sympathy for the young child, but a sense of fear.

"I don't mean any disrespect, but don't take me to that church again," demanded Season as she slammed her aunt's door. They had finally made it back home from church that afternoon, and Season couldn't get over what had happened earlier out of her mind. It bothered her so much that she couldn't even listen to Pastor Hollis' sermon. Everyone at the church was treating the poor girl as if she had a sickness. The numerous people speaking in tongues when the pastor placed his oily hands on Serene's forehead was enough for Season to get up out of her seat and run for the border. She didn't know how to take her aunt's face when looking at her, but something deep inside told Season that her aunt disagreed with the church's actions as well.

"Season, I'm not about to have this conversation with you," sighed Autumn as she got out of her car. "Let's just go in the house, and I'll prepare Sunday dinner."

"Don't tell me that you agree to this blasphemy of a church! How could they do that to the poor girl?"

Autumn sighed once more and said, "No, I don't agree to certain things in church; today was just one of them. I can agree with you that it was distasteful to do so."

"So why would you go to a church like that?" asked Season.

"Honey, I've been going to that church since I was little, and so did your mother. I can't leave a church that my parents helped build with their blood, sweat, and tears. Besides, it's not too many churches here in Hollins to choose from. I guess old customs die hard," she responded, saying the last sentence quietly to herself.

Season couldn't understand the excuses that were spewing from her aunt's mouth. Clearly, she had some attachment issues, not only to this town but also to her church. The more she thought about it, the sicker it made her feel. "How far is the beach from here?"

Autumn, who was in a thinking state, finally looked at Season. "How far is what?"

"How far is the beach from here?" asked Season once again.

"The beach, yes! It's walking distance from here. You can cut across the backyard field, and it would be 10-15-minutes walking distance from here straight across. Do you want me to take you?

"No, I can manage," retorted a disgusted Season as she made her way to the backyard.

"Be careful out there," yelled Autumn. "When you get back, there are some things I do need to discuss with you."

Oh gosh, now what? This place never ceases to amaze me, thought Season as she walked past her aunt's garden to get to the fields.

Season approached the ocean with her head hanging down in deep despair. She was still in awe of the situation she was brought into, a strange town with strange people she was growing to despise, not to mention an estranged militant aunt who wanted things her way. Season sensed this as a way for her father to punish her for her wrongdoings.

"If only my mother was alive to witness such things, she would have never exposed me to this craziness," she said to herself. She looked up to take a view of the ocean and was in an immediate standstill. All the negative thoughts that were in her mind swept away as the tropical scenery pushed in comfort. The sun's rays rested gracefully on the patterns of each wave's patches, emphasizing the value of its richness and fluidity. Strangely, she felt she was on hallowed grounds. As if she was told by a small voice, she obediently took off her open-toe shoes and embedded them into the smooth sand. She swayed to the ambiance of the sea and breathed in its allurement of distinctive smells of saline and algae. The voice once again told her to run, so she ran. She was jogging at first, enjoying the cold, smooth grain of the white sand beneath her feet as she imprinted on it. As she began to pick up speed, a cool breeze from the wind welcomed her, and she returned it with a smile. For the first time since she came to Hollins, she felt welcomed and relaxed, unburdened from the pain she was receiving in life. She ran as fast as she could along the coast, not being cautious as to what she was stepping on or what hurdle was coming her way. She felt free.

After having a moment to run freely, she began to retire to the great sea. As she approached the oceanfront, she dropped to her knees to take a closer look at her reflection in the water. The water wasn't as clear and glistening as the water in Jamaica. She took a family trip there with her parents when she was around eight and had a marvelous time there. To say the water there was wondrous would have been an understatement. To Season, it was magical having both of her parents there to enjoy each other, and the setting was bigger than going to Disneyworld at her age. The water she was gazing at now was almost close to the feeling, but not quite.

As she looked at her reflection, the small ripples gave her face a sort of distorted look. It embodied her existence, a slanted and foul reality that was mistreated in life. She took her hand in anger and slapped the water vigorously until some splashes landed in her eyes. Forgetting it was saltwater, she rubbed her eyes but made it worse. As she looked down to open them wider, she saw her reflection again, but only this time, it wasn't distorted. It was placed in a small unsolidified square surrounded by other patched squares. It seemed the ocean stopped moving so she could clearly see herself. Then suddenly, there appeared a reflective form placed on a squared right next to her reflection. The form looked to be a human being, considering not only its head was being reflected but its whole body. She turned around slowly and noticed a young boy standing almost beside her, looking down at her.

"Oh, I'm sorry, I didn't know anyone else was here," said Season as she quickly got up and wiped the wet sand off her dress.

The stranger looked a lot younger than she was with a small, frizzy afro on top of his head. He had a browned caramel shade that accentuated his thick eyebrows and droopy eyes. He was a little on the short side, around 5'2, couldn't possibly weigh more than 105 pounds. His arms were long and lanky, like a praying mantis. He was dressed in pure white, from a white button shirt to a white bottom capris. His clothes fitted too small on him, like he was wearing a younger sibling's clothing. Not to mention how malnourished the poor child looked. To Season, he wasn't all that attractive, but wasn't unappealing. He looked as if he was a poor ward of the state and needed a good tending to.

Season waited for the boy to respond, but he didn't say anything. She decided to try again, hoping he could respond back.

"Hi, I'm Season, Season Holidae. I know my name may sound sort of funny, and yes, my parents named me that to go with the last name. They had a weird sense of humor," she stated as she rolled her eyes. She held out her hand for a handshake, but the poor boy looked at it surprisingly.

Season gave him the same look back, surprised the boy didn't understand what a handshake meant. "You're supposed to shake it. It's called a handshake. It is a common sign of a greeting gesture to most people."

The boy hesitantly held out his right hand to touch her hand, and she shook it. She noticed how small and soft his hand was, as if he soaked and moisturized it for hours. It felt so strange and so fragile that Season quickly let go of it.

"You see, no biggie," she replied, faking a quick smile.

The boy returned the smile.

"So, um-do, you have a name?"Season asked.

The boy looked down as if he was thinking of answering her question. He slowly looked up and responded, "Yusef."

Season did not expect such a deep voice to come from a young boy, but she was glad he responded all the same.

"Yusef, huh? Well, how old are you, Yusef?"

Once again, he hesitated before giving a response. "I'm-I'm fifteen, I guess."

"You guess? How do you 'guess' you're fifteen?" Season inquired in a puzzled tone.

"Yes, I'm fifteen," he said, now confident.

"Are you sure? You know, you don't have to lie about your age."

The boy gave Season a look of discernment. "I don't lie. I can never tell a lie."

Season figured she probably hit a nerve and didn't want him to feel like she was offending him. "I'm sorry, Yusef. I'm not calling you a liar," she quickly apologized.

"Then why mention the word 'lie'?" he questioned.

"Well, I assumed you didn't know how old you were or if you were thinking of telling me an age. I apologize for my ignorance."

"It's okay," he smiled once again.

Whew! That was close! Season thought, this time returning the smile.

"You're not from around here, are you?" Yusef asked.

"Let me guess, my dialect told on me?"

"No, I just have never seen you around before."

"Well, that's one thing you got right. I'm from Columbia."

"Columbia? Where's that?" Yusef asked with a confused look on his face.

"You haven't heard of Columbia? Are you serious? It's like the capital of this state," answered Season in bewilderment.

"I'm sorry, I can't say I've heard of such a place," Yusef replied, dropping his head as if he failed at knowing something so trivial.

Season felt sorry for the poor guy. He was totally clueless and ignorant of the world around him. *Living in this place could absolutely confine you to ignorance. Case in point, this guy standing in front of me,* she thought. She knew she had to make one good friend in this God-forsaken place if she was going to survive the whole summer here. She might as well start with him.

"So Yusef, what is there to do in Hollins? What do you like to do?"

Yusef gave her a dubious look and browsed around. "I guess hang out here. I don't live too far."

"Oh, really? Man, it must be cool to wake up early in the morning to have a view like this."

"Oh, please, this is amazing. Of course, my dad does have his timeshare at Myrtle Beach; we would go there every summer."

"Myrtle Beach?"

"Oh gosh, don't tell me you haven't heard of Myrtle Beach."

"No, can't say that I have."

"Whoa, dude! You need to get out more. Where's the furthest place you have been?"

"Me? Well, I haven't stepped foot out of Hollins before."

"Oh, my gosh! Are you serious?"

"Sadly, yes. I do wish to do so one day."

"Well, tell your parents to hurry up and plan somewhere to take you."

Yusef hung his head once again. Season sensed something was wrong, but she didn't want to open that door, so she changed the conversation. "So, how's school down here? What is it like?"

"School? Nah, I'm homeschooled," Yusef responded quickly.

"Homeschool? Are you kidding? I would literally die if I had to stay at home all year long to learn about the world around me. What about your social skills?"

"Well, the kids here are few, not a lot of them around. The few that are here clearly don't want to be my friends. Instead, they ignore me. They don't even care to acknowledge my presence."

"Mmh, that's not nice," Season frowned.

"Well, kids can be cruel, but the grownups can be the worst!"

"Tell me about it. You should've come to church service with me. The way this old woman humiliated her own grandchild because she was a pregnant teen. Like that's an uncommon sort of thing! Teens get pregnant every day. I'm not saying I condone it, but I don't condone grownups embarrassing and provoking adolescents as well. It's like we can't make any mistakes in life, only adults. That's so hypocritical of them to think so."

"Well, I can tell you right now, Season. This sort of thing is frowned upon by the ole' folks here. It is strictly forbidden, and they will not tolerate it," Yusef warned, giving Season a solemn look.

"So, what are they going to do? Cry to the pastor about it? Drag pregnant girls to the altar so they could cleanse them of their evil deeds? The action has already been done, so what could they possibly do? Beat the baby out of them?

Yusef whispered one word that made Season's skin crawl. "Worse," he responded. "Much worse."

Chapter 5:

WORKING TO BUILD CHARACTER

a week in Hollins passed slowly but bearably as Season spent most of that week on the beach with her new friend, Yusef. He was really growing on her, in a big brother kind of way. The more time she spent with him, the more he became a mystery to her. He never spoke about where he lived or his family. He told her that he lived with his alcoholic father and never knew his mother; she walked out on them when he was just a baby. After hearing this, Season grew closer to him.

Almost similarly, but her mother died and left them alone, but she also knew the massive void of a missing parent and how it can affect any child. She made it an obligation to visit him often and learn more about him. She discovered that they both love to swim and read books, so she brought some novels along with her so they could read together. It was her father's idea for her to bring her 8th-grade summer reading list to complete before school in August. She didn't mind at all, considering her avidness for reading classical and contemporary young adult novels. It was a good way to pass the time besides spending the entire summer getting into mischief with Suki.

For the past week, Season nor Autumn spoke about what happened. Instead, Autumn gave Season the option to stay home and clean up. Season wasn't going to argue because she would rather chop wood or clean toilets than go back to that satanic church. So, Season stayed home, did her chores, and went to visit Yusef at the beach. She could sense her aunt was curious as to why she was spending all her time there. *I guess she understands the concept of minding her own business,* she thought with a smirk.

She got up early, showered, and put on a t-shirt and shorts. She was hoping to bypass her aunt but couldn't bring herself to leave out the door without the smell of her aunt's cooking entrapping her to sit down and eat. As she sat down, her aunt's back was facing her as she was busy scrambling some eggs. Season scowled at her, despising how much she loved Autumn's home-cooked meal but not her attitude.

Autumn turned away from the stove with a pan full of scrambled eggs and faced Season with a weird smile on her face. "So, where are you venturing today? Oh, let me guess, to the beach again?"

Or maybe she didn't get the concept, Season thought

again, slumping in her seat as her aunt placed the steamy eggs beside two thick slabs of bacon, creamy yellow grits, and one homemade golden croissant on Season's plate.

"Yep, is that a crime?" Season retorted.

Autumn looked at her niece with a smile. "No, I'm just getting clarification. To be honest, I would like to know as to why you want to spend all your time over there."

"No reason." Season replied quickly as she mixed her eggs with her grits.

"Well, I was off all last week, so I could've spent some time with you. Now, I have to start work in about an hour or so, and I would like to talk to you before I leave."

Interestedly, Season gave her aunt her undivided attention. She didn't know a thing about her, only that she was a damn good cook and a committed gardener. Not to mention, worshipped with evil, old people. "Where do you work?"

"At a home health care agency called *Heaven Sent*. I'm a certified RN there," she beamed proudly.

"Oh," Season replied as she went back to her meal.

"Besides gardening, I love nursing. It makes me feel like I'm giving back to a community that helped raise me when I was a young girl like yourself. Giving back builds integrity inside. It makes you appreciate what you have and not take anything for granted. You'll learn to appreciate your hard work and the sweat and tears you put into something just by earning your living," she remarked, sitting down at the table to eat her breakfast.

Season didn't respond. She knew her aunt was trying to get at something but was unsure where she was heading with the conversation.

"Which leads me to my next point of discussion. I talked to Mrs. DeVeau, who is the chief librarian at Hollins Public Library downtown. I put in a good word for you to help her out at the library. I told her how much you love to read books, and it would be a good opportunity for you to work there to earn your keeps."

"You did what?!" Season squealed, dropping her fork on the plate. She couldn't believe her aunt's initiative to go behind her back to find her a job, especially at a library! Yes, she loved books and wouldn't mind reading a massive novel during long rainy days, but to have her first job working at a library? Her aunt was getting on her last nerve.

"What? I don't see a problem with you helping out at the library. Besides, you are trying to build character while you're here. It will prove to Xavier that you've tried to win back his trust. You can't spend the rest of your summer break lounging by the ocean," pointed out Aunt Season as she lifted a forkful of grits to her mouth.

Season thought about her aunts' rationale for a minute. Of course, she wanted to win back not only her father's trust but his love. To her, it was like the magic of "family" disappeared into thin air after Holidae's passing; yet ironically, Season lived in the literal season without as much love and nurture coming from her father. Maybe her aunt had a point in all this, but still…. a library?

"Mrs. DeVeau wouldn't be so interested in me once she hears about my kleptic-past," she snapped as she got up from her chair to put her empty dish and fork in the sink. "She wouldn't dare hire someone like me to tend to her precious books."

"Oh, don't worry. I've told Mrs. DeVeau everything about you," Autumn fired back with a smile.

Season was revolted, to say the least. Her aunt never ceased to amaze her. She was uncomfortable with her aunt sharing her business with a perfect stranger.

"I wasn't going to let you work there without informing her about you. Honesty is a narrow pathway where others can't seem to walk on. There are no shortcuts in life, Season. You will come to realize how the truth can hurt, but it builds trusting relationships. My advice to you? You need to make better choices to avoid humiliations. Mrs. DeVeau is a dear and trusting friend. Don't worry, you can rely on her. She's different from the others in Hollins. She's been a friend of this family for a long time, and when it comes to her word, it's bonded. Honest people deserve the honest truth. She would never hold your past against you; instead, she gives people time to grow and learn from their mistakes. Trust me, you will absolutely love her! You will start on Wednesday from 9 am to 3 pm, so you can't be late on your first day." Autumn beamed.

"Yeah, okay. Whatever," Season snapped as she was about to head out the door.

"Um, one more thing," Autumn responded hesitantly. The mellow tone she had went away quickly and was replaced with a voice of dismay.

"Come sit down; this is very important," her aunt instructed her.

An annoyed Season dragged her feet as she came back to the dinner table. She decided to entertain her aunt — anything to get out of this house to see Yusef.

"There were some things that I meant to tell you once you were here, but I was sidetracked in other matters, and you were always on the go," Autumn explained with a look of wariness in her eyes.

After sensing her aunt's suspicion, she could tell this part of the discussion was worth hearing. Summer used to tell Season that she had more senses than Spiderman; she could sense anything from a mile away. Season had to hand it to her mother; she was right. There was a chilling cloud hovering over the kitchen table, and it didn't sit right with her.

"When I gave you the few house rules last week, I failed to mention other rules."

Season gave her aunt a perplexed look. "What other rules? You mean, there are more house rules? Are you serious?"

"No, no, no, Dear. There's no more house rules," she chuckled nervously. "However, there are some rules set by the town of Hollins.'

"Huh?!" Season gasped.

"Yes, there are some rules set by the mayor of this town for everyone to follow. Most of those rules were made before I was even born, and a few were added last year, especially after what happened," explained Autumn, nearly more to herself than to Season.

"Hold up! What type of rules? And what happened last year?"

"Oh, don't worry about that, Season. Just know that there are rules we must abide by, and while you are here, you must abide by them as well. Since you love going rogue on me, I would rather for you to know so you won't get yourself into any trouble with the locals. You're a very stubborn girl, Season Holidae, and learning that about you scares me to death," she croaked while revealing a tear from the corners of her eyes.

"What are you talking about? I don't know what you're saying. What are the rules?"

"To begin with, curfew for children starts at 9:00pm. Street lights come on way before then. So, to avoid any consequences, I need you home before those lights come on.

"WHAT?!" Season shrieked.

"I'm sorry, but it's the only way to guarantee you're in by then. I will do check-ins."

"What's the meaning behind this?" Season demanded.

"I'm not finished," Autumn replied while putting both hands up. "You're to come to church with me every Sunday. There will be no muss, no fuss. I gave you a break last Sunday and told the members that you had a terrible cold."

"I'm sorry, but I'm not going back to that church!"

"It's not optional, Season. Long dresses or skirts with stockings are appropriate. No open-toe shoes, no skin showing, nothing."

"How—"

"If there's a boy you meet in this town, or if you've already met him at the beach, you might as well forget about it because the congeniality between you two will only result in consequences you won't be able to pay!"

"Is this because of that girl? Because she got pregnant? Who would make up rules based on a teenager's bad choice to have sex?"

"It's more than that. More than I could care to get into."

"No, let's get into it. What's going on with this town? I'm sorry, but this is ridiculous. How do you expect me to meet anyone?"

"There's nothing wrong with meeting new people. I can imagine being in a new place with no one to talk to. It can put a strain on your social life. Season, heed my words. Everyone here is not what they appeared to be."

Season was beginning to get agitated with her aunt's idle warnings. She could tell by Autumn's distress counsels that something was unsettling about this town, but until Autumn explains the whats and whys, Season would have to walk blindfolded.

"So, baby curfews, strict dress codes, and no cooties. Got it. Now, may I please leave?!" Season snapped, jumping up from the table.

"You think this is a joke, Season?"

"I'm not laughing, Aunt Autumn. You're the one giving commands, so it's your world, your way."

"Then why do I feel as if I'm throwing caution to the wind?"

"Maybe because you're not explaining the reason for the caution."

Aunt Autumn shook her head at her attempts. She didn't want to explain more than she had to. Doing so might make it worse for her niece. "You're just like Summer, never wanting to listen or take heed to anything."

Season snapped, "Well, maybe that's why she was able to leave this blasphemous town!"

Autumn was about to counteract what Season threw out but decided against it. Instead held her head down. Once again, Season walked to the door and was about to turn the knob.

"One more rule, don't ever let the sun catch you down at that beach. So, no trespassing after 8:00 pm, or they will spot you."

Season was about to ask who were "they," but that would be another dead-end question with no response. She hurried out of the house successfully.

"So, what I'm hearing is that you're in Creepville, South Carolina with a crazy-ass aunt who thinks someone or something is out to get kids?" asked a confused Suki on Season's phone.

Season decided to FaceTime Suki to rant about her disadvantages of staying off from home. She was on the woodland pathway to the beach. It had been three days since she contacted her best friend, and she needed to rave. Her dad seemed to not want to hear her out. After calling him numerous times, all she got from him was, "Stick it out." Suki, on the other hand, was her ace. If anyone left could understand her situation, it had to be Suki.

"Pretty much so. I don't know what's going on in this town, but I gotta get out of here, Suk. This place is driving me mad!"

"I would say, 'stick it out,' but your dad beat me to the punch," joked Suki as she laughed.

"That's not funny, Suk. If you were here, then you would agree that something is rotten in the town of Hollins."

"Okay, okay, enough with all the Shakespeare, drama queen. Let me think."

There was a pause on both ends of the line. Season picked up a twig to throw it as far as she could in the open field out of anger.

"I have a cousin who goes to USC Beaufort down there. Maybe you two can link up. She's really cool; we spent last summer together."

"Are you talking about Darhia?"

"Yeah, remember her? She took us to the Gamecocks homecoming that time."

"Oh, wow, I haven't thought about that!"

"Maybe she can rescue you. How far is Hollins from Beaufort?"

"About fifteen to twenty minutes, I want to say,"

"Awesome! Just give me the word, and she would be there."

"Thanks, I'll let you know when to bring the Calvary."

"Sure thing, speaking of Calvary, when are you going to tell me more about the mysterious Yusef?"

"Oh, it's nothing," replied a sheepish Season as she walked toward two sand dunes leading to her destination site."

"Yeah, right, girl. I haven't spoken to you in three days. I guess Romeo is getting all my friend's attention."

"He's definitely not a Romeo…more like a Mercutio."

"Hold up, partna! I'm like your Mercutio!" Suki exclaimed with a feigned look of jealousy.

Season laughed. "You're a mess. You know you're my day one since the sun, so don't trip."

"I'm not tripping, just saying," said Suki, returning the laugh. "So, what's wrong? He's not dreamy enough?"

Season looked around to see if she could spot Yusef, but there wasn't any sign of him yet, so she spoke freely. "No… he's just—"

"Just what?"

"He's just weird, but a good weird. Not the type of weird you don't want to associate yourself with, but the type of weird that makes you want to know more about him."

"Interesting…" Suki chimed in with a thoughtful look.

"I know my aunt warned me about meeting anyone here, especially guys. But he's totally different. It's something about him that I can't put my finger on. I'm not attracted to him at all, but I feel attached to him. We have a few things in common. We both love to swim, maybe him a little more than I do. I have to drag him out the water sometimes before he drowns."

"Wow, a person who loves swimming more than you do? That's crazy!"

"Right? He's not that literate when it comes down to reading. He enjoys picture books more than he enjoys reading it. He absolutely loves it when I read to him. He would lay down in the sand and place his arms behind his head to relax. He looks so peaceful doing just that."

"Hold up! I'm confused. What kind of love jones is this? First, you say you're not attracted to him, but you're watching this fifteen-year-old fall asleep as you're reading. He's not a comprehensive reader, but you're reading him bedtime stories?"

"Wait, Suki! What are you talking about? I'm not reading him bedtime stories."

"You might as well be. You're reading, and he's relaxing. You're acting as if he's your child, and you're his mother."

Season frowned after thinking about what Suki was insinuating. "I don't get that at all, Suk."

"Well, it seems to me that you want to be a protector," claimed Suki.

"And what's wrong with that? Besides his alcoholic father, he doesn't have anyone," explained Season.

"Except you, right?"

"What's that supposed to mean?"

"Maybe you should listen to what your aunt is telling you."

"Wait, I thought you were on my side."

"I am and always will be. But what you told me about these people, just be careful out there, Season."

"Look, I think I'm a good judge of character, Suki. Besides, Yusef is harmless."

"Maybe so, but remember what your aunt told you. You're down there to build your character."

"Meaning?"

"Meaning, as you are building character, you have to be cautious of the characters around you," Suki warned.

A hot breeze aroused the temperate air as the clouds revealed the early afternoon at the beach. Season and Yusef were having the time of their lives, not allowing grief to have any authority over their present childhood being spent. They played tag while trying to run in the silk sand, they built a massive sand castle surrounded by a deep filled water moat, and they swam closely together like a school of fishes in the ocean.

Later, they walked along the coast for a while, talking about their dreams. Season wanted to be a world-renowned professional swimmer and Yusef, a captain of a huge ship, circumnavigating the rambunctious seas searching for real treasures. Season thought his dream was sort of infantile, reminding her of children's aspirations of unicorns, Easter bunnies, Peter Pan, and Captain Hook; stories parents used to impart hope and courage in toddlers. Of course, she didn't want to be the one to blow out his candle of imagination. Perhaps, that's what she loved most about him – his innocence. After her mother's death, the courage to dream the impossible was placed on hold. So, what right did she have for taking one's dreams away?

They ended their enjoyable late afternoon sitting in the sand, facing the water with Season reading *The Giver*, by Loris Lowry. It was one of the books from her summer reading list she had to complete. Yusef, lying in the sand, was in a deep thought after Season finished the last page of chapter four.

"Truly amazing," remarked Yusef to himself.

"What is?" asked Season as she placed a bookmark between two pages and closed the book. They began reading the book a couple of days ago; two chapters a visit was what they agreed upon.

"It's amazing how one person can interpret your views

or feelings of a place where you're living, as if the person lived in the same place as you."

Season thought on what Yusef was saying but didn't comment. Instead, she looked out upon the ocean where the tides were harshly coming upstream.

"The civilization that was described in this book seems to be pretty strict and unpleasant," continued Yusef. "As if the author was talking about Hollins."

Season let out a small chuckle in agreement to Yusef's comparison. "I haven't thought about it like that, but you may have a point. The deception of the setting is placed as a Utopian community, but it's clearly a dystopian."

"What's the difference?" asked Yusef.

"Well, utopia is more like a heavenly place where people can live harmoniously together without causing issues. It is like a dream island with endless resources satisfying everyone. Dystopian is the total opposite. It's dark… it's bleak… it's a systematic prison ruled by overambitious assholes with only one single concept and endless set of rules."

"Is it kind of like Heaven and Hell?" asked Yusef, giving Season an innocent look.

"I guess you can say that if it helps you to know the difference between the two."

"You know the young boy in the book? Jonas? He reminds me of you," Yusef stated with a smile.

"How so?"

"Well, kinda. Jonas was born and raised in his

community, so that made a difference. But you both experience feelings and situations differently than the citizens in both communities."

Season was a bit surprised by Yusef's comprehension and analysis of the main character. This was in no way a simple bedtime story for this guy. Suki was wrong.

"You're both in a place where nothing makes sense, including the rules. What your aunt told you was just the tip of the iceberg."

Season's eyes grew larger from what Yusef was telling her. "You mean there's more?"

Yusef looked away from Season and shook his head.

"Who comes up with these rules?"

"Beats me," Yusef shrugged. "Let's just say that this town is more than what meets the eye, and you don't want to get involved in any sort of way."

"Try me," Season dared.

"Well, have you noticed the insufficiency of children here?" Yusef inquired.

"You know, I have wondered about that and asked my aunt about it, but she told me that Hollins is predominately a senior citizen zone, and many of the younger generations moved out after reaching eighteen."

"Mh," Yusef mumbled, picking up a fistful of sand. "By the time a child reaches thirteen, he or she is groomed to be adults. Meaning no after school playtime or activities. They are expected to have a job in town. There are children here, but they just act and dress more maturely than you and me. It's a way to 'grow character,' they would say."

Season was taken back by the term 'character' and covered her hand with her mouth as she realized her aunt's words being played back as a recorder. "Wait, how is that mandatory? How is that legal? South Carolina Child labor laws don't ring a bell for anyone here?"

"Well, did that law stop the community Jonas was living in?" asked Yusef.

"That's different, Yusef! The book is fiction."

"A book has a way of revealing the truth through fabricated elements, Season," Yusef pointed out. "If you asked me to write a fictional story, I could write it, but my ideas had to be inspired by some kind of truth in the real world."

Season nodded her head in agreement and realized this guy was very astute and sincere in how he felt. Clearly, she was the one who felt ignorant for undermining his intelligence.

"As the teenagers begin to mature, they are to continue their lessons in adulthood by attending services in Hollins New Deliverance Holiness, which is also known as the "Grand Chapel." In this way, they are raised not only by their parents but by the community. Not only are they raised but assigned to their lifelong partners."

"Excuse me? You mean to tell me that the church assigns arranged marriages?"

"Well, yes. It's Hollins's custom to oversee who should marry who. The only befitting suitor should come from the Grand Chapel. No outsiders. If so, that person will be ostracized from the community."

"So, there's only one church in Hollins?"

"Yes," replied Yusef, "Why are you surprised? Isn't it like that for all communities?"

"Oh, no. You see, there are many religions and many different cultures. People are not confined to one space like a cult. We all have choices to serve whomever we want to serve."

"Well, not here. Here, it's ruled by one thumb under God, so there should be one church to unite everyone."

Season gave Yusef a crazed look as if what he was saying only made sense to him. "Who's the mayor of this town?"

"Mayor?"

"Yes, the elected bobble-head in charge of this place."

"Oh, you mean Pastor Hollis?"

"Wait! Hold up. You mean to tell me that the mayor of this town is also the pastor of Hollins New Deliverance Holiness?"

"Why, yes, only we don't refer to him as the 'mayor.' He is Hollins leader, a position inherited to him from a long lineage of the Hollis' clan."

"Oh my God!" Season exclaimed as she quickly jumped up and brushed the sand off her body. "Oh, no-"

Alarmed by her reaction, Yusef jumped up quickly as well. "What? What's wrong?"

"This town is an outrageous incubator for breeding a

demonic cult. I can't believe this! What was my dad thinking? I have to get out of here," yelled a hyperventilating
Season as she turned to make her exit toward the sand
dunes.

"Wait!" called out Yusef as he grabbed Season's wrist.

"Please get off of me!"

"No, wait…calm down, Season. There's no need to get
carried away. Don't leave."

"What do you mean 'no need to get carried away'? Are
you listening to what you just told me? Now, this funky
town is making some sense to me. It's telling me that I
need to get the hell out of dodge. I don't belong here," she
asserted.

"Please don't leave me. I can't stand it here by myself,"
cried Yusef as he let go of her wrist and walked away.

Season, surprised by Yusef's emotional outburst, followed Yusef. "What do you mean you can't stand it here?"

He slumped down in the sand and cried softly. Season
got on her knees and offered a sympathetic look.

"You don't understand, and you never will," spoke
Yusef softly as he looked out at the horizon.

"Then make me understand. What is it?" asked Season
once more.

"You have a home to go to. You have an aunt you can
go home to. I don't have anyone."

"But your dad—"

"My dad doesn't see me, Season. No one sees me. I'm
an invisible drifter to everyone here, except you. What

makes you so different?"

Season had a hard time comprehending what Yusef was saying, but it finally hit her. He didn't have anyone, and his drunk father failed to notice he had a son to raise into a man.

"Maybe because I'm invisible too, Yusef," she acknowledged as she looked out at the horizon as well.

"How so?"

"Before losing my mother, my father and I got along just fine. In fact, he gave me the name Season. You want to know why?"

"Why?"

"He told me that the word 'Season' is a reminder of a temporary sequence of good and bad. I must comprehend the two to appreciate humility."

"Your dad seems to be a Nurturer like Jonas' dad," Yusef stated with a genuine smile.

"Yeah, only Jonas' dad cared to give up a strange baby to be 'released.'"

"What do you think the book means by 'released'?" Yusef inquired.

"What do you think it means?" asked Season, giving Yusef a grim look.

"I don't think the idea of it is as good as its word."

"It's not. Let's just say it's a bad way of ostracizing someone from society."

Yusef thought for a moment before he spoke something that made Season tense again. "You mean, how the community comes together out to the beach some nights for the Righteous Ritual?"

"What?"

Yusef's face lit up as he got up quickly. "I-I um, just remembered that Dad likes his place cool before he gets home. I must go, or he'll get angry. Please, meet me back here around noon tomorrow! I want to hear more of the story," Yusef began running to the opposite place.

"Wait, Yusef, what were you saying about this ritual? Don't leave!" she yelled but could only see a speck of Yusef's white linen shirt.

She looked up to the sun and realized how rapidly it was coming down from the skies, leaving the beach to appear quite grayish and dull, and the wind began to pick up rather severely. As she looked to the ocean once more before leaving, she could not help but notice its waves. It appeared to take the form of giant white claws unclutching its hands as it traveled quickly up the oceanfront and collapsed hard as it hit the shoreline, leaving Season's feet flooded in water. It wasn't just any tidal waves a person witnessed on a day at the beach. These waves were unnaturally angry and were trying again to flood where she was standing. Attempting to turn around, she ended up slipping as the small current was trying to gravitate her back toward the ocean. She was terrified. She decided to quickly and vigorously crawl back to the dry sand, but not until she heard a faint sound coming from the sea. It was either a sound of cats meowing or of babies crying out loudly in her ears. It was not the type of cries for attention or fussiness or aggravating colic from a late-night bottle. It was cries from excruciating pain and demise. It was cries that terrified Season…cries that were imprinted on her heart and mind. She ran until she passed the divided dunes and made sure to not take a single look back, or whatever was out there would capture her.

Chapter 6:

A REPLACED SOLACE

*A*fter the horrific day at the beach, Season wasn't able to sleep. When she made it home that early evening, she locked every door in the house, including her room door. She sat in the room and tried calling her dad but was too traumatized to unlock her phone.

A tired Aunt Autumn came home from work around seven and decided to check in on Season. Autumn noticed her niece wasn't lounging around the front room, so she knocked on her door to see if the girl was in her room. She knocked a couple of times, but there was no response. She tried opening the door but realized it was locked.

"Season," she called out, "Why is this door locked? There should be no locked doors in this house. If you can't abide by—"

The door opened quickly, with a terrified Season coming out of the room. She hugged her aunt out of fear, making sure to not let her out of her grasp. Autumn, shocked and confused to finish her sentence, slowly returned the gesture and noticed how much Season was shaking.

"Hey, what's wrong, Season? What happened? Did something happen?"

Season, too disturbed to say anything, just held on to her aunt for dear life.

Her aunt didn't push the issue. Instead, she made her some hot cocoa and sat down with her at the table to watch her. Season felt a little better after taking a few sips but didn't want to be left alone. Sensing Season's vulnerability, Autumn ran Season a hot, lavender bath and tucked her into bed. She made sure not to leave Season's sight until Season was resting safely.

During the middle of the night, Season would toss and turn, hearing the same horrendous cries she heard earlier. When it became unbearable, Season woke up in a cold sweat screaming. Autumn, who was asleep in a rocking chair not far from the bed, woke up and went to the poor child's side, wiped the sweat from her face, and asked her again what happened. Season did not want to revive the scene. Instead, she decided not to fall asleep.

It was the same routine for Tuesday night as well. Sleep was irrelevant. Season opted not to go back to the beach the next day, despite what Yusef wanted. He wasn't there to witness such a horrific event. Season decided to listen to her aunt and not return to the beach until she gets some answers.

It was a sunny Wednesday morning and Season was in bed with her eyes wide open, with her feet tucked under her, and her hands clasped to the comforter she was under. There was a time when she believed and feared the boogeyman or a paranormal entity she watched in movies. *Maybe it was just my imagination. There are no such things as monsters, sadistic killer clowns, or ghastly cries from the ocean. Perhaps it was the sound of how the waves came crashing that made me fear for my life. Yeah, that was it! But it seemed so real,* thought Season. She was never great at rationalizing anything that didn't make sense to her, which made her fear what she did not understand.

She grabbed for her phone on the nightstand beside the bed. She scanned through her contact list until she saw her dad's number appear and tapped on his name to make a call. As she placed her cell next to her ear, she began thinking of ways to tell him everything wrong with this place, but it seemed outrageous to her.

"Hey, Sunshine!" spoke a voice on the other end of the phone.

"Dad! Hey, I'm surprised you answered," Season retorted.

"I'm sorry, sweetie. I've been swamped with work. Sorry for not returning your calls, Season. I know you're mad but—"

"Dad, I want to come home."

"Why? What's wrong?"

Season took a deep breath and told her father everything. She told him about her time at Hollins New Deliverance Holiness, her Aunt Autumn's decision for her work in a library, the rumors about the town (leaving out the fifteen-year-old boy who she befriended on the beach), and what happened while she was on the beach.

"Hold up," demanded her father, sounding as if he was about to have a panic attack on the phone. "Were you on the beach by yourself?"

Lie, Season, Lie... don't tell him you were on the beach with a strange boy you just met a week ago. But then again, it's not as if you were going out with him. He was a friend, or so you thought, when he left you high and dry, she thought.

"Not exactly-," hesitated Season, trying to come up with a reasonable explanation as to why she was alone on the beach in the first place.

"Okay, so you were with Aunt Autumn?" he asked.

She wanted to lie. Her dad gave her the golden opportunity to use Aunt Autumn as a false alibi, but where would that get her? Being dishonest led her to this hellish place. If she wanted her dad to trust her again, she must tell him the truth. Could it hurt any less to do so?

"I was with a friend," she responded quickly.

"A friend?" her father repeated skeptically. "Honey, you've only been there a little over a week. Who is this friend?"

"Don't freak out, okay? It's a boy. I met him on the

beach. It's nothing serious, very platonic!"

"Season Belle Holidae," stressed Xavier, fuming on the other end of the phone.

Oh gosh! Not the whole name! Season stated in her head.

"Are you out of your thirteen-year-old mind? What are you doing on that beach? Especially with a strange boy you don't even know? Where was your aunt? Did your aunt know about this? Who is this boy?"

Season didn't know which question she should answer first since her father was firing them like cannonballs. She decided to avoid the "boy" questions and answer the latter.

"Dad, Aunt Autumn didn't know. I didn't tell her. I sneaked out a couple of times when she was at work. It was the only sane thing I thought was okay to do. She tried taking me to this cult-like church where everyone in town goes to. Did I mention that the pastor is also the mayor? Dad, you must come get me. I can't stay in this prison. I'm—"

"Season, don't you dare change the subject. Don't play games with me! Who is this boy?"

She was puzzled by her dad's response to what she was telling him. As if he wanted to avoid the real issue and talk about something as minor as a boy. She couldn't understand her father's fixation. "His name is Yusef, dad."

"His name is what?" asked Xavier.

"Yusef. Y-U-S-E-F," sighed Season.

There was an odd silence on the other end of the line, not a second interval, more of a thirty-second intermission before the fireworks started. *Maybe, he's thinking about taking a trip down here. Why is he so silent?*

"Where is your Aunt Autumn?"

"Oh, she's probably in the kitchen cooking breakfast."

"Let me speak to her."

Season thought for a moment before granting her father's request. What was he trying to prove? Why does he sound anxious and bizarre? What's going on with him?

"Dad, I'm sorry, but I need to charge my phone," she lied, hoping he could not pick up on it.

"Fine, I guess I will have to call her cell phone!" Xavier snapped as he hung up the phone without a goodbye or a 'talk to you later.' Season couldn't do anything but looked at her phone screen. Something weird was happening. She could feel it in her bones, but what? Why hurry off the phone to talk to Aunt Autumn?

She could hear Aunt Autumn's phone ringing in the house. The phone rang for seven seconds before it stopped. She could also hear Aunt Autumn's voice clearly saying the words "Hello," and Season listened to her aunt's room door closed after ten seconds. Whatever was being said behind closed doors was obviously for her not to hear, mostly when her aunt was still on the phone with her father after the next thirty minutes. Season did not know what to make of this situation.

Aunt Autumn drove Season into town so she can begin her first day at the library. After having a long talk with her dad, Aunt Autumn made no effort to talk to Season.

The only words that came out of her mouth were, "Get ready for work, or you'll be late." Nothing else, no emotions. Nothing. This made Season very uncomfortable and vulnerable. There was no one else to talk to. The verdict was still out on Yusef. She didn't know if she could trust him or not. Maybe he really had to go. Perhaps his father would get upset if he didn't have the house cool enough for him to come home to. Whatever the reason may be, it was still fishy for him to bring up something like the 'Righteous Ritual' and then finally remember that he had something important to do without explaining himself. Weird.

"We are here. I'll be back around 3:30; my break is around that time. I told Mrs. DeVeau to make sure you'll be at the library when I return. I don't want you wandering off, especially in this town," stated Autumn as she was looking around to see if anyone was listening.

"And why can't I? Why can't I just wait outside?' asked Season in a nasty tone while unbuckling her seatbelt.

Autumn gave her a cruel look as she shifted the gears from park to drive but had her foot on the brakes so her niece could hurry up and get out of the car. "All I know es dat ya betta get outta da car and have ya rass in da library 'round da same time I cum background," she asserted rapidly in that strange dialect she used whenever she got upset.

Season opened the car door and got out. She was careful not to slam it to avoid any more eruptions from her aunt. She turned to go into the two-story white stone building that looked like a poor emulation of a castle.

This is by far the craziest stage of my life, groaned Season as she opened the door to the library.

Inside did not look as clichéd and senseless as the outside. In fact, it looked normal. The place brought in a whiff of mothballs and moldy books to Season's nose. There were tall bookshelves covered from wall to wall with books, graphic novels, magazines, and newspapers. To the far-right end of the library, she noticed a sizable children's nook for children to read books, browse information on computers, and create puppet shows in a small puppet theatre stand. When she looked up, she could see the balcony of the second floor. From what she could see, most of their technology devices were located up there. The library was not too shabby. Seemed a bit normal.

Season walked up to the circulation desk and noticed the backside of an older woman who appeared to be busy organizing some books that were left on a long table. She had on a long, flowery silk Mumu that looked ridiculous, especially considering the old fashioned grayish, curly short-cut wig on her head. She wanted to get her attention, but the lady appeared to be talking to herself as if she was a nervous wreck.

"Um…excuse me, Ma'am?" Season spoke, clearing her throat to get the lady's attention.

"Now I know I've seen this book around here. Where is it?" asked the lady to herself as she held a single catalog card in her right hand as she was looking for the book it belonged to.

"Could you please tell me where I can find Mrs. DeVeau? I'm new, and I was told she was the librarian here."

"Well, no need to look any further, dear, I'm Mrs. DeVeau," she announced, finally turning around to greet the voice behind her.

Season wanted to laugh at how much Mrs. DeVeau looked like Thelma Mae Harper from the early 1980's show *Mama's Family*. Her mom loved that show and made Season watch reruns of it until she became fond of it herself. She had the same type of wig, the small string pearls, and the eyeglass straps (only hers were decked out in gold beads). Her glasses were perched on the brink of her nose, and her puffy cheeks were covered with black freckles. Unlike Mama Harper, Mrs. DeVeau had a smooth caramelized complexion, looking almost like a mulatto. The nasolabial folds located on each side of her full lips seemed to reveal laughter and happiness, exceptionally for a librarian.

"Well, let me guess... you're that gal Autumn can't shut up about," she let out a crazy laugh as if she made a hilarious joke.

"Excuse me?"

"Excuse me, honey, where's my manners? I'm Mrs. DeVeau, and you are Season, am I right? Season Holidae."

"Yep, that's me."

"Well, come here, sugar. Give me a big one," Mrs. DeVeau hurried out of the vast, round desk with her arms opened wide to give Season a hug. Season, who was too oblivious to the kind gesture, just stood there as the woman squeezed her senseless.

"I guess you're wondering, 'Why's this crazy woman hugging me?' Honey, I'm more like family to your kin, and not to mention I love to give hugs instead of handshakes. Handshakes seemed to be more formal, which I'm not. Also, no offense, honey, but people don't wash their hands nowadays. You just got to be careful, ya know?" Mrs. DeVeau chuckled.

Season couldn't help but to smile at the wild librarian. She liked her, and felt comfortable being in her presence. It was something about Mrs. DeVeau that reminded her of her mom, sweet but silly. *Maybe, I can let my guard down just a little,* she grinned.

"C'mon, let me tell you what needs to be done. Oh, I can't believe I see Ola Mae's grandbaby," she said, waddling really fast as she led Season behind the circulation desk.

"Ola Mae?" Season repeated with her eyes scrunched.

"Yeah, child, that's your grandmamma and my dear friend."

"Oh, I didn't know," Season responded softly, ashamed by not knowing her own grandmother's name. Her mother never talked much about her parents. Just that they died right soon after she left Hollins.

"Summer ain't told you a thing, did she? Gawd, that child could be unruly at times, but boy, was she smart! I guess her dreams were too big for Hollins to handle. Mh. When I heard about your mom's passing, it was the day after I learned they buried her. Man, it hurt me to find out about Ola Mae's oldest child's passing, and I couldn't at least attend the funeral. Your mama and your aunt were like my own children. I helped raised them, and they spent time here in this library with me almost every day."

Season looked around the place once more and imagined her mom and aunt playing and running around as kids. She could almost see her mom resting at one of those kiddie tables and reading a book. *Boy, did she love to read.*

"Could you tell me more about my mom? What was she like as a child?" she asked impatiently.

"Gal, I can tell you a lot, but we got a lot of work to do! I have some inventory in the back, and you have to do some card cataloging! Cindy, my assistant, will be back in a moment to train you, but let me show you how to check books in and out."

"Um…Mrs. DeVeau, you know there's a digital way to do card cataloging, right?"

Mrs. DeVeau looked at Season offensively and placed her hands on her hip with a discerned look on her face. "Why, yes, I do, Ms. Season. Cindy oversees those digital things, and I prefer to do things the old fashion way. Gawd forbid, if a whirl storm came and knocked all yall precious technology offline, what will happen then? That's the problem with you young folks, always putting your trust in a robot and in a man," she ranted, walking away from the desk to a room adjacent to it.

Season didn't take offense to what Mrs. DeVeau was saying. In fact, she thought she was humorous. Season smiled and shook her head as she picked up the catalog card Mrs. DeVeau was holding earlier.

"*The Giver,*" she read, smiling at the idea of simple coincidences life tends to bring to people. She sorted through the stack of books on the table and realized the book she was looking for was near her left foot. She picked up the book and placed the card in its card pocket.

Yea, this place might be a suitable replacement for the beach, she thought.

"Had fun?" asked Aunt Autumn while picking Season up from the library.

"Matter of fact, I did. I really like Mrs. DeVeau. She can be over the top with things, but she's hilarious."

Aunt Autumn smiled as she drove away from the building. "I'm glad you find her interesting. I told you she was wonderful. Man, your mom and I had great times at that place. It seemed to be the only place that kept us from leaving this town."

Season looked up at her aunt with sympathy. "Why didn't you?"

"Why didn't I do what? Leave? Where would I go? I didn't have any future goals or a purpose for leaving town. I guess your mother was the smart one to leave. I felt indebted to take care of your grandparents."

"But I remembered mom telling me that your mom passed shortly after she left," replied Season, being careful how she spoke. She learned pretty quickly how sensitive her aunt can be when discussing anything relevant to the past. Season didn't want to risk a cancellation of any discussion or a change in the conversation.

Autumn carefully agreed, "She did, but there was your grandfather. I had to take care of him, not to mention I had to work to pay off the bills because we were in debt. It was the burden for being the youngest," she frowned while stopping at a light.

"That was pretty unfair," stated Season quietly, looking out her window. She spotted three young girls who appeared to be around her age, dressed as if they were going to church with sheer flowery dresses and white dress hats on their heads. They wore laced gloves and carried a small tote at the smallness of their wrists. Season also noticed how each girl was wearing sheer stockings and were mechanically walking down the sidewalk to reach their destination. After seeing the girls, her mind went back to where she worked. Everyone, including the children on up to the adults, were sophisticatedly dressed. The females wore dresses, and the males wore slacks, dress shirts, and penny loafers. As if it was a thought, she looked to her aunt and realized she had on a smock top with a pleated long, dark skirt. She never paid any attention to what her aunt wore to work until now, and it was absurd. When she worked in her garden, she wore overalls. Perhaps because she was on her own land, and wasn't anyone close by to ridicule her on her clothing.

"Am I missing something here?" Season asked her aunt as she pointed to the young girls.

"What do you mean?" replied Autumn as she looked to where Season was pointing. "And stop staring and pointing. That's so impolite!"

"Why are they dressed? Is there an event in town?"

"No, Sweetie, it's not. You see, Hollins is a different place than most places you are used to."

"Tell me about it," groaned Season.

"Well, down here, people believed that both men and women should carry themselves differently. It doesn't matter what their age may be. Young girls should be groomed to be refined ladies, and young men should be groomed to be chivalrous gentlemen."

"So, what you're saying is that girls should be submissive housewives, wear dresses, be silent in church, and be men's toy dolls? Ha! And to think American women, especially Black American women, thought fighting for their equal rights would be the ideal American Dream for all humans. To think the Me-Too movement was finally getting everyone to wake up to the inequality of genderism and sexual assaults, but you guys want to go backward in time."

"That's not entirely true, Season. What's wrong with upholding moral discipline?"

"Everything if a town has absolute control over how you look, what you wear, and what you do!" Season pointed out.

"Well, I don't agree with everything this town does, but it has shown growth in the less crime rates, prostitution, drugs, theft, and anything imaginable in the outside world you call home. Hollins just has its way of cultivating virtues by eliminating sinful deeds."

Season rolled her eyes and responded, "Oh, pray tell, how one could eliminate sinful deeds?"

Autumn grew quiet by Season's question and pretended to concentrate fully on the SUV ahead of her. Season did not expect an answer, so she went back to looking out her window. A strange town with strange deeds strikes illegal actions. There was no doubt in Season's mind that she would get an answer to her question sooner or later.

Suddenly, Season's eyes bulged out of her sockets as she watched two familiar pedestrians getting into a confrontation outside of what seemed to be a general store. One was the young girl she saw in church, getting banged in the head with a pocketbook by an elderly woman.

It can't be, Season thought, straining to see the two people with her naked eyes. *Is that Serene and her grandmother....Oh! What's that old devil's name? Mrs. Winnie! That's her name!*

"AUNT AUTUMN, STOP THE CAR NOW!" yelled Season.

Autumn, distracted by Season's voice, came to a screeching halt as she slammed on her brakes. Thank God a car wasn't behind them, or they would've been in quite a crash!

"Gal, what's wrong with you? You were about to give me a heart attack! What's wrong?" Autumn panicked.

"Look! That girl Serene is getting clobbered by that mean Mrs. Winnie!"

Autumn looked out at Season's window. "Oh, my God! Hey! Mrs. Winnie!" she called out, but Season's window was up. Immediately, Season wound her window down so Autumn could be heard. "Mrs. Winnie, stop it!"

There was a car honking behind them, trying to get them to move on ahead. Instead, Aunt Autumn found a nearby parking space. Once she parked, Season automatically jumped out of the vehicle with a look of anger on her face as she walked toward the confrontation. Autumn waited until it was safe for her to open her car door, got out of the car, and slammed it shut. She rushed in the same direction, making sure she was ahead of her niece so she would not do anything crazy. Autumn dived right into the middle of Serene and Winnie, taking the volatile hits from the pocketbook so she could protect the pregnant teen.

"Autumn Shepherd, get outta da way!" yelled the crazy old woman as she stopped swinging her enormous, bulky purse.

"You know I can't let you do that, Mrs. Winnie. Calm down!" Autumn asserted, levying her arm down. "This child is pregnant. You can't be swinging your purse at her like that. What's going on?"

"Ya stay outta da way, chile. Dis matta don't concern ya. Dis es 'tween me and me grand chile, ya hur?"

"I'll tell you what's going on, Ms. Autumn," replied the store clerk coming out of the store they were in front of. "This child was trying to rob me blind!"

Season looked at Serene as she was huffing and puffing angrily. Tears were gradually coming down faster than she could wipe from her face. She didn't say anything to defend herself.

"Well, that doesn't give you the right to assault her in the street like she was trash," blurted out Season, who stood in front of the poor girl.

"Gal? Who ya tink ya talkin' to like dat?"

"I'm saying this to you, Mrs. Winnie. You were wrong," said Season in almost a whisper.

The old woman was callous and scary. Her eyes were bloodshot red, and the grey strands of hair that were once placed in a neat bun were scattered everywhere. Season took a step back because of how the old woman's chest was heaving up and down. She could have sworn two horns would appear from the top of her head.

"Season, stay out of this," warned Autumn, as she took a step closer to Mrs. Winnie, but the old woman took a giant step back.

"Ya need to control dis rug rat ya call a gal, Autumn. She's ale' mannered and needs a good whippin' herself."

"Mrs. Winnie, I do apologize for my niece, but she's right. You must have some sense of control. I'm pretty sure there are other ways to handle this matter. She's just a child," explained Autumn with a cracked voice. For the first time, Season witnessed her aunt's ability to be empathetic and stand up against people like Mrs. Winnie or Hollins.

"Ya right, and she will learn in tree days," spitted Winnie as she held out her three fingers to emphasize her point. "Da devil is tryin' ta get to me grandbaby. It won't sleep til it's done corrupt every last of em chullen. Da Lord knos me doin da right ting. Ya was raised betta tan tis, Autumn. Ya parents would be disappointed in ya for defyin' me."

Autumn held her head down in defeat. Season was trying to make sense of what Mrs. Winnie was saying. What will happen in three days? What did she mean that her grandparents would be disappointed in her aunt? For what? Stopping a crazed lunatic from abusing a poor child?

"The only devil I see here is you!" snapped Season.

For a split second, the atmosphere became quiet as the old beast took in what the rebellious child told her. Like a running back trying to reach touchdown, the old woman hobbled over to Season, cocking her purse to knock the insubordinate taste out the child's mouth. She nearly succeeded, but Autumn was a swifter defensive lineman. She grabbed ahold of Mrs. Winnie's wrist with the purse before it could reach Season.

"Mrs. Winnie," Autumn stated calmly, still holding on to the lady's wrist. She locked eyes with the old goat so she could express her solemnness. "I have never in my life disrespected any of my elders. After growing up, I tried every day to follow in my Savior's footsteps, obeyed my father and mother, and played the obedient and righteous servant to this community. But I promise you, on my parents' grave, if you lay any hands on my daughter, you will see the wrath of this devil put you in a tailspin the Holy Father can't bring you back from."

Both of the teen's mouths were ajar. No one ever spoke to Mrs. Winnie how Autumn spoke to her, and the way she sounded, she meant every word of it. Season was too flabbergasted to notice how her aunt mentioned her as "her daughter." She was also concerned about the look on the old lady's face as if she saw a ghost. Autumn placed the fear of God in her heart, and she couldn't do anything about it.

After some seconds of reeling, Mrs. Winnie snatched her wrist from Aunt Autumn's grasp. She gave Season and Serene a deathly stare before she replied, "Ya wait til Passa Hollis hears bout dis!"

"Grandma?" responded a weak Serene as she walked towards her grandmother.

"Get thee behind, Satan! Ya not cumin' wit me til ya wash wit da blood of Jesus! Find ya own way, home!" she snorted, hobbling off in a different direction.

"Autumn, you shouldn't have done that," intervened the store clerk as he shook his head defensively at the poor woman.

Autumn, who was staring continuously at Mrs. Winnie, finally broke away from her mood. "Yea, well, it's about time for someone to stand up to her and others. Even adults sometimes forget to do what's right."

"Yet, they're over cultivating values?" asked Season, walking away to get back to the car.

Chapter 7:

CINDY LOU'S PROJECT

*A*fter Mrs. Winnie abandoned her grandchild, Autumn offered to give the poor girl a ride back home. Of course, Serene was too frightened to go home to a surly, old woman, and Season couldn't blame her. In fact, Season pleaded with her aunt to take Serene home with them for one night so it would give both parties time enough to calm down from today's disastrous event. Autumn was hesitant at first but realized that stress would not be wise for Serene or the baby. So, she agreed to one night only but grounded Season for being disrespectful toward Mrs. Winne. *Oh well, you must take the good with the bad, especially when doing what is right,* Season reasoned.

That night, Autumn cooked a pot of delicious gumbo with sweet cornbread to soak it in. It was the best tasting meal Season had since she got there. Having seconds was not an option for her, but for Serene, she was trying to eat the entire pot. Autumn and Season were both surprised at how much the fifteen-year-old could devour so much. Season took it as Serene's way of feeding for two, but it was an indication of neglect to Autumn.

"Okay, Serene, as much as I enjoy people eating my cooking, I can't let you eat yourself silly. You're going to get sick," Autumn replied as she took Serene's fourth bowl away from her.

"Oh, I'm sorry, Ms. Autumn. I just couldn't help myself. Ya cookin' is real good! I had to savor as much as I could," Serene apologized shamefully, looking down at her stomach."

"Hey, no sweat, honey. There's no need to apologize. Just don't want you to get nauseous, is all. All this gumbo is not too good for the youngin' you're carrying," Autumn smiled.

Season finished her second bowl and noticed how gentle and careful her aunt was with the young girl. She couldn't help but admire her aunt for that. *Maybe she wasn't a monster*, Season thought. As she smiled, she reached for the basket of cornbread located in the middle of the table.

"Okay, Season, I need that little bit of gumbo left to be put up. Use the-"

"Tupperware. I know, Aunt Autumn," Season smirked.

"Hm…yeah okay, smart mouth. Serene, I'll make sure to leave a nightshirt out for you; it should be able to fit you. Season, if you want to sleep with me and let Serene take your bed, I think that will be fine. However, I do have an air mattress I can blow up if you can't take my snoring. I thought about going to bible study tonight, but after what happened today, I think that's totally out of the question."

"Good idea," the girls called out simultaneously, then laughed at each other.

After the laughter died down, Season looked to her aunt and then to Serene before she answered, "I think I'll go with the air mattress if you don't mind."

"Suit yourself," responded Aunt Autumn, making a beeline out of the kitchen.

"Aunt Autumn,"

"Yes, Season," she answered, turning around.

"Thank you," Season smiled.

Aunt Autumn returned the smile as she left the room.

"Ya aunts a cool person, and a bad-ass fa talkin' to my grandmother like dat," Serene complimented, getting up from the table.

Season smiled as she began cleaning up. "Yeah, I'm starting to notice that myself."

"Here, let me help you with the dishes," offered Serene, heading over to the sink.

"Um, no, I can't let you do that, Serene. Take a load off; it's okay. It's part of my 'building character' chores," Season stated mockingly as she ran hot water in the sink.

"I have to find some way of repaying ya. I thought sure I was going ta die if ya haddin' stepped in the way you did."

"Well, no offense to your grandmother, but what she did by hitting you in public, not to mention embarrassing you in church, it was uncalled for. You can break a person's spirit like that."

"Yeah, well, I have gotten used to grandma treatin' me this way. It's no big deal. People 'round here gives her a pass because she's da mother of da community and is Pastor Hollis's right hand."

"Hm…well, that's not reality, Serene. Old people can go to jail just as well as young people. If we have breath in our bodies, then we all are held accountable for our actions."

Serene looked at Season and gave her a respectful smile.

"What?" Season asked dumbfounded.

"Ya not from round here, are ya?"

"What gave it away? Is it my lack of morals?" Season replied sarcastically as she rolled her eyes.

"Naw, just different from the rest is all. Ya have an 'I don't care' attitude toward everything. Ya lot braver than me."

"No, I'm just more aware of my surroundings to know what's right and wrong. Sometimes my mom would call me 'Fight-Night' Season," she chuckled, thinking back on the times she loved getting her point across to her parents. Her parents would even go out of the way to keep a point system to see who will win such debates as her having a cell phone, drinking coffee, lifting her bedtime sched-ule to watch television, reading in the dark with only a flashlight, and other simple things any young child would dispute over. Oh, how she yearned for those years to be revived.

"Used to? She doesn't call you that anymore?" Serene asked.

"No," she responded, bringing herself back to reality. "She's dead."

"Oh, my! I'm so sorry, Season," Serene apologized.

"It's okay. She passed last year."

"I bet it hurts, huh?"

"More than you'll ever know."

"I can imagine so. I mean, I have a crackhead for a mom. Haven't seen her in months!"

"Must be really hard for you and your siblings," Season hinted, remembering Mrs. Winnie's testimony about having to raise three grandchildren.

"Yeah, well, life is full of disappointments, ya know? Here I am, preggo, and me and my siblings can't half raise ourselves, let alone eat."

"Well, you can't raise yourself. You're kids. Your grandmother isn't taking care of you?"

"She's old and set in her ways, Autumn. Ya heard her in church. She's on a fixed income, and her' college children' she gloats about could give a rat's ass about her. They don't even come down here to visit her. There's a saying here around kids our age, once you find a one-way ticket out of this hell-hole, don't pack anything. Just leave and don't look back!" she explained with tears appearing in her eyes.

Season began to understand some of the reasons her mom left and why most of the younger generation left. There was no life here. Instead, there were just old totalitarians who had taken the bible out of context to appease their evil minds. Too bad her aunt thought she owed this place her life. She didn't deserve it. Suddenly, a question came to Season's mind as she finished washing up her last plate.

"Hey, Serene, do you know a young guy around your age that lives near the beach named Yusef?"

She thought long and hard for a moment before she answered, "No, I don't think so. You say he's around my age?"

"Yes, he's a bit smaller for his age. Scrawny dude…a little darker tan than I am. He loves to wear white linen shirts and pants," Season described.

"No, I haven't heard or seen anyone like that before. If he doesn't look presentable, then he's probably an outsider."

"No… can't be. He says he lives not too far from the beach with his dad."

"Who's his dad?" Serene inquired.

"You know? I didn't even ask him about that," Season realized as she dried her hands on the dish towel.

"Maybe I will know him if ya can get the dad's name. I know everyone from Hollins. Anyway, why ya asked? Is he ya boyfriend?" grinned Serene, moving her eyebrows up and down seductively.

Season laughed at Serene and tapped her playfully. "Nooo, he's just someone I met on the beach, is all."

"Oh, okay," Serene dismissed as she stretched her arms out.

"Hey, have you heard of this thing called 'Righteous Ritual'? Yusef told me about it and—"

"Shh!" interrupted Serene. "Ya shouldn't speak of such things. Who told ya something like that?"

"I just said Yusef, but you shut me up," Season hissed, confused at Serene's response.

"Well, what does Yusef knows 'bout it?"

"I told you that Yusef is from Hollins," Season stressed.

"Impossible," she said, more to herself than to Season. "Well?"

"Well, what?"

"Are you going to tell me, or aren't you?" inquired Season, growing impatient.

Suddenly they heard someone clearing their throat. It startled the girls as they turned around to see a serious Aunt Autumn near the doorway.

"Ladies, enough of the chit chat. It's time for bed. Season, you sleep with me tonight. I'm too tired to find that air mattress. Let Serene get a good night's sleep in your bed. She has to go back home, and you have to go to work tomorrow."

Such an impeccable timing, and right about the time I thought I would get some answers. All this time, she could've found the stupid air mattress. What are you really hiding from me, Aunt Autumn? She thought as she glanced back at the sink.

"Season?" called out Aunt Autumn.

"I hear you…well, Goodnight, Serene."

"Goodnight, Season," Serene responded weakly, biting her bottom lip.

"Gal, what's wrong with you?" asked Mrs. DeVeau, eating some boiled peanuts out of a soaked paper bag. "You look like you've lost your puppy or something."

It was Thursday morning and Season's second day at the library. She didn't appreciate her aunt's dismissive behavior last night, and especially this morning. Sure, she cooked breakfast for the girls but remained tight-lipped as they all sat in silence at the dinner table. Season realized how predictable her aunt can be when she felt insulted or felt she needed to conceal her feelings. It was beginning to get old and annoying to Season.

"Oh, it's nothing. Just woke up on the wrong side of the bed," she responded, thinking literally and figuratively, giving how her aunt kept her awake most of the night with her loud snoring and snorting.

"Well, cheer up, gal! This is the day that the Lord has made!" Mrs. DeVeau preached as she playfully pushed Season.

"Yeah, you're right," smiled Season.

Cindy, Mrs. DeVeau's assistant, entered the library, walking with a serious look on her face. Season never paid it any attention yesterday when Cindy was training her to work the circulation desk. Maybe the young girl took her job seriously, or perhaps she was too tired and was ready to leave. Today, she had that same grim look with no type of life in her eyes. She was biracial, very tall, thin, and looked to be fresh out of college. But why work in a library, in Hollins?

"Hey, Miss Cindy Lou. Happy to see you this morning," greeted Mrs. DeVeau while offering her some boiled peanuts, "Would you like some?"

Cindy's corner right lip tweaked a little to acknowledge Mrs. DeVeau's kind gesture, but she delightfully declined the offer. Cindy reminded Season of a porcelain doll she once had when she was around six. Her soft, dark auburn hair was spruced up in candy curls with a neatly tied blue ribbon holding up a small ponytail at the front of her hair, which matched the baby blue maxi dress she had on. She was a gorgeous young lady with attractive, protruding hazel eyes and very fair skin. She could be absolutely stunning if she would just smile.

"All right, Cindy Lou, you know what you have to do. You have my gal, Season, to train. Me, I have a huge gas problem that I need to let out! Don't want the library to start smelling like a gas station. Then I have to change my career from a librarian to a town pump clerk," crackled Mrs. DeVeau, heading to the bathroom.

"She's a character, isn't she?" Season asked Cindy as she laughed and shook her head at Mrs. DeVeau's joke.

Cindy, who wasn't at all flattered by the joke, had a look of disgust on her face. "Character is not the word for it," she said as she placed her big, black book bag underneath the counter.

"Excuse me?" asked Season as if she missed an insolent moment.

"It's not proper for a lady of any age to announce her gastric hiccups aloud," Cindy snapped as she sat adequately in a seat.

"It wasn't as if she announced it to the world, Cindy. Relax, it's not that serious.

"It is imperative to maintain the proper respect as a lady, but why do you care? You wear jeans like you're a boy or something," Cindy snapped.

"Um, Cindy. I know we just met yesterday, but you're acting as if you know me, and you really don't. So, let's get reacquainted with each other. Hi, my name is Season, Season Holidae, and I'm not from '*prim and flocking, where's your stockings*' Hollins," she retorted, giving her best antebellum voice to insult Cindy.

"Hm, you're quite the comedian, or 'joke,' aren't you?"

"Huh? I'm a joke? You're trapped in a late 19th-century idiotic version of Ibsen's *A Doll's House* town. It's obvious you have never stepped foot out of this place, or else your porcelain face would crack!"

"See how much you know, little girl…I graduated

from USC Beaufort with a degree in Sociology and a minor in Psychology," Cindy acknowledged with a friendly, nasty smile.

Despite being skilled as a pompous bitch, Season was surprisingly impressed with the girl's academic resume. "Why come here?"

"Well, I could give you a sorry excuse of 'this is my hometown,' but I'm currently working on a project."

"What kind of project?" inquired Season.

"A project which doesn't concern you," retorted Cindy.

"Why are you so clandestine about a project?"

"Because I don't trust you."

"Of course not, I hardly even know you. So who could I tell your project to?"

"Well, for starters, your aunt."

After Cindy's remark, Season could not help but be more curious about what this girl was up to. Why would she care if she told her aunt? Then bells began ranging in her head.

"Okay, so listen, I'm not from around here. As a matter of fact, it was against my will to even come to this stupid town. I got in some trouble and my dad saw this as an option to punish me. He sent me to live with an estranged aunt I hardly even know," explained Season.

Cindy took a good look at Season before responding, "I'm truly sorry to hear that. Moreover, for your father to think that this place would be the ideal juvenile detention habitation to send you. What's your point?"

"My point is that I'm not happy, and I don't belong here. As you can see, I don't dress, talk, or act like the residents from Hollins. Something weird is going on in this place, something I can't even explain. I have to get out of here, Cindy," Season expressed with a look of desperation in her eyes.

"How do I know if I can trust you, Season?" asked Cindy.

Season looked down at her hands as she tried to recall the event that haunted her for some days. "I met this boy when I was at the beach shortly after coming to Hollins. For the first time, I felt relieved that I could adjust to this place, especially after having this sync connection to this guy. By all means, I wasn't in love or attracted to him. He was just relatively easy to talk to and to pick up the shattered pieces of a joyous time I used to spend with my best friend or my mom, who died last year. One afternoon, he left me abruptly after remembering something he had to do for his father. After he left, it seemed as if the atmosphere left with him…all around me was like a scene from a place where nightmares are kept. It immediately became bleak, grey, and just creepy. I remembered how the waves were coming in from the ocean. It wasn't natural. The wind began to pick up, provoking the waves to manifest into some sort of monstrous hook to capture me."

Cindy's eyes widened as it was glued to Season. Season, oblivious to Cindy's facial expression, continued revealing her experience while reviewing the scene in her mind. She stopped talking for a moment to wipe a tear from her left eye and said, "When it came to shore, the water came up to my ankles. I tried to make a run for it, but I fell. I could have sworn there were hands that covered both of my ankles and wouldn't let me go. With sand landing in my eyes and my mouth, I couldn't see or couldn't scream for help...but I heard something."

"What did you hear?" Cindy asked shakenly.

Season smirked, too embarrassed to say. "You wouldn't believe me if I told you."

Cindy gave Season a stern look. "Season, what did you hear?"

She looked at Cindy with fear in her eyes. "I heard the cries of babies. Not just the sound of the wind howling, but the actual sounds of babies crying. It was the most terrifying sound I have ever heard in my life. The pitch of it all outweighs fingernails scratching on a chalkboard."

"How did you manage to escape this?" asked Cindy, breathing deeply.

"I fought. I clawed my hand through the sand, refusing to give in, until it let me go. Sounds crazy, right?"

Cindy didn't comment. Instead, she reached for her big black book bag under the counter. She unzipped it and took out an old, dusty azure-colored hardcover book. The book's spine stitches were coming apart, losing its purpose of bounding the pages inside. Cindy hesitantly handed Season the book. Season, exhibiting the same gesture, reluctantly took the book and looked at the risen gold-colored Victorian font size entitled: *HOLLINS WUDU PROCLAMATION* written by *Marion Hollingsworth II (1905).*

"What's this?" asked Season as she traced a finger on the title.

"It's a book on Hollins' history," Cindy replied.

"What? There's a history book for this piece of a town?"

Cindy sighed. "There is important detailed information inside that you should be made aware of. You have to keep this out of eyesight because Hollins' folks do not take kindly to outsiders understanding their history. I know it sounds dumb, but they are very secretive and territorial. They feel it's in their right to protect and not taint their way of living to the outside world. That's why there's only limited copies given to the loyal subjects of this town."

"So, what will happen if they catch me reading this book?" asked Season.

Cindy gave Season a more pressing stare. "Just don't get caught."

"Then why give me something that will cause trouble for you and me both?"

"Because Season, you should know the truth about this place. I don't think it's fair for you to be in a place you don't know anything about...especially when it's dangerous."

"What do you mean dangerous?"

"Just read the book, Season. The book can help explain what I'm saying without too many listening ears. Read it in secrecy and don't trust anyone," Cindy replied, lowering her voice and looking around an empty library.

Season was beginning to fear for her life. She didn't know what to make of Cindy's warning. It was all too overwhelming for her to comprehend. On the other hand, she was curious about what she could learn from this ancient, twisted literature. But on the other hand, she was terrified to open the book.

She cleared her throat and asked, "What's the purpose of your project, Cindy?"

Cindy looked at her for a moment before responding, "To expose them, even if it means risking my life."

Chapter 8:

"MARION HOLLINGSWORTH I"

"Okay, Ms. Season, it's the weekend, and I'm off. You want to help me in the garden?" Autumn asked as she placed on her garden hat.

It was a scorching Saturday afternoon. The temperature was scaling up to the upper nineties. On a day like this, Season would enjoy taking a swim, but there wasn't any way she was going to go back to that beach again, whether Yusef was there or not. Let him be alone with the wickedness of that place, the same place where he left her high and dry. It would serve him right. Besides, she had other things on her mind, like finding the time to read the book Cindy gave her. Before, she could never find the day or time to do so with her aunt watching her every move.

"Um…No, thanks. I think I'm going to watch a rerun of *Dancing with the Stars*, if you don't mind," Season answered, with an innocent smile.

Autumn had a look of disappointment on her face but decided not to address it. "I bet you are a great swimmer, huh?" she asked.

Season thought for a minute as to how that question derived from watching a dance show. "Oh yea, I was pretty good. Just haven't been practicing for a while."

"Is it because of Summer?" Autumn asked somberly.

This time, Season did not respond. She did not want to relive that dreadful summer last year or talk about it with her aunt. Some things were left better unspoken.

Autumn smiled weakly as if she understood. "Well, if you need anything, I'll be in the garden." She turned around and headed out the door.

"Aunt Autumn," Season called.

"Yes?" Autumn asked, turning around.

"Thanks for understanding," she replied.

Autumn gave Season a smile and a nod as she closed the door behind her. The coast was clear. Season hurried quickly to the bedroom to get the contraband from underneath the mattress. She was glad to know that one of the bedroom windows faced the backyard where Autumn's garden was located. She could see her aunt's back walking towards it. Season would have to be on the lookout and read all at the same time. This way, she could race to the living area and watch television.

"Okay, let's see …," she said merely to herself as she sat on the bed and placed the book on her lap. She rubbed the title once again before opening the book. Season sneezed when the dust greeted her nose, and it reeked of moth-balls and mold. On the dedication page, it read, "*Hollins Independence circa 1866. The honorable Devotees will guard this decree with full sincerity and loyalty. Thus, foreigners who are caught with the possession of this book shall reap the con-sequences of a cleft tongue and will be cut down lower than a serpent. Alas, if thy brother betrays another for a foreigner, he too shall reap the same fate as the latter and be cast out from Hollins,*"

Season froze. She placed her left hand to her lips, imag-ining how excruciating it would be for someone to snip her tongue like a pitched fork. *Should I really be reading this? No wonder Cindy was bent on being discreet. If limited copies were given to particular citizens, how did she get her hands on one?* Season thought. Her mind was working overtime with questions and possible answers. She managed to skip a few pages until she came across a section called "The Historic Hollins." On the left-hand side of the page was a picture of an antique black and white cabinet card of an old black male who looked to be in his seventies. His long, greyish beard covered most of his lips, and his head was completely bald. What was so weird about the picture was how stiff the guy looked. His eyes were closed, and he was propped on some sort of furniture. The caption read below the photograph: *Post-Mortem Photography of our great Leader, Marion Hollingsworth I (1833-1900). The Founding Father of the town of Hollins.*

"Oh, my," Season cringed as she quickly turned the

page. She didn't expect to see a photograph of a dead corpse. What purpose did it serve? Why not use a picture of the guy when he was alive and well? Season turned the page and read the headline:

"THE CAUSATION OF MARION HOLLINGSWORTH'S VISION"

"Mmh, this looks interesting…" she said to herself as she continued flipping through more pages. There were photocopies of several journal entries belonging to Marion Hollingsworth. At the end of the last entry, a page read, *"Our great founder was known to write thousands of journal entries. These selected entries from his first journal were chosen to highlight the foundation of Hollingsworth."* She looked out the window to check on her aunt before flipping back to the first entry:

October 12, 1850

 I told my poor mother that I wish to remain the ignorant Negro my fellow counterparts desired me to be. Her response to my explicit request was literally a slap to my face and hours of chastisement. She asked, "Why would you want that, boy? Why would anyone like you want something like that?" If my face wasn't in so much agony from her blunt force, I would answer her, "Is there anyone like me? Could I identify with anyone who's 'like me?" I was an unrequested product bred from a vicious rape that left my mother

barren. John Hollingsworth, my dear father…my oppressor…my "Master" was the devil the Bible would
describe as being wicked.

Everything, from his appearance, sickens me. He
was a big, tall man in his early fifties who prided
himself on being one of the county's wealthiest men.
I thank the good Lord for not inheriting those cold,
blue eyes, but I was cursed with his nose, mouth, and
height. I was the only child "white" enough to live in
the big house, but not white enough to eat with his
white wife and his two white daughters at the dinner table. When riding into town, I was the trusted
"negro" who steered the horses, not the son who could
enjoy a carriage ride inside with his father and be
indulged in a meaningful console. My flamboyant
trends with hand-me-downs such as white frocks, silk
ties, and long overcoats spelled out "betrayer" to the
enslaved. It was a far cry from two suits worn all year
round, holes in the sole of the shoes (if you're lucky to
have anything to protect your feet), and potato sacks
to wear for bedtime. I lived in the big house as a property, not a member of the Hollingsworth's household. I
was in training to be over the enslaved house servants.

Sure, he had a few illegitimate litters after me,
but they were all flawed due to their hue being a tad
bit darker than mine. Moreover, something else set
me apart from my poor brothers and sisters, and that
was education. John Hollingsworth prided himself

on being one of the wealthiest croppers on this side of Beaufort County, investing his money in slavery. So, for him to hire a French tutor to teach not only etiquettes but literacy to his daughters, I was fortunate enough to be present if I offered "my sisters" Maryanne and Lorraine, my servitude when doing so. That's when I encountered her…Madame Cherie Moreau.

The tutor, Miss Moreau, was different from the other whites I've met. She was striking, with a firm posture when she walked. Her skin carried no tint at all, for she was pale as powder. The brunette hair she so proudly flaunts was placed in a bun with two braids as chains securing it and curls in the front to accentuate the beauty of her oval-shaped face. On the upper left side of her lips, stamped a beauty mark as approval for being a refined Madame of her rank. She was cordial but formidable; strict but fair. She didn't treat me any differently from Maryanne or Lorraine. At first, I thought she was deceived by my complexion and my name, for she couldn't see that I was a Negro, but of course, "father" was there to set the record straight. She was under strict instructions to give only Maryanne and Lorraine the best of her knowledge.

Maryanne was an eleven-year-old perfectionist. The only thing we shared in common was our father's obvious distaste of our existence. His cruel reason for mine was evident; for Maryanne, she wasn't a male heir. It wasn't a myth that all white masters wanted their firstborns to be white males. A young, innocent infant in training to hate every color in the rainbow. A successor to carry on their predecessor's powerful torch. I pitied Maryanne as she tries daily to compensate for her imperfection in masculinity but loathe her willingness to idolize her father.

Lorraine was an unruly, rebellious, and gluttonous nine year old who would instead feed her stomach than feed her brains. That was one of my difficult tasks as well, to see to it that the young miss didn't gain a pound or go skulking into the kitchen somewhere in an eating frenzy. I couldn't count how many times I received a lashing for Miss Lorraine's intense appetites.

When Madame Moreau taught, she would cut her eyes at me to see if I understood. She would hand me the same learning materials she gave my sisters and demanded that I sit instead of stand. To not complicate matters, I sat near the doorway in fear of my life. But in all honesty, I was involved....I was engrossed with learning my letters and numbers; how I should present myself as a proper gentleman or how a decent woman should present themselves to gentlemen; how to conduct the French etiquette 'Les moeurs' or etiquette manners at dinner tables; and how to dance elaborately to the Forbidden Waltz. Unlike Lorraine's savory, I engorged knowledge. Every morning, I woke up anticipating Madame would provide me with enough wisdom to understand what was going on outside of my father's South Carolina plantation and the United States, extending to different countries I would love to someday venture. Being sated wasn't enough to fancy my covertness for enlightenment. I didn't care for what the consequences may cost. I made up in my mind that it was worth dying for.

It was hard to say at first, but it became evident that she was intentionally teaching only to me over some days. At first, I wondered: why would this pale, sophisticated stranger care to entertain me? I couldn't wrap my mind around it. She seemed more determined for me to understand what she was instructing rather than care what her pupils were getting from it. She included me in her modeled instructions and called me her "Doux petit garçon négre," or "sweet little negro boy."

So, what led me to wanting to cease my intellects? It wasn't because of fear; fear was the furthest thing from my mind. It was because of shame. I was ashamed about the wealth of knowledge I wasn't privy to in the first place. My mother taught me not to steal anything I couldn't pay for, but I guess stealing wisdom was acceptable for her. I was so much on a rise that I couldn't look down from my pedestal to see the conditions of the same people I was in bondage with. I was getting reprimanded and spat on from both sides of the line. If it wasn't Master Hollingsworth getting upset that I didn't do something to his liking, or I didn't answer when Lorraine or Maryanne beckon for me, it would be the field hands taunting me or calling me a "white negro" under their breath. My mother told me not to listen to them, but it's hard not to. She didn't know how it feels for your own people to look at you with damnation in their eyes or shake their heads at you when you passed them. Even the house workers gossiped or were spiteful by dropping dishes to see if I would run and tell them. It was upsetting. It made me regret I was ever born!

January 2, 1851

I felt awful waking up this cold morning with a furnace providing me heat in the lower part of the house. I couldn't say the same for my mother or the ones living down in the quarters. The wooden cabin walls were not insulated enough to keep out the deadly cold drafts. It didn't help that a few were sleeping on rough timbered floors to accommodate the children sleeping on hard cots with scratchy blankets to cover them. The fire they acquired came from the same open fireplace they used to cook in giant cauldrons and pots. Throughout all the hardships, cold weather, and living conditions, Master Hollingsworth put all his cares on his wife, who was now with child. After witnessing his wife's cravings, vomiting after every meal, and her fickle behavior, he decided to call Dr. Jasper and the local midwife, Lowie, to confirm his suspension.

They predicted that she was, in fact, a few months along, not to mention examining the smallness of her protruding belly. Master couldn't be more thrilled but also perplexed. I couldn't understand or give reasons for the confused look he portrayed on his face, but it wasn't long for the Misses to assure him that he will finally have the son he hoped for. Ironically speaking, I was his firstborn son.

If I may be candid, The Misses never took a liking to me. In fact, she despised me. I could always feel her eyes stabbing right through me as if I was a diseased pestilence that must be exterminated. Poor Misses, if she only understood the disadvantages of being a bastard child to the wicked likes of John Hollingsworth, she wouldn't waste time being resentful towards me. Jealousy is the most terrible malevolence state to be in. It chokes the light out of anyone's spirit and turns them into a dark void. If it fancies her to exhaust her body for her husband's attention, then so be it! A real father doesn't play a God who dictates with evilness and tyranny.

January 14, 1851

Master Hollingsworth and I went to an auction in Charlestowne a few days ago to find the strongest, top-notch "nigger" who can swing a "lightning bolt with his bare hands," whatever that analogy meant. However, I knew what he wanted in a slave. A Negro who is weak in the mind but firm in the muscles. A Negro who could follow orders with a flick of the wrist or a look in Master's eyes. A breakable Negro who knew the consequences of defying his owner if he thought one second to step out of line.

I had to wait with the horses as Master Hollingsworth ventured out on his vindictive retail to trade two young children, ages ten and twelve, and a young maiden, for what he wanted to buy. His rhetoric delivery? "Two little Negros to help out in the field and one fine breeder to increase the owner's pockets." What a distaste for humanity! Even if I was permitted to follow Master Hollingsworth, I would rather have a bird peck out my innocent eyes. I could imagine the event without being there. An assembly of white males having a cheerful time with spirits and cigars. The different coloration of darker skins labeled as black cargo being housed in barracoons, who were confused, uncomfortable, disheveled, and worse of all…terrified.

Time went by, and the scorching heat signaled the late afternoon. My father arrived, but not with the "merchandises" he sold, but with one single purchase; his perfect, dark night Herculean. To me, he didn't look like an average Mandingo…in fact, he looked ordinary. By the revolted look on Master's face, I could tell it was a deal gone wrong.

"Marion, meet Omo," he replied with a gruff.

I looked at Omo with inquisition. He was tall

and lean with no shirt to cover the scars he possessed on his hairy chest. He looked as if he had been rolling around in a field full of grass burrs. My mother always told me that you can tell the mannerisms of slaves. You have to look at their physical scars and rigor beneath his or her feet. I looked down to see the cakes of mud on his feet. He, too, looked at me critically but with a smug look. As if he knew I was the "special" Negro, or the "One-eyed Charlie" who was fortunate to ride my Master around because I was literally his biological product. Yes, I've seen that look plenty of times before.

Master Hollingsworth grew impatient at my scrutiny and scolded me for not starting the carriage on his demand. He chained the innocent man to the back of the wagon as he marched straight inside the coach. I quickly made haste by grabbing the reins and clicked my teeth to move the horses. After seeing Omo, I couldn't take my mind away from him. It was something about him…. something conjuring but exciting at the same time. How the sun glistened on his locks, as if it was lead of fire burning from his head. How his eyes burned right through my oblivious soul. He was different. I couldn't put a finger on it, but he was.

Season was so engrossed in the journal that she had forgotten about aunt. She looked out her window but didn't see Autumn. She quickly stashed the book back underneath the mattress and dashed to the front room to see if she could locate her aunt's whereabouts. Suddenly, she heard the backdoor open from the kitchen area and was finally relieved. Autumn, whose overalls were covered in dirt, closed the door and took off her garden gloves.

"What's going on?" she asked with a smile.

"Um…nothing, just got tired of watching television and thought maybe I could join you in the garden," Season lied.

Autumn looked at her niece hesitantly as she walked up to her. "Mh, you look as if you've seen a ghost."

"No, I'm fine, Aunt Autumn, really," Season smiled, hoping her good girl act was selling.

"Mh, well… I'm heading out to go grocery shopping. Any kind of knick-knacks you're craving?"

"Naw, I'm good. Thanks, though!"

"You are welcome to join me. I would rather you come. I'm trying to play nice, so I can perhaps persuade you to come with me to church tomorrow."

Season raised an eyebrow at Autumn's proposition. "I don't think so. I'm sorry, but I'm not about to worship with those hell-mongers, no offense, Aunt Autumn."

She expected her aunt to raise hell with that funny dialect, but to her surprise, Autumn didn't. Instead, her aunt walked by her calmly, heading out of the kitchen. As soon as Season let out a sigh of relief, Autumn turned around.

"You're going," she retorted, leaving dismissively.

By then, it was evening, and Season sat in her bedroom. She found herself thinking back on Marion Hollingsworth's journal entries. To say he was a slave back in the mid-1800s, he was clearly intelligent. His writing held so much depth when it came to expressing his feelings on the inequality of captivity. Season sympathized with the writer's pain and wanted to know more about him. What happened after the last entry she read? How did he become the founder of Hollins? And what was his connection to these diabolical people in this town?

Before getting up to shower, she looked across at a single item placed on her tall dresser. She sauntered over to pick it up. It symbolized the connection she shared with her now-former friend, Yusef. The vintage paperback of *The Giver*. She caught herself smiling and reflecting on Yusef and just the idea of fun, but then, she reflected on their last dreadful dialogue:

> *"What do you think the book means by 'released'?"*
> *"What do you think it means?"*
> *"I don't think the idea of it is as good as its word."*
> *"It's not. Let's just say it's a bad way of ostracizing someone from society."*
> *"You mean, how the community comes together out to the beach some nights for the Righteous Ritual?"*

Season tossed the book back on the dresser as if it was possessed. When she looked at the mirror above the chest, she screamed loudly as it reflected a worrisome Yusef, who was standing outside her bedroom window. Reacting to the scream, he let out a short shriek. Season ran to her window in haste, confused as to why he would be peeping at her.

"What is wrong with you? What are you doing here? How do you know where I even live?" Season scolded, firing questions as if she was his mother.

"I...I'm sorry, Season. I didn't mean to frighten you," he stated apologetically.

"What are you doing here, Yusef?"

"Well...I haven't seen you in a while, and I was worried. I thought something might've happened to you," he replied shamefully as he looked down to avoid eye contact.

"What do you mean, 'something might've happened to me?' What could possibly happen to me?"

"Yeah, you're right, just my imagination, I guess," he grinned sheepishly. "I'm sorry I left rudely. I had to leave."

"Oh yeah? Well, I didn't sweat it one bit," Season said dismissively, knowing well she was lying.

"I'm really sorry, Season. Truly I am...I missed our fun times on the beach, especially you reading to me. I couldn't stop thinking about you," he muttered.

Season began to soften to Yusef's apology. She couldn't stay mad at him for so long. Besides, there were still some unanswered questions that were pounding away at her. "Yusef?"

"Yes?"

"When we last talk, what did you mean by the 'Righteous Ritual'?" she asked softly.

Yusef gave her a look that made her shiver a bit, but she embraced herself so she could finally get the answers she deserved.

"Oh, it's just a silly thing folks do around here. There's nothing special about it," he laughed nervously.

"Uh-huh, I see…Well, I guess I will have to find the answer to my question elsewhere."

"What does that mean?"

"You know, you're just like everyone else around here. Too cautious, too eerie, and unreliable. Just leave, Yusef,"

"But…"

"Go!" Season yelled.

"Could I say just one thing?"

"You have ten seconds, Yusef,"

"Don't trust anyone here."

"You're telling me as if I didn't know this already," Season replied sarcastically.

"Please, just listen to me…stay away from the beach, Season. Don't go near it, okay?" Yusef begged, with terror in his eyes.

"Wait, what?"

"Just stay away," he warned once again. He turned and rushed off into the thickness of the night.

From that moment, Season was too stiff and fearful to move away from the window.

Chapter 9:

INDEBTED

Travelin' shoes, y'all
(Got on my travelin' shoes)
Travelin' shoes y'all
(Got on my travelin' shoes)

Once again, Season was back at the demented place of worship, where she claimed she wouldn't ever step foot in again, and once again, the Mahalia Jackson's doppelgänger was bringing the walls down with her fierce voice, making everyone stand up to their feet. Season could care less for praising in her traveling shoes, considering how her traveling stockings were making her itch.

This morning, Aunt Autumn won the war. After Season's insolence, she waived the proposition to the point of no negotiations. She purchased stockings and a long sheared and dreadful yellow dress for Season to wear to church. There wasn't much fight left in Season, especially after seeing Yusef last night. The combat was less of a battle after Season got to thinking that maybe being with her aunt was safer than being home alone.

The guitar carried the tune as the drums filled the sanctuary. Serene sat in the same spot in the lion's den. She gave Season a quick smile and a wave when she turned around, and Season returned the gesture. Season couldn't help but notice the bowling ball she had as a stomach. It never occurred to her how far along Serene might've been. Serene looked as if she could go into labor anytime now. Not far from where Serene sat was Mrs. Winnie, prancing around the altar. Season watched the ridiculous sideshow Mrs. Winnie was performing. Her stretched, bloated lips were pursed to her nose as if she was smelling something terrible, and her back was arched like a gazelle. She closed her eyes as she slowly strutted around in a circle, holding both sides of her dress an inch below her shiny black flats. She looked like a pedigree of a proud secretariat with a big, flamboyant sky-blue hat, who had just won first place. It certainly didn't help that the congregation was cheering the old woman on. Season stifled her laugh, for she knew her aunt kept an eye on her from the choir stand.

After everything died down, it was time for Pastor Hollis to deliver the sermon.

"Amen, Church!" he called out.

"Amen," the congregation responded.

"Whew, Sister Dorsey, ya done it again! Ya brought the

spirit back with dat voice of yours. Can I get an amen?"

"Amen," the congregation repeated.

"I don't know about you, but I'm feelin' good this here morning. The choir showing out, my beautiful deaconesses looking lovely in that corner over there, my men folks looking dapper as ever, and my congregation lookin' lovely, ain't I'm blessed, y'all?"

The rush of "amens" and "yes, pastor" rang simultaneously in the sanctuary.

"I'm telling you, ain't nothing like being blessed by our dear Savior in his holy temple. Sister Dorsey, you're blessed, child. You hear me? God blessed you with that voice to use you. He wants to use you to bring in his flocks, am I lying?"

The middle-aged woman was blushing from the choir stand as the other choir members beside her reached out to touch her shoulders.

"Ha, I wish I had a voice like that. I would be winning so many Stellar Awards, I think I'd get the big head and switch over to the devil's music," Pastor Hollis joked.

Everyone laughed at his joke as if it was the funniest thing they ever heard.

"I ain't lying, or as them young folks would say, 'I ain't cappin,'" he laughed so hard that he was beating his hand on the podium as the other members followed suit. "Mh, that happened to many of them stars out there. Started off singing in their home church…their roots. Then they got the big head and maneuvered over to the devil's music.

The Bible tells us in Romans 12:2, 'Do not be conformed to this world, but transformed by the renewal of your mind, that you may prove what that good and acceptable and perfect will of God is.' So those singers you listen to on the radio about 'Baby, you all I need,' the devil is a liar because GOD is all you need, can I get a witness in here, folks?"

"Amen, passa, preach on," the elderly deacon shouted.

"Y'all play 'round wit God, and don't obey him. He'll strip all that talent he has given you. What use is you when ya can't be a soldier of da Lord? Huh? What's your purpose on this here Earth? Last night, I had to wait on da Lord ta give me a message to say in front of y'all. I was stuck in a tailspin. I had to ask him, 'Lord, what message do you want me to give to your flocks this Sunday morning? I waited and waited…and he brought this memory of my dear brother to my mind. I ain't lyin."

Season wished that he could just eliminate the term "lying" from his vocabulary, as if he needed confirmation to know if he was telling the truth. Clearly, if it came out his mouth, and he believed it to be accurate, wouldn't he take his own word for it?

"My younger brother….mmh hmm… he had the brains to do whatever he wanted to. God blessed him with a long ride through college, and after college, a position in running this here town. And what did he do instead? He brought himself a one-way ticket out of this place to venture into the sinful nature of this world."

Like anyone could blame the poor guy, thought Season, with a frown on her face.

"When the Lord brought this matter to my attention, I wanted to cry for my brother. I wanted to cry because the world loves to turn its cold shoulder to a person like my brother and give him its behind to kiss…. Like drugs, alcohol, gangs, sexual diseases, theft, tramps, slumps, gambling, you name it, that's its evil behind."

Some people in the congregation were shaking their heads and giving looks of disdain at the mentioned topics.

"But y'all know? God told me…he said, 'Son, don't you worry 'bout dat. As sure as da foundation your mama and papa built for you, like a tree planted by the waters, he shall not be moved. Give him to me, Eddie. Let me secure your worries, and I'll bring him back like the prodigal son coming home to his father."

"Yaasss, passa….Believe that he'll do it!" Mother Winnie cried out with one arm in the air as if she was grasping for relief.

"I do believe he will do so, Mother Winnie. You want to know why? Cause I have the faith to believe my God can do anything but fail! Right now, he's being stripped of his talents because he's not using it wisely. And when he's done spending and falling, he's going to come back as the prodigal brother, and you know what I'm going to do?" Pastor Hollis asked with a smile.

"What?" the congregation asked.

"I'm going to welcome him back home with open

arms and say, 'Brother, you once were lost, but now, you're found!"

The crowd cheered wildly as if they were at a football game. Season and Autumn appeared to be indifferent to the pep talk Pastor Hollis was dictating.

"Now, let us pray for my brother, and keep the faith, y'all. Bow your heads for the words of prayer," he commanded.

Everyone obediently bowed their heads... Everyone except for Season, who was praying for the opposite. Praying that his brother has the good sense that God gave him not to return to a place like this ever again.

It was precisely three o'clock when Pastor Hollis finally decided to do the benediction. Season thought he would never finish his sermon topic, "Lost but Found." The craziest thing was that he continued talking more about his brother than directing his "flocks" on how they should apply the concept to their lives. After the last amen, she was so happy that she quickly jumped up and approached Serene, who seemed delighted to see her again.

"Hey girl," Season greeted as she was careful not to hug Serene tightly.

"Hey Season, how's it going'?" Serene asked.

"Man, I'm just happy that service is finally over. I don't know how you can endure this every Sunday.

Serene let out a small chuckle. "I guess if you were raised to do so, it starts becoming natural, ya know?"

"Mmh, well, I can't get used to this."

Serene looked Season up and down before commenting, "What! Are you wearing stockings?"

Season frowned.

"Looks good on you, Season. Look at ya, looking like a young lady."

"Yeah, right, more like an elderly lady."

"Oh, stop it," Serene chuckled.

Aunt Autumn came quickly to the young girls, looking as if her mind was working overtime.

"What's wrong?" Season asked.

"Who me? Oh, nothing," Autumn replied with a simple wave. "Just been thinking about something is all… Hey Serene, how's everything?"

"Everything is fine, Ms. Autumn. How's everything for you?" Serene asked politely.

"Everything is good, I guess," Autumn smiled. "You look as if you're about to burst."

"Yes, ma'am, it's getting close to the time."

"Nervous?" Season inquired.

"Umm, yes…I guess. More afraid than anything else. Afraid of what could happen after I deliver," she frowned while looking down.

Season was confused by her response. "Wait, how you could be afraid…"

"It's going to be alright, baby. Hold on to God's

unchanging hand, okay?" Aunt Autumn interrupted as she quickly held Serene in her arms.

Season couldn't understand what was transpiring in front of her. It was as if another conversation was going on without her knowing so. Surprisingly, Pastor Hollis came quickly into the small circle like a whirlwind, with a wide grin on his face.

"Praise da Lord, saints," he responded.

"Praise da Lord," Autumn and Serene responded.

"How are you this blessed day, Serene?" he asked.

"Fine," she replied, barely in a whisper.

"That's good, and you must be Season, am I correct?" he asked as he gave Season his right hand to shake.

"Yes, that's me," she replied with a thin smile, shaking his hand.

"Well, I'll be…" he smiled back as he stared at her intently.

"Pastor, that was some sermon you preach today," commented Aunt Autumn, clearing her throat.

"Huh? Oh yes, thank you, Sister Autumn. I had to speak what da Lord gave me," he said absently.

Season noticed how closely the pastor was eyeing her, and she felt uncomfortable. It wasn't a flirtatious look, but a look of familiarity. Either way, she didn't like him staring at her.

"Speaking of which, Sister Autumn, I need to talk to you briefly in my studies if you don't mind."

Autumn pretended to be surprised by his request. "Oh?"

"Yes, just for a brief minute. You don't mind leaving the young ladies here to talk for a minute, do you?"

"Sure, I'll be with you in a minute."

"God bless you, and nice seeing y'all, Season and Serene."

He made his way up to the front to greet more parishioners before exiting out a side door that led to the other side of the church.

"Season, if you will, please have a seat and wait for me; I'll be right back," Autumn assured.

"But…I want to go home," Season groaned, although she was curious as to why Pastor Hollis would want to speak with her aunt.

"Season, for once, please follow instructions. It won't be long, now," Autumn begged, then left the girls to follow the same route Pastor Hollis went.

Season couldn't take her eyes away from the door. It was an exit she was contemplating on taking. She knew what her aunt told her to do, but deep down, she knew she had to follow her.

"Ya wantin' to go see what they're talking about, don't you?" Serene asked with a sly grin on her face.

Season nodded.

"And if I told you to not go, would you go anyway?"

She nodded again.

"C'mon, let's go," Serene demanded, taking Season's hands.

"Go where?"

"To where you shouldn't go."

"Why would you want me to go?"

"I'm just figuring you out, Season Holidae. From what I can gather, you're like dat gal from the television show, *Nancy Drew*. You can't mind your own business to save your life. It's in your nature."

"You don't know me, Serene."

"Well, tell me I'm wrong. Tell me that you don't want to know what they're talking about in his study. If ya say I'm wrong, then we won't go."

Season bit her lips, trying hard not to admit Serene was right. She quickly surrendered and let Serene lead the way. The sanctuary was getting less crowded as people were making their way to their cars.

The door led to a long, narrow hallway with two entrances to the right and left and a door that stood at the end reading, "Pastor Hollis' Study" in gold letters. As if it was a reaction, Season began shaking, taking smaller steps than before. Serene turned around.

"You okay?" she asked, barely in a whisper.

"Um, yes…" Season whispered back.

"Sh! Ya have to be very quiet to listen," she instructed while placing a finger over her lips.

"Okay," Season agreed. She placed an ear to the door to listen to what was being discussed on the other side:

"I take it Mother Winnie told you about what happened the other day with Season?" she heard her aunt stated coldly.

"Yes, she did, actually, and I can't say I'm happy to hear what she told her," Pastor Hollis responded in a disappointed tone.

"Mh, and I take it that she didn't tell you how she was beating her pregnant grandchild like she stole something?" Autumn argued.

"Sister Autumn, you should know already, what happens in a family, stays in the family. You should have never gotten involved."

"Oh, so beating a poor pregnant child upside the head should be looked over, is that what I'm hearing?"

Pastor Hollis sighed, "Look, Sister Autumn, what Mother Winnie does is her business. She's raising that child, not you."

"Well, I don't feel it's right, Pastor."

"You don't have to feel anything when it's nonya business," he snapped.

Everything got quiet after that. Season pressed her ear near the door to see if her aunt would make a rebuttal. It was as if she was listening to an important debate at her old school again. If she could, she would've joined in to shut down Pastor Hollis.

"Look, Sister Autumn, I apologize," he said, softening his tone. "You can't bring trouble where it's not wanted. You know how things work around here. Mother Winnie is one of the few pillars left to uphold our integrity and traditions in this town."

"Why must things be the way they are, Eddie?" Autumn questioned, almost crying. "Why not do the *right* thing? I know how we were raised, but who's to say that it was the right way?"

"And what's the right way, Autumn?" he asked boldly. "Huh? What is the right way? By letting our sins get the best of us?"

"Eddie, I read that Bible through and through, and in no way, shape or form did it say anything about what we're doing is right. Trust me, sooner or later, we all got to pay the consequences."

"IN CASE YOU FORGOT, WE'RE IN TRANS-ACTION!" he yelled.

Season couldn't believe what she heard on the other side of the door. What did her aunt mean by "pay the consequences"? What did Pastor Hollis meant when he mentioned "transaction"? She looked to Serene for answers, but Serene turned her back towards her. She quickly placed her ear to the door once again.

"Did you forget, Autumn? Did you forget what happened nearly fifteen years ago? After what you've done to tarnish our ritual?"

"The hell with the ritual, Eddie!"

"The hell with what? It was you! You brought shame to your own family's name. Ya mother and father died, carrying the heartbreak of the both of ya to da grave with them!"

Season could hear her aunt sobbing slowly in the background. She wanted to intervene but wanted to hear more.

"You leave my mama and pa out of this, Eddie!"

"The hell if I do, Autumn. It's because of you that my brother ran away too. Your mama and pa understood the consequences, and that's why they left *you* to pay the debt. So, as far as I'm concerned, you indebted to Hollins…you indebted to me! After what you pull all those years, you have the same blood on your hands as we all do!"

Suddenly, the girls heard the opposite door from the other side of the hallway. Serene pulled on Season's arms so they could leave. Season, too revolted and puzzled to move away from the door, yanked her arms back.

"Gal, you're goin' to get the both of us in a world of trouble. Let's make haste," Serene whispered as she grabbed for Season's arms again.

This time, Season followed Serene as they tried to rush down the hallway. As they were halfway between the two doors, Mother Winnie stood at the exit with her arms placed on her hips. She looked like she was auditioning for a western movie and was ready to draw at any moment.

"Where y'all comin' from?" she demanded, squinting her eyes, trying to look fierce.

Season was too scared to answer, but Serene thought quickly on her feet.

"Um, we had to use the restroom," she answered as she placed her hand on the closest doorknob to the left.

"Uh-huh, I bet," Mother Winnie snapped as she

ambled to the girls. Season and Serene slowly began to back away from the aggressive old woman.

"Ya know what they say about curiosity? It kilt that cat!" she said, wielding an invisible knife in front of the girls.

"Yes, ma'am," Serene gulped with a nod.

"Ya scared of me, child? Aren't ya?" Mother Winnie asked Season.

Season stared at her with fear, refusing to respond to her question.

"Well, ya should be. Ain't got all dat mouth now? Do ya? Ya try dat stunt again, and see where ya end up, gal," she threatened.

Suddenly the door to Hollis's office opened, and the Pastor and her aunt stepped into the hallway.

"What's going on?" Autumn frowned.

"Dem gals sayin' they goin' ta-da restroom, but I think they want to listen in on grown folks' conversation," Mother Winnie replied, with a cruel look on her face.

Season expected her aunt to scold her right then and there for her disobedience. Instead, Autumn displayed a look of defeat, disappointment, and hurt.

"Let's go," her aunt said quietly as she placed her hands tenderly on her niece's back and led her back to the exit.

Season turned around to see a sad Serene waving goodbye to her and a strange, satisfying look on both Pastor Hollis's and Mother Winnie's face.

Chapter 10:

THE RIGHTEOUS RITUAL

The rest of the afternoon went by slowly. Instead of taking Season straight home from church, Autumn drove into town to an old-fashioned ice-cream parlor called Ian's Frozen Cream. Inside the small place, the decorum looked like a 1950's furnished diner shop. The long island bar had a baby blue marble top, completed with six shiny red barstool underneath it. The topping bar to the left side of the place was enticing, filled with any toppings you could think of to put on some tasty cold treats. Six booths were placed near the parlor's far wall, with Autumn and Season occupying the last booth near the restroom. Season had three scopes of Aquamarine Mint Chocolate in her bowl, whereas her aunt had two scopes of Pa's Praline Cream.

The mood was quiet but uncomfortable as they sat in silence, shielding their ice cream and their thoughts without any eye contact. Season looked around the walls to see the big black and white printouts of what seemed to be old pictures of African American teens appearing at the same establishment to what appeared to be over fifty years ago. They looked to be having the time of their lives, with the girls' long poodle skirts and white button-up shirts, and handsome guys appearing dapper with conks or a short cut with a huge part in their hair, wearing a schoolboy sweater. One picture showed one guy swinging a girl over his neck. Another couple shared a huge ice cream sundae while looking at each other with admiration in their eyes. The images of these black faces were captivating and treasured, as they definitely symbolized the epitome of Black American love.

"The pictures are fascinating, aren't they?" Autumn asked, noticing Season's engagement with the murals.

"It's beautiful. Never would have depicted us at a diner sock-hop kind of joint," Season admitted.

"Well, I guess if there's one positive thing to say about Hollins, it's primarily black-owned."

"Yeah, one out of ninety-nine isn't bad," sighed Season as she dug into her ice cream.

"That's one of the ironic reasons why I like coming here. It seems so rich with our culture, as if the happiest times for us happened in these establishments we were banned from during segregation. Instead of doing sit-ins or boycotting, the older generation believed we should have the same equal rights and institutions as the Whites."

"True, but we shouldn't have to add separation to everything. It just gives validation to the Southern racist pricks who started this whole segregation mess to begin with. America is not a color or race, but a gumbo melting pot full of ethnicity to give all a satisfying feeding of freedom. When we start separating or leaving out the ingredients from the gumbo, then it's a recipe for disaster," explained Season.

"I haven't thought about it like that, Season. But what's wrong with black-owned businesses?"

"Nothing is wrong with black-owned businesses. I think it's imperative and prominent to do so, but we shouldn't only cater to Blacks, is all."

"Well, I don't think that was the concept behind it, Season. Our race has always been so receptive to other races when it comes to buying, selling, and supporting since I don't know how long. If it wasn't for black-owned businesses, we couldn't survive or repress or pay for the over-priced items that were being sold in those White establishments."

"I wonder what the Black innovators of America thought about when creating their inventions. Did some think their inventions would be useful? Or sold to only Black people or White people? What about Black scientists or doctors who discovered expedient ways to send a man into space or even heal people? Black writers amusing and expressing the emotions we all feel as humans? Or Black entertainers suppressing and exposing the pain by singing the blues or performing with hurt? It wasn't intended for just Black people, but for all races to be receptive of us, as we of all them. As African Americans, we helped build and contribute so much to this country, which made us the stock in that gumbo soup," Season declared.

Autumn, too stunned to reply to Season's concept of the American Dream, gave her a slow smile then ate some of her ice cream. "Summer raised one hell of a smart child. I'm so glad to have you in my life."

Season gave her a weak smile as she went back to her now melted ice cream.

"I know you eavesdropped on us earlier," Autumn stated nervously.

Contritely, she looked at her aunt to confirm the claim.

Autumn continued, "There are some things you wouldn't understand, Season. Things I wasn't so proud of in the past."

"We all make mistakes, Aunt Autumn," assured Season, hoping deep down that her aunt could tell her more on what was being discussed in the office. "Just keeping it hidden makes matters worse."

"Yeah…you're right, but still…Some things are left better unsaid. The repulsion of it all, you shouldn't have to be exposed to it."

"What did Pastor Hollis mean when he said that you were indebted to him?"

Autumn slumped in her chair overwhelmingly. She slowly pushed her bowl away from her and clasped her hands tightly together on the table. "I did something that I thought was right at the time, but I put shame on my family's name. In the end, I had to pay for it. I'm still paying for it."

"What did you do?" Season inquired.

Autumn looked at her niece but shook her head to signal her silence on the matter.

Assuming the answer wasn't going to be so easy to get in the first place, Season asked, "If you're not going to answer that question, then answer this, was it worth it?"

As she wiped tears from her eyes, she stared back at Season and replied, "Yes, every bit of it."

"All right, Miss Season, time for bed," said Autumn standing outside the room door, watching Season as she pulled her covers back to get in bed.

"Yep, I have to get up in the morning since I'm a 'working woman' now," Season chuckled as she rolled her eyes.

Autumn chuckled as well as she came into the room to sit on the bed. "I know it would be hypocritical of me to ask any questions, considering how I foiled when you asked me questions earlier at the parlor. But there's one question I've been dying to ask you since you got here."

Season sat up in the bed with anticipation. "Ask away, I am an open book," she declared, hoping her response would cause a little sting to her aunt.

"Why swimming? Why do you love the sport of swimming?" she asked with a look of interest.

Season was a bit startled by her question, not saying that she wasn't asked that before, but the way her aunt asked seemed a bit strange. She thought about her response, and it made her smile. "Because it's refreshing…when I'm in that water, I feel as if it's a part of me. I know I sound a bit corny, but I feel as if it's my destiny to do so. It's funny; you have people who fear drowning, but not me. I drown my sorrows and hurt when I'm swimming. It's my security blanket when all else fails on this land, you know?"

Autumn was lost in thought after Season's response, but she gradually nodded her head with a smile. "Season Holidae, you are one amazing thirteen-year-old girl, you know that?"

"I'm okay," Season smiled.

"Well, I'm about to hit the sack. I have to get you to the library tomorrow and me to my own job," Autumn yawned as she got up to stretch and walk out of the room.

"Aunt Autumn?"

"Yes, honey?"

"Do you mind if I read for a bit? I have to finish up this summer reading list before school starts back, so I have to get a head start," Season pleaded.

"Sure, sweetie. But don't stay up too late, or you won't be able to get up on time."

"Oh, do you mind closing the door? I think I'll be okay."

"You're sure?" Autumn asked with concern.

"Yeah, it's okay."

"Well, if you need me, I'm right down the hall. Goodnight," Autumn assured, closing the door gently.

"Goodnight," Season called back.

As soon as she heard her aunt's footsteps down the hallway, she crept out of her bed to lock the door quietly. She went quickly to the mattress to retrieve the forbidden book. Reading the rest of the entries was all she could have thought about today, and now, she had the chance to finally do just that.

March 29, 1851

I am fervent with rage! I cannot explain the extent of my wrath or what I can do if provoked by even a single blow of wind. The one thing I found pleasurable in all my young adult years was stripped away from me by my father's unsettling and despicable libido. What drives this man so much to know not only his wife but half of his female slaves and a few white mistresses in town? He's a monstrous God who is impossible to satisfy. He exploits all women and defeats all the little "white gods" who dare to cross him. I've never experienced the absolute term of "hate" until I witnessed what I saw today.

"Nigger!" he yelled… "Nigger," as he thundered in the house with red disdain on his face. He slammed the door, and the wife came to comfort him. He

calmed down long enough to reveal to her how the town's mockery of him was unbearable. When they both spotted me by the door, the Misses slapped me in the face, called me a "house pet," and "to never eavesdrop on private conversations on others." She ordered me to go out back with my mother in the quarters. Father, too blinded with vengeance to say anything, pranced back and forth in the common room, mumbling something under his breath.

I rushed out of the house in fear of falling victim to his hostility and walked down to the quarters to visit Mother. When I got there, I saw a few of my siblings playing outside. When I opened the cabin, my mother, her sister, and my two uncles were at the table indulging in a serious exchange.

As I greeted them, they did not return it at all. Mother had a look of trouble on her face as she told me to sit down. At first, I was hesitant to do so, but the seriousness in one of my uncle's eyes told me I better think smart and fast.

She asked, "Why ya didn't tell me about that negro 'ooman?"

I felt confused and cornered with this type of question as if they were blaming me. But for what?

"Ya know what I'm talking, don't act dead. That negro ooman who was teaching them gals and you them letter and numbers? Ya didn't tell me she was a Negro!"

At that point, I was in total shock and confusion. Miss Moreau? A Negro? It can't be! I tried to explain to my mother how ridiculous she was sounding and how Miss Moreau was a heartwarming white French lady who showed nothing but compassion toward me. She was the only white woman, I guess you could say, who treated me as an individual and not as a diseased animal. Mother wouldn't hear it; instead, she slapped me on the head and told me to open my eyes. One of my uncles, Uncle Coffey, told her to take it easy on me. He used the term "white smart" and not "bible smart" to explain my ignorance. I was slightly offended by his choice of words, but it did stop mother from chastising me.

Uncle Jack took over by explaining what he heard from the other workers from different plantations of a group of "free black educators" from Cincinnati to infiltrate Southern states. If they passed as "white," they were taught to learn a foreign language and culture to deceive the Southern whites into thinking they were refined, foreign teachers. If they couldn't pass as white, they were to go in as what they ran away from in the first place, as a slave. Miss Moreau was the latter. Their primary purpose was to not only free the slaves, literally, but to free them mentally. By doing so, it enlightens us to make the risky trip up north meaningful. I had to contest that Miss Moreau did just that to my mind. My dear uncle also said how

Miss Moreau's true identity was exposed by a Judas in her camp. After learning the truth from folks in town, Mr. Hollingsworth was not only ashamed but livid.

Mother, who was troubled with the news, left out the cabin weeping in sorrow. Maybe because she felt sorry for Miss Moreau, or perhaps frighten for me if Master Hollingsworth caught wind of knowing I was one of Miss Moreau's targeted pupils. Later on, I would figure out that it was the latter.

The rest of us sat still for a long spell, dictating only silent thoughts in our own minds and watching the fire in the chimney place devouring the logs. I glanced at Uncle Coffey a few times, shaking his head, and Uncle Jack mumbling obscenity under his breath. Maybe they were thinking, why would any liberated Negro sacrifice his or her freedom to help the enslaved? There's a thin line between heroism and insanity, but I believe what separates the two was the passion.

It was over an hour when Mother finally came flying back into the door, as if the wind pushed her in. The look on her face spoke hysteria as she broke into an emotional episode to tell us how Master Hollingsworth took Miss Moreau captive inside one of the broken cabins where he usually goes to do his "business." As an impulse, I rushed out of the house, despite my family's cries to come back. I had to see if she was okay. I had to get her out before that ole' Hollingsworth gets his way with her.

When I got there, I thought I would have some struggles with the door, but the door was half-closed, to my surprise. That was a bad sign. After witnessing the scene that was laid out before me, I was too late.

When I was with my family, he had sufficient time to enact his evil plan. He stood over her lifeless, dismembered corpse with pride in his eyes and wickedness in his smile. His pants were loose, and his shirt was smudged with Miss Moreau's blood. In his hand was a soaked pickaxe he used to butcher pigs. To him, Miss Moreau's life was equivalent to such a nasty animal.

He noticed my presence and looked at me with insanity in his eyes and spoke, "That'll teach 'em not to pull one on me. Albino rats need to stay where they are. No one makes a fool out of John Hollingsworth! Now round up my properties and the other pick ninnies to see what betrayal looks like, boy!"

I couldn't move…I was frozen in place with tears rushing down my face. Suddenly, like Moses parting the red sea, my knees gave out, and combustion rose from my soul. Everyone in the quarter, including my mother and uncles, probably heard me because they came rushing toward the cabin. Master Hollingsworth hurried over to me and knocked me on the head with the butt of the ax. I couldn't remember anything after that.

Tonight, I write because I want this to be known.

I will not sleep or dwell in any happiness until Master Hollingsworth's life is as equivalent to a pig!

April 21, 1851

For the last couple of entries, I wrote about Omo and the new marks he received on his body from unlucky endeavors. It's something about his presence that vexes me but excites me as well. I can't hardly explain it. Whenever Omo refused to obey or did something not to the master's liking, Pony, the overseer, had to punish him. Strangely enough, all the lashings this poor human endured, it didn't break him one ounce. He was as strong as an oak tree with limitless strength and power. He couldn't be brought down by the fierceness of man. Even the others saw this and thought it was something supernatural about him. What was even stranger was the fact that Master Hollingsworth didn't intervene when it comes to "setting him straight." Usually, he would chastise us without a second thought. But when it came to Omo, his boldness seemed too weakened. I didn't quite understand the reluctances until last week, when Omo finally encountered me.

As I mentioned in my past entries about how distraught and disturbing I was after Miss Moreau, I allowed vengeance to consume me. My last attempted plan failed after my mother apprehended me for mixing poisonous berries in his tea. She told me, "Let the

Good Lord handle him," but the Good Lord wasn't working fast enough for my good. I wanted my father to meet his evil maker in hell that day, and it cringes me to know that I was almost one step closer to helping him get there.

That fateful day while I was tending to Hollingsworth's prized horse, Eugene, at the stables, there appeared Omo by the door, stocking some hay off the trailer. He couldn't stop looking at me with those deep eyes of his. I felt a bit uncomfortable. What did he fancy about me? Did I look familiar to him? Or was it the same look as the others when they look at me…a privileged mulatto?

His first words, "Was that your teacher yo' daddy Massa killed?"

I didn't know how to answer the question, considering how he called Hollingsworth "my daddy massa," and she wasn't technically my teacher. I replied, "I didn't know she was like me."

He stopped what he was doing, and looked at me intently with the same serious eyes, this time with empathy. "I heard you want to get even with him, your daddy massa."

"He's not my 'daddy master,' and he's going to get what's coming to him."

"You want that to happen?" he asked.

I nodded.

"Then lemme take you under my wings. There are

ways far betta than killin.'

I thought about what he said, and it interested me. I implored to know more.

"Killin' him would be blood on ya hands you have to clean. Our sins will cause us to suffer slowly and painfully. Eventually, he would die a cruel death."

"You're just like the rest of them....wait on the Lord to punish him for his evil deeds," I cried out profusely as I turned my back to him.

He came to me with comfort and said, "No, I was taken away from my Akoko. I was angry and upset. But she saw to it that my anger wouldn't be in vain."

I was confused about who he was referring to as his "Akoko," but I found out later that he meant his mother.

"Clean this man's sinful heart by taking away something he loves in return," he continued. "Killing him means putting him out of his misery. Make him suffer!"

I gave him a look of confusion, for I did not know what my father coveted so much that it would make him suffer.

"If you let me fix this, you in return have to do me a favor," he insisted.

At first, I wondered what favor he would want from me, but I was too irate, and I walked right into his cleverness without thinking. I accepted this proposition, realizing later my soul was snatched from God's grace.

Season was in awe at what she was reading and looked at the clock to see that it was getting late. Who was really this Omo character? It was moments like this where she wished she wasn't so intrusive in matters. She was about to close the book until she turned the page and read two words that caught her attention. These words and this entry was the answer she was looking forward to in solving this mystery:

April 24, 1851
"The Righteous Ritual"

After spending a couple of days with Omo, I began to understand his life's earlier exposition. He wasn't human. He wasn't God. There was no category to describe who or what he was. His origin traced back to a small village located in Nigeria. I will try to communicate this story to the best of my knowledge, praying that writing it on paper would make sense to whomever reads this journal.

Omo claimed his biological mother was of the great Orisha, or Goddess of the ocean named Yemaya. She was a water deity who brought fertility and cleansing to women in his village, where most women were barren at the time. She had him as a gift to sacrifice to any poor woman's soul who longed for a child to raise as her own. To Omo's luck, there was an old ajẹ, or witch by the name of Akoko, who prayed for a child to call her own.

As she sat by the river to ask Yemaya for a child (something she was doing for many years), a small wave carried a wooden straw box along the sea. As she spotted the box, she rushed in to fish it out of the ocean. As she reached the sand, she placed it on the ground and opened the box to see what was in it. Covered with straws and water, laid a beautiful boy child, who appeared to be lifeless. She took the small corpse out of its carrier and breathed life into him, realizing Yemaya wouldn't harm something of hers. After bringing life to the child, she thanked the Goddess of the ocean, took off her shawl to swaddle him in it, and took him home to raise. She called this boy child "Omo," which meant baby.

Akoko raised the child as if it was her own. She taught him the way of the land, the family practice of necromancy, and how to defend himself in case of any danger. Since she was the village witch, the villagers respected her only out of fear. They knew the consequences for disrespecting her and her son, or else they wouldn't live to tell the story. It was during harvest time when the village men went on a quest to hunt the fiercest game. Akoko thought it would be a great plan to teach the now young man, Omo, how to be a man by joining the others on their quest. What was meant to be a rite of passage for predators led to the predators being the prey.

In the wild, Omo noticed unfamiliar men riding

on horses. They were pale, loud, and spoke in an un-accustomed tongue. Their intense, invasive visit set off a confrontation, which ended up with four of the warriors dying from gunshot wounds. Because of this, not to mention the gun smoked air, the native men realized their bows and spears were no match for the long muskets the interlopers were carrying. They sur-rendered under their enemies, including Omo. The white human poachers clasped long rusted iron shack-les on each of their necks, making sure their hands were bound in shackles as well. They marched them along the woods to the clear ocean blue water, where a huge cargo ship filled with human cargo from their village awaited their presence.

Not too far from the seaside, Omo could hear his mother calling and wailing out his name. Afraid the men would spot his Akoko if he called out to her, he kept in his yells and cried instead. Nothing prepared him for this day, to see his mother for one last time. The invisible umbilical cord was now cut loose, and there was hell to pay. Omo could see his mother's arm reach-ing out to him from a distance, coveting his embrace.

For many days and nights, underneath the cargo holds, Omo tried reaching out to his mother based on a ritual she taught him. He tried meditating throughout the nights, although being compressed into a contami-nated and confined space didn't help matters at all. All he could get from his visions were rambunctious red *waves and young children crying from back home. He didn't quite understand what was going on or what was going on with his mother. All he could think about was if she was okay and did she escape.*

Days turned into long weeks as they journeyed on from place to place, being fed soggy rice, defecating and urinating on themselves, being plastered in their own vomit from seasickness. There were some deaths below, which made the ship heavy with deadweights aboard. To relieve the extra weight, the crew members began throwing the lifeless corpses to the sea. The detainees below salvaged the small amount of energy they had left to sing in their native tongue the song for the dead. Omo did not partake in the sad, communal spiritual. It was a sign of weakness. It was a sign to foreshadow his departure from the Earth. He went against his better judgment by following suit with the others, and looked where it got him? Constrained by ruthless men who wanted to do God knows what to him. Inside, he was afraid, but he would not let anyone around him see those emotions. Therefore, he showed no remorse for the dead and no weakness for the hopeless.

When they finally reached the new world, they were placed in a small room with no ventilation, where there were no doors, just the open air. From what I gathered, in barracoons as they were called, where they were trapped there for weeks in chains.

One fateful day, they were forced to make space for more slaves to come in from another ship. In this group, he met a familiar face by the name of Jimoh. Jimoh was a child under him, and it seemed the brutal trip took a lot from his health. As they spoke in their native tongues, Jimoh was desperate to tell Omo what became of his mother:

"When she watched you drift away from her, she became hysterical. The Orishas seemed to be on her side as she cast a spell over the village. She blamed the villagers for your capture. She played with the mothers' minds and drove them all to sacrifice their babies to the ocean, as she felt her gift was taken from her. She said, 'A sin for a sin leaves hands clean only for a passing mood, until the heart is either faint or satisfied!' Then she perished in the sea"

After hearing this, Omo vowed to cleanse his vengeful heart by returning the gift Yemaya had given women to reproduce.

The sins of the father and mother would only be cleansed by the sacrifice of their first newborn. To be honest, I was disturbed and petrified after hearing this out of Omo's mouth, but sooner or later, a seed began to grow inside me. A seed that sprouted out poison for the innocent. Maybe it was his doing. Perhaps Omo cast something upon my heart to only see the vengeance I craved so much. My innocence left the day Hollingsworth took Miss Moreau away.

Season read the last paragraph over again to see if her eyes were deceiving her. *Sacrifice? Newborns? Is this reality? Clearly, this Marion Hollingsworth had to know this purpose was far below getting some silly revenge for a woman who he was acquainted with as his teacher. Could Omo possibly have spelled him to believe in such a craft?* Season closed the book and threw it on the floor as if it was burning her hands. *Is this the same "righteous ritual" these crazy people are practicing? If so, they need to be stopped!* Season got up and pranced back and forth in her room like she was a ticking time bomb. She wanted so much to react to this madness, but what could she do? There's no way they could get away with something huge like this. Was her aunt involved in all this too? There were so many questions generating in her mind that she had to take a breather.

She unlocked her door and crept quietly down the hallway so she could get a glass of water. She did not want to wake up her aunt…her alleged homicidal aunt. The very thought of her aunt keeping a secret so deadly, it gave Season chills. What if her aunt found out what she knew? What would she do to her own niece to keep something like this from surfacing out of this town? As she reached for a clean glass in the cabinet, she slowly turned on the faucet to fill her glass with water. Before she could drink her water, she heard the door from her aunt's room open and slow footsteps coming towards her. It startled her so that she accidentally dropped the glass on the hardwood floor. The water splashed all on her bedroom shoes and pants as the glass was now broken into pieces.

"Season, what happened?" Autumn cried, looking at the accident on the floor.

"I…I…I wanted a glass of water. I didn't mean to break the glass," Season stuttered fearfully.

"Oh, honey, you have to be careful! Walk around the glass, I'll clean it up. Just go to bed. It's late, and you have to get up in the morning," Autumn replied as she reached for the broom and dustpan near a corner.

"Yeah, I am a bit tired," Season agreed as she tread carefully around the glass and around her aunt.

"What's wrong with you, child? You look like someone scared the jeepers out of you! Is it the book?"

"Huh? What book?!"

Autumn gave Season a skeptical look. "The book that was on your reading list, silly."

"Oh yeah, that book! Um…yeah. That's it."

"Well, that's enough reading for tonight then; you don't need to have any more bad dreams."

That's for sure, Season thought.

"Goodnight."

"Um, goodnight."

Chapter 11:

THE SACRIFICE

*M*onday morning awaited Autumn and Season with a heavy fog. While Autumn made a light breakfast, Season took her time to wash up and do her hair. After reading the diary entries from last night, having breakfast with her aunt was far from what Season wanted to do. By the time she got ready, Autumn had made her an egg toast sandwich and told her to carry it with her in the car. Season, loaded with questions and concerns for Cindy, made sure to slide the book in her backpack.

"What's wrong with you, gal?" Autumn questioned, driving Season to work.

"Nothing, just a little sleepy," Season answered, trying to avoid her aunt's eyes while pretending she was sluggish.

"Well, I told you about staying up half the night, but you didn't listen," Autumn warned as she stopped at a stop sign.

"Next time, I'll listen."

"Today is the day for the unknown," Autumn quoted, more to herself.

"Why would you say that?" Season inquired.

"All this fog is not good for people who can't see very well. Sooner or later, something unexpected may come."

"It's not going to be like this all morning, Aunt Autumn. It will clear up by the afternoon."

"Maybe."

Autumn instructed her to call whenever she was ready to get picked up as they reached the library. Season was to work from eight to two that day, so she would have to wait until her aunt came to get her on her break—enough time to read another entry. Season waved goodbye as she got out of the car and rushed inside the building.

As expected, it was empty, but surprisingly, Cindy was early today. She had on a fuchsia and grey plaid dress with a headband to match. She had small gold buds attached to her ears to complement her stylish but conservative style. She was wearing glasses as she was reading what looked to be an article.

"Hey, nerd…I need to talk to you," Season teased as she went behind the circulation desk to place her backpack behind the counter.

Cindy looked up as she took off her glasses slowly, using both her pointer fingers. "What do you want, Miss Heathen?"

"We need to talk about this book you just gave me!"

Cindy looked both ways before responding, "What about the book, and please keep quiet."

Season groaned at Cindy's paranoia before continuing. "I finally read up to the part where it discussed the 'righteous ritual.'"

"Oh."

"Oh? You're acting as if this is a normal, ceremonious action. This is serious! Please tell me that the righteous ritual isn't about killing an innocent child. Please!"

Cindy looked ahead as she concentrated on the exit door. "It's normal to Hollins. It's something we were born into, Season. Instead, I had never gotten used to the idea of infanticide. It seems all this world will ever do is kill off anything or anyone innocent, just to make your life a living hell. You think I'm proud of my hometown practicing such a thing?"

"Then why haven't you reported it, Cindy? Why hasn't anyone reported it to the authorities?"

"Because…I'm afraid, Season. That's why," she cried, wiping her eyes. "It's like the whole town is brainwashed and driven to do madness. They literally think they're being purified of their sins, but it's the total opposite. They got everyone fooled around here."

"Who's 'they'?"

"Hollins' Devotees. The pillars of this community."

"Pillars like Mrs. Winnie and Pastor Eddie Hollis?"

"There's more…."

"You mean, my aunt? Autumn?

She nodded her head.

Season was hoping for Cindy to say no to her question. "Who else is involved?"

"As far as the pillars of the community. They all are, in fact, the descendants of John Hollingsworth's slaves. Pastor Eddie Hollis is his great, great, great-grandson.

"Why am I not surprised by this?" Season asked.

"I guess it can be obvious by the partiality of the name. Once freedom presented itself, most slaves kept or shortened their oppressor's surname."

"If it was me, I would've changed my name," snapped Season.

"They worked, sweat, and bled by that name. Having a distinguished surname was credibility back then," interrupted a voice from the back.

Season turned around to see Mrs. DeVeau leaving out her office with a serious look on her face. She then began to panic out of fear. She didn't know whether to trust the dotty librarian or not. Season turned to see Cindy's face, but Cindy didn't share the same emotion oddly enough. It was as if she was comfortable with Mrs. DeVeau interfering with what they were talking about.

"Like Tina told that lawyer on *What's Love Got to Do with It?* She worked too hard for that name," chuckled Mrs DeVeau, finding a seat near a corner.

Okay, I'm confused. What is going on? Season thought.

The witty librarian caught on to Season's puzzled face and began to smile. "I took it you read the book?"

Season remained silent, refusing to answer any questions that could put her in harm's way.

"I told Cindy Lou to give you that book. At first, she didn't want to, but I knew better. I've been friends with your family for a long time. Ola Mae and I didn't agree on everything, but one thing we did agree on is this town's appetite for serving the devil. Your mother and aunt were good girls. They knew what was right and what was wrong. If you're anything like them, then I know you'll agree to this also…that this town is heading down damnation!"

"So you knew Mrs. DeVeau was in on this the whole time?" Season asked Cindy.

"Yes, I knew. At first, I didn't trust you. It's hard to trust tainted minds these days, but Mrs. DeVeau was the only person I could trust. She noticed how different and standoffish I was towards everyone. I was currently researching to write an article about this town's fatality practice, and she advised me to play the role so I wouldn't stick out like a sore thumb. If it wasn't for her, I wouldn't have found the strength to do so. I only have my mother and sick brother to tend to. If Hollins knew what I was doing, my family would pay. This article is my chance to get my family and me out of here for good. That's why I came back home. I couldn't just leave them here."

Season began to feel sympathy toward Cindy. She finally understood her purpose for coming back to Hollins, and she couldn't blame her for doing so. Yet, there was still one unsettling question that was tearing away at Season.

"You said my mom and aunt were good girls," Season clarified to Mrs. DeVeau.

"They were," she admitted.

"Then why is my family one of the pillars of the community? Were they descendants of Hollingsworth's slaves as well?"

"Oh, dear child…you can't help or change what family you were born into. You can only make good choices in the present to dictate the brightness in the future. I wish I could tell you more, but it's your aunt's job to do so," coaxed Mrs. DeVeau.

Season lowered her eyes. She knew her chances of her aunt having this conversation was zero to none. "She will never do so."

"Only because she wants to protect you, dear. These people are perilous. Trust me, I know, and I understand your aunt perfectly. But, it's only right for her to tell you the truth."

"The truth about what?" asked Season, now more irritated than before.

"How you and your family are the descendants of the great Yoruba *brujo*, Omo."

After hearing Mrs. DeVeau reveal the most revolting truths, Season fainted. Cindy and Mrs. DeVeau fanned her and waited until she was conscious of consoling her, but she refused their kindness. Instead, she grabbed her back-pack, headed straight to Mrs. DeVeau's office, slammed the door, and locked it. Cindy was about to unlock it with one of her keys, but Season heard Mrs. DeVeau commanding her not to. The news hit her like a tidal wave. Never in a million years would she expect to be related to an evil warlock who pardons himself by killing innocent babies. Was this why Summer was so quiet about her side of the family all those years? If so, she had every right to be, but she could have let her own husband know about this as well. Maybe he wouldn't have been so quick to send her here.

"Can't be…can't be…," Season muttered as she reached for Hollingsworth's book in her bag. She found her page where she left off to start on the next journal entry:

May 29, 1851

Some slave masters detested having their slaves' soul's being saved. They would laugh as if it was the most preposterous thing anyone could think of. A slave having souls? That's like saying wild beasts have souls. Does that mean we should pray over every animal in this world? The only souls they have are their sole purpose of submissiveness to their masters. Ironically, Hollingsworth would disagree. He was a very superstitious and somewhat religious white man who wanted his slaves to receive the "word." Only not because he cares, but he saw it as a fear tactic for us to honor and fear him. He would usually send Pastor Euling to come pray over us and give us a word in his own interpretations. Unlike my other counterparts, I knew better than to listen to Pastor Euling's crude analysis of 'what thus sayeth his Lord.' He would always elaborate on one key phrase for us, "vengeance is mine, saith the lord".....If only the Pastor could attest to what happened the last few days up to last night, he would've given up being a shepherd for his own master.

It seemed once I lost one teacher, I gained another one in Omo. He taught me a lot, but not all he knew about dark magic. At first, I was skeptical about it; even my mother told me to be careful around Omo. She said she felt uncomfortable in his presence, and her spirit didn't agree with his. I was only keeping him in my company to see if he would keep his word...to see Hollingsworth suffer. In the end, it paid off.

One night I followed Omo to the edge of the woods. He asked me to retrieve something closely related to Hollingsworth. I was able to sneak into the master bedroom, get a few hairs from his brush, and wrap it up in a handkerchief. When I gave it to him, he told me not to follow him, that this part was for him to perform only. I watched as he disappeared into the dark, thick wilderness as the moon reflected a blue light on his back. I was anxious to know what he was up to, but I knew better than to go against a man like Omo.

The next day, I woke up on my uncomfortable cot in the basement. Like clockwork, I was to report upstairs and tend to my normal duties. Hollingsworth was already up and out the house, probably on one of his hunting excursions. Usually, I didn't have to attend with him while he sports. He would take two young slave boys to scare some birds so he could shoot at them. My sisters were not there as well, for they were visiting some distant relatives. Mrs. Hollingsworth was ordered by the doctor to stay on bed rest until it was time for her to deliver.

I can honestly say, being in the house with Mrs. Hollingsworth was an absolute pain. She would ring that little bell she had near her as if there was no tomorrow, demanding the house servants to do this for her or do that. The woman was resilient in making our lives a living hell. That same day, she asked Big Hortense, the chief maid, to send for her son, Ben, the blacksmith. Master Hollingsworth fancied Ben for his remarkable talents when making adequate farming tools to profit from farmers. Come to think of it, Ben has been coming to the house more than once before. By the troublesome look on Hortense's face, I knew Mrs. Hollingsworth was up to no good.

As the afternoon sun greeted the skies, Mr. Hollingsworth came back with a canvas bag full of dead ducks. By that time, Ben left the master suite and was heading out the door. When Hollingsworth *spotted him, Ben told him that he came to see Hortense. Obviously, Mr. Hollingsworth smiled and patted him on the back and said, "Dear boy, you sure do love your mama, don't you? Well, you keep that up, and you will almost be a respectful man for your people to look up to." Nasty? Isn't he? Almost a man? As if he wasn't looking at a fine twenty- year- old specimen in his face? I'm pretty sure his wife felt differently.*

"Aye, boy," he called out to me.

"Yes," I answered.

"Get Omo and me here a tall cold glass of water here, so he could tell me about his savaged tribe back in Nigeria," he said, laughing at the thought of being entertained by it all.

"Sir?" I asked, confused. I looked over his shoulders as I saw Omo boldly enter the house, knowing he was a wanted guest. He looked me dead in the eyes as he gave me a knowingly smirk.

"Ya deaf, boy? I said I need two cold glasses. And after we are done, throw his glass away, please. Can't wash away negro germs!"

"Ye...Yes, sir, right away!" I stuttered, not believing what I was witnessing. I ambled past Omo, and he turned around slowly with his hands behind his back, watching me head straight to the kitchen. He was definitely up to something, but I didn't know what.

I grabbed the two glasses from the cabinets and

washed them thoroughly as I listened to both men laughing and talking in the background. They laughed and talked as if they were well-known acquaintances, minus the degradable colloquialism coming from Master Hollingsworth. It was still implausible to witness such a thing.

As I filled up the glasses with cold water and placed them on the service tray to give to the gentlemen, Master Hollingsworth took his without a thank you (a typical behavior), but Omo gracefully took his glass and said "thank you" with a look of assurance in his eyes. Was this just a ploy from the plan we started? Or was he genuinely trying to be flattering to him? He served to be a great performer in my eyes.

After a few days, Omo's plan appeared to unfold. As God as my witness, I've never seen anything so paranormal or phenomenal. Master Hollingsworth was indeed under Omo's mind spell. Omo was right behind him every step he took, demanding every move he should make: when he should eat, when he should sleep, what to say to his workers when they were getting restless or overwhelming (which surprisingly worked out in our favor). You would think, with the power to control this white man's mind, Omo would command him to set all of us free from this heinous life of slavery, but he assured me that it wasn't the time to do so. That Master Hollingsworth needed to suffer slowly, and by suffering slowly, he needed to see the truth and destroy it, whatever that meant. The next day revealed it all.

It happened after sunrise when Hollingsworth called for the doctor and the midwife when the Mistress was in labor. He sat in the living room with a small glass of whiskey, waiting to hear his newborn's first cries and the doctor and midwife's yells and praises. Poor Master, Omo's witchery really took a toll on him. He didn't look like his old, high, and mighty villainous self. His eyes were bloodshot red with anxiety, and the extra skin beneath them hung low out of desperation of sleep. His face was drawn in, and his weight was gradually deteriorating only after a few days. The stubble of grey hairs on his face grew like weeds as he neglected to shave. For a minute, I began to feel sorry for the poor brute, but it wasn't stronger than my enmity for him. Omo wasn't by his side this time, whispering in his ears. I looked out the window to see where he could be, and strangely enough, he was standing at the front door of the house. He didn't find any need to knock or come in, yet he stood there as if expecting someone to answer the door for him. He held his head down the entire time. Possibly praying to whomever God he served. I didn't bother to see what was going on with him, partly out of fear. Whatever the case may be, it wasn't with good intentions.

All at once, the sound of wailing and the doctor's and midwife's voice rung through the house. Master Hollingsworth's head came up from a quick slumber after hearing so. He accidentally dropped his whiskey on the floor and barked at me to clean it up. He got up slowly, as if he was experiencing pain from working in a field too long. I quickly attended to the mess as he hobbled across the room to get up the stairs. Big Hortense came down the stairs around the same time, like the mighty wind, huffing and puffing. She was also in the room with the others, helping them bring a new life to the world. It was her most extraordinary zeal in duty to do, but the look on her face was far from the opposite.

"Massa Hollingsworth, the doctor recommends you stay down here for a while," Hortense panicked.

"What do you mean, 'stay down here for a while?' My baby boy up there crying his heart out, and you 'spect me to stay here and not see him? Ya tell that doctor that I'm not his patient, and this is not his office for recommending anything," he snapped, climbing a couple of steps. Hortense placed her body as a blockade on the fifth step while holding on to the banister.

"Massa, I can't let you do so," she said strictly.

"Hortense, if you do not get out of my way, by God I will…"

A couple of hard knocks at the door interrupted Hollingsworth, and we all turned to look at the door.

"Boy," he directed to me, "Get that door, now."

I remained stationary for a while, confused at Hortense's sense of boldness and afraid of the aftermath *of what her disobedience may cost her. The baby's thrilling screams were still resounding throughout the place, and everyone was on edge.*

"Did you hear what I said, boy? Get the damn door now!" he yelled, pointing.

I quickly made haste and opened the door. It was Omo. The rugged look on his face looked immoral and sharp. He looked at me with a smirk on his face... A daunting smirk, then he looked up to Hortense and said, "Let him go!"

"Ha! Ya heard him. Let me go, ya big wretch," he yelled as he shoved a confused Hortense to the wall, almost knocking her down. He held onto the banister as he slowly made his way up the stairs.

Instead of following him, Hortense decided to descend down the stairs. She held out her hands for me to comfort her. Omo just stood at the doorway, refusing to come in.

"Ya don't understand," she cried to Omo and me. "Ya don't see what I've seen."

"What's going on?" I asked her out of anticipation. Hortense looked disturbed as she shook her head with uneasiness.

"It's not right....it's not right," she kept repeating.

"What's not right? What's wrong with the baby?"

She looked up at me with tears filling her eyes. She wouldn't say anything. She looked upstairs, looked at me once again, and then she gave Omo a nasty look. "It was you," she accused. "Ya cause all dis here trouble, and now what? What ya got going, devil?" She asked.

Omo had a foolish, wide grin on his face, refusing to answer whatever Hortense was accusing him of.

"Ya don't play smart with me, ya witch! I've seen the likes of the devil's work many times before. Even in Hollingsworth's soul, ya fool him, but ya ain't fool me!" she pointed out.

Suddenly, a yell from Mr. Hollingsworth thundered through the house, overshadowing the baby's cries and the doctor's voice to calm everyone in the room. I looked at Omo as he bowed his head down again. I let go of Hortense as I dashed up the stairs to see what all the commotion was about. As I reached the room, I saw Mrs. Hollingsworth apologizing hysterically to her husband, and the midwife was trying to hold her arms down. The doctor was held up in the corner, shaking his head with disbelief as he was getting a syringe ready to insert in her arm. Mr. Hollingsworth, who was in great despair, leaned heavily on the white bassinet with the baby inside, who was now cooing. Quietly, I crept to where the baby was and took a peep. To my surprise, I was disturbed by what I had seen. Inside the little bed, I saw…me... A miniature me.

His caramel skin was smooth and flawless all over. His small cheeks were puffy and wide, along with his *button nose. On top of his head was a hefty amount of slick black hair. He looked up at me with purity in his eyes, wondering if I was his father. Obviously, the child couldn't connect to the disheveled, old white man who was scrutinizing him. For a little while, I found satisfaction in Hollingsworth's tribulation but sorrow and pity for the little one who came into this world looking exactly like me.*

"Give me those sheets," demanded Hollingsworth to the midwife.

"What are you going to do?" she asked hesitantly while giving him the blankets.

"That's none of your damn business," he growled, snatching it from her hands.

"Sir, I'm going to give your wife a sedative first, so she could be calm enough to deal with the distress," recommended the doctor, afraid of what Hollingsworth would do next.

"The hell with that woman! Knock her out if you have to. I will not be the laughing stock of this town ever again! And this evil spawn she birthed will not destroy my family's name!" he spat while picking the baby up to swaddle him with the blankets.

"Honey, wait! What are you going to do with my baby? Where are you taking him?" Mrs. Hollingsworth asked in desperation as she attempted to sit up.

"You mean your nigger baby? It's not mine! After you sedate her, doctor, make sure she's well enough to

leave my house. That's the only sympathy she will receive from me!"

"Oh yeah? What about him? Huh? What about this nigger son you raised in this damn house? Oh, you forgot about that," she cried, pointing to me. "You think you can create these ugly spawns and think I would tolerate it? Having him sleep in this house and play 'daddy' to you like you're some God doesn't give you the right to take away my baby! You're evil, John Hollingsworth, and the people in this town are already laughing at you. You are the laughing stock of this town. You're just too blind to see it," she yelled as she laughed hysterically.

Hollingsworth quickly gave the baby to me as he walked fiercely to his wife's bedside. He threw a mean punch, knocking her unconscious. The midwife let out a loud gasp as she held her hands over her mouth.

The doctor, too stunned to say anything, put down the needle.

"I told you to knock her out, and your way took too long," Hollingsworth responded as he snatched the baby away from me. "If any word leaks out about what happened here today, your practice with medicine will not be the only thing you need to worry about."

He stormed out of the room with the baby in tow. Too shocked by his actions, I followed him to see what he was up to. He went down the stairwell, past *a praying Hortense, and was met by Omo at the door. Omo gave a slight nod to him as he gracefully stepped out of Hollingsworth's way. Hollingsworth carried the small bundle in his hands, refusing to look at the now crying infant. He marched across the courtyard with evil intentions in his heart. The workers who were tending to the lawn stopped what they were doing as they watched Master Hollingsworth passed by them. Their curiosity quickly developed into urgency to follow him, for they heard the turmoil from outside of the house and knew what was coming wouldn't be pleasant.*

He walked down to the quarters where the children stopped playing and followed along to see what he had in his arms. The adults inside took a peep through their windows or doors and saw their children and the house workers in the procession Hollingsworth was leading and decided to follow them. I was behind him, terrified. I didn't know what he was going to do, but I knew it wouldn't be amusing. The better question was, what did Omo order him to do? I looked behind me, and it seemed almost the whole plantation was here, following us, but where was Omo? Could it be possible that he fixed all of this? Or could he have us all under his control?

We walked and walked for a long time until the grounds went from a grassy knoll to a widespread white sand and the blue sea. We stopped at the knoll as he continued down the pathway to the ocean. No one dared to cross over the sand but him. Somehow it was put in our minds to not cross it, like a spell that kept our feet station there; however, it didn't stop the others from whispering, mumbling, crying, and praying. I wanted to cross over. I tried to snatch the baby away from him and save part of myself, the only piece that had a little bit of humility left. It was a battle inside my head, and the darkness was taking over. It was too late to turn back. The deal I made with Omo was completed, and retribution done signed my name under the devil's contract.

He didn't stop until he was in the water knee-deep. He appeared to be talking to the ocean, and as a huge wave came roaring across the vast sea towards them. Along with others, I shouted for him to show mercy, but he was prone to what he was set out to do. As the current got more vigorous, its monstrous white gateway leaped high in the air and cascaded down to devour both Hollingsworth and the baby. The young one cried and was no match for the horrendous crashing of the destructive waves. It was one of the most appalling scenes I've ever witnessed, and I may have to pay for the rest of my time here on Earth.

Season couldn't hardly breathe or say anything. Her face was covered in tears, and her nose couldn't stop running. Her hands began to shake as she thought to herself, *am I a descendant of this monster?* She couldn't bring herself to look at the other entry that was on the next page. She slammed the book shut and threw it across the room. The more she thought about it, the more she began to hate herself. As if on cue, Mrs. DeVeau unlocked the door with her key.

She gave Season a look of sincerity as she ventured toward her. Season, too distraught to acknowledge her presence, hung her head to the ground and cried loudly.

"Oh honey, I am sorry," she said, taking some Kleenex from her shirt pocket to give to the poor girl. She then grabbed a chair and moved it to sit next to her. "You can't unravel yourself over something that wasn't in your control. Everyone had someone in their lineage to cause harm to others or shame their own legacy. You're not the only one, and you certainly won't be the last."

"Why did I come here?" cried Season. "I should've fought my father with tooth and nails if I knew it would come down to this." She rested her head on Mrs. DeVeau's lap.

Mrs. DeVeau used one hand to brush through Season's big, tangled puff. "Well, from what your aunt told me, your father thought by bringing you here, it would keep you out of trouble. Not to mention, learn more about your mother's side. I guess you didn't expect the terrible truth behind it all."

"My mom was one of the sweetest people in the world.

She couldn't harm a fly," Season remarked.

"That she was. Both her and your aunt. They wouldn't dare hurt anyone. Time of the righteous sacrifice, they wouldn't participate with the others. Instead, they would come right here to this place and hide in this same office and cry their eyes out the same way you're doing right now. That's why you can't be too hard on your aunt. She's trying to keep you safe and out of harm's way. You can't keep fighting her every chance you get, Season."

She looked up at Mrs. DeVeau with perplexity in her eyes.

"Oh yeah, I know what you are doing. Autumn tells me about your rebellious behavior. How you like to challenge her every chance you get. How much she tries to connect with you, but you shut her down at times. The saddest part is how Autumn talks so highly of you. About how intelligent you are and how proud she is of you. That child loves you! "

Season couldn't do anything but frown after listening to Mrs. DeVeau. She didn't realize how much of a brat she was toward her aunt. The worst word to use "rebellious." After reading Marion Hollingsworth's entries, she didn't want to be consumed with negative energy. The type of energy that led him astray.

"You can't change the past, Darling. You can, however, change the future. Starting now, your aunt needs you more than ever. The truth doesn't stop here. Ask her for it. Beg if you have to," asserted Mrs. DeVeau, perching

Season to get up and held on to her shoulders tightly. The once lively spirit she usually had was now replaced with sincerity in her eyes.

Season asked, "What do you mean?"

Before Mrs. DeVeau could open her mouth, Cindy appeared at the door with anxiety on her face. "It's Serene," she said, placing her hand over her heart.

Mrs. DeVeau and Season exchanged a glance of discomfort as they hurried out of the room to see what was going on. Serene, who looked as if she was crying all the way to the library, now looked upset.

"What's wrong?" asked Mrs. DeVeau, coming from around the desk to comfort her.

"I'm next."

Chapter 12:

THE FALSIFIED TRUTH

*a*fter a long time of comfort, Serene was able to calm down and tell the others how frightened she was about the ceremonial ritual coming up this Saturday. Season was at a loss for words. How she felt a couple of minutes ago didn't compare to the turmoil where Serene was placed. Season wanted to help her, but she didn't know how. For the first time since her mom's passing, she felt utterly helpless.

"It's going to be okay, Serene," Mrs. DeVeau promised, holding her tightly. "This baby will live, you hear me? This baby will strive many days after he or she gets older. God will see to it!"

Season frowned after listening to the godly librarian.

"No offense, Mrs. DeVeau, but I think this situation is way bigger than God. Don't give Serene false hopes in what's to come. It's very hypocritical of anyone, including you, to go to a church and praise the one true living God but turn back around to sacrifice a lamb to a demonic water monster."

Mrs. DeVeau looked at Season with sadness. "Oh little one, O ye of little faith? There's nothing too big or too small for my God to do. He's the alpha and the omega, the beginning and the end. A demonic water monster is no match for my father. What you need to understand is that there's nothing new under this here sun," she proclaimed, as she pointed up. "People have been conjuring and worshipping evil spirits since the bible days; nothing has changed. You failed to realize that God's amazing, and the truth is in the living testimonials people speak daily. I'm not supposed to be the one to tell you, but you're living proof of a testimony, young girl!"

Cindy and Serene looked to Season as if she had three heads. Season, who was confused, felt as if a thousand bricks hit her chest. "What do you mean, a living proof?"

DeVeau let out a sigh as she took Serene to the bathroom to fix her face. Cindy was still staring at her with a look of disbelief.

Season called out a little louder, "What do you mean, Mrs. DeVeau?"

Mrs. DeVeau didn't turn to answer the poor girl. She opened the door and went in with Serene.

"I'll be back in an hour," Cindy interrupted, as she placed her pocketbook strap on her shoulders.

"Where are you going?" cried Season, who was barely

holding it together.

"I'm taking a lunch break. Look, just continue working at the desk and pretending everything is okay. We will get to the bottom of this, I promise. Fix up your face; someone is coming through the door."

Season covered her face with both of her hands to let out a low growl. She was not a great actress when it came to revealing false emotions, but she would have to try to make it work in this case.

"How was work today?" Autumn asked in a cheerful tone.

"Work was okay," Season replied nonchalantly.

It was precisely three o'clock on the dot when Autumn came to pick up her niece. Season was too thrilled to see her aunt after having a talk with Mrs. DeVeau. Aunt Autumn had a lot of explaining to do if she ever wanted peace with her. For now, Season played it cool and decided not to bring up anything just yet.

"Well, I have an idea," continued Autumn, "Since I don't have to go back to work, why don't we head over to Hilton Head Beach and relax by the water. I just love the horizon when the sun sets on it."

"Why not go to the beach here? It wouldn't make any sense to visit another one," Season acknowledged.

"Well, I kinda figured you would like to head out of

town for a while. I know you see this place as a prison. Maybe you need a different kind of fresh air," she proposed, hardly sounding convincing.

Season shook her head, "Naw, I'm okay. I'm just not in the mood,"

"You're not in the mood? Are you okay?"

"I'm fine, why do you ask?"

"Just a couple of weeks ago, you've asked me what people do around here that's fun. I'm offering you a 'get out of jail free card' here, but you're revoking it. Obviously, something is bothering you."

"I'm fine, okay?" she snapped.

Autumn looked hesitant at Season and responded, "Okay…sorry if I'm pestering you."

"You're not pestering me. I'm just tired, is all."

They continued to ride together in silence as they reached home. Season got out of the car first and used her key to open the door. Autumn stayed in the car, wondering what could possibly be going on with the girl.

Season went straight to her room and closed the door. Suddenly, a ping sound came from her pocket. As she reached for her phone to look at it, she noticed Cindy sent a video to her messenger. It read, "Righteous Ritual 2016-The Truth." Season clicked on the link to watch it.

The person who was filming appeared to be in a safe spot, looking down on the ritual. The camera quickly zoomed in to get a better view of what was going on. There were about thirty members dressed in white on the same beach. The men were dressed in white linen shirts and pants, and the women wore white linen dresses. They were gathered around a huge bonfire, praising and singing to whomever they were evoking. Season recognized most of the members from church, including Pastor Hollis, Sis. Winnie, Sister Applegate, the deacons and deaconess board, and surprisingly the Mahalia Jackson woman. They all wore white turbans wrapped around their head. As far as she could tell, her Aunt Autumn wasn't there, which was quite a relief!

After the praising and singing died down, Pastor Hollis began speaking in a different language, a very foreign language to Season. Sister Winnie's eyes were rolling around in the back of her hand as she was chanting to herself near the open fire. The other members followed her lead. Behind the pastor's back was a vast wooden family table decorated with gold chalices and a grass basket placed in the middle. Sis. Applegate padded out of the camera focus and came back seconds later with a young girl following behind her. The girl was so tall and thin that the white robe she was wearing was swallowing her figure. She looked to be around eighteen or nineteen. Season scrunched her eyes to get a clear focus of the young lady and placed two fingers on her phone to zoom in on the girl's long, dark auburn hair and fair complexion, and held her hand to her mouth so she couldn't shriek. The girl was Cindy! This was Cindy's sacrifical ceremony! Which could only mean that Cindy had a baby!

"Oh my God!" Season cried.

Cindy looked very frightened as Sis. Applegate was holding her by the arms to walk her to the table. Sis. Applegate appeared to be quarreling with Cindy to take out whatever was in that basket, but she simply shook her head. The woman looked a bit annoyed by her answer and slapped her on the face for disobeying. By then, Cindy hesitantly picked up a baby…*her baby*, wrapped in a blanket, and dragged her feet toward Pastor Hollis, who took the baby. Sis. Winnie came up to the front with a sharp object in her hand. Season was afraid to even watch the part of her using the sharp object to slit the child's arms. The other members crowded around the wooden table where chalices were placed, and Pastor Hollis visited each one by placing a drop of the baby's blood into a cup. They turned to the ocean and chanted a few words simultaneously, then drank. Cindy, too helpless to save her baby, fell to the sand and began to mourn. Season recognized one of the chanted words, *Yamaha,* and immediately connect it to Hollingsworth's diary entries.

"These people are insane," she whispered to herself with tears in her eyes. Because she didn't want to bear witness to the poor child's fate, her finger approached the stop symbol on the player… until she saw a young person dressed in white linens that was far behind the cult. It was a young teenage boy who looked to be crying at what was going on. As the pastor went to the edge of the water, the boy held out his hand as if he were trying to stop them, but no one paid him any attention.

"YUSEF?!" shouted Season.

Suddenly, the door opened, and her aunt stepped in with a frown on her face. Season tried to get rid of the video by hitting the "x," but it was too late. Autumn heard everything, from the pastor's loud voice to the praises from the cult, rejoicing and throwing their drinks on themselves. Season looked at her aunt like a deer caught in headlights. She knew she was in deep trouble.

The night skies were spacious with a surplus of stars in all directions, forming different shapes parallel to the afternoon skies. It was a wondrous sight, but to Season, it reeks of the little lost souls that were petrified in the ocean about a few miles east of the house. She sat with her aunt on a porch swing. Their eyes were fixated on what was above them, trying to find the right words or the right answers for the discussion that was inevitable to avoid.

On the bottom porch sat a brown package wrapped tightly in plastic. It caught Season's attention, wondering what was in it. Autumn, noticing where her niece was looking, decided to break the silence.

"Fresh Water Hemlock. Very poisonous if exposed openly. Shouldn't use your bare hands," Autumn answered, responding to a nonverbal question.

Season asked, "Why is it on your porch?" There was a

sudden chill to her response, thinking of possible ways her aunt would want to use the plants.

"Calm down, silly. I'm not trying to hurt you if that's what you're thinking. I could never hurt a soul if I could. The plants are for my friend, Bart, who's a botanist. He lives in California."

"Why would you send something poisonous to a friend?" Season frowned.

"Well, I spotted them outside of a ditch not too far from here and did some research. As destructive it can be, it can also be useful."

"Like how?"

"Well, from what I gathered, it can help with females' menstrual problems or asthmatic issues. You asked before about my hobbies, and researching exotic plants are one of them, especially if they're dangerous."

"Why dangerous?" asked Season

Autumn looked at Season warily. "Because even something supposedly beautiful can be labeled as dangerous with perilous intentions. Sometimes, we have to find something good in all things, including us."

Season took in what her aunt was telling her and sighed. It was easier said than done when it came to finding the good. The only question was how?

"I met this boy on the beach," Season admitted while twiddling her thumbs.

"Oh?" Autumn responded, shifting her body toward Season.

"Yeah, that's why I had such a fascination being at the beach. I met him, and he was so...so different. Not different in a bad way, but a good different. For the first time since I came here, I felt I could relax and be myself around him, you know?"

Autumn didn't say anything but listened as Season continued.

"After that day, what happened near the ocean...how he left me, and the piercing sounds coming from the water, I was upset with him. He even came to my window one night acting weird."

"Wait, you mean to tell me this boy came here? And you didn't think to tell me?"

"I'm sorry, but he didn't stay for so long...just to warn me is all."

"Warn you? About what?" Autumn asked, raising her voice.

"I honestly don't know. He just seemed freaked out about this town, not that I don't blame him, but to be honest, I'm freaked out about him also."

"Why?"

"Because not too long ago, before you caught me looking at that video, I saw him on it. He was standing off in a corner, trying to stop the ritual, but no one was listening. He was crying his heart out and couldn't help that poor baby when those crazy people finished what they started."

Autumn looked complex and a bit anxious. She told Season to show her the video to see for herself what Season was trying to explain. As the video played, Season wished she could read her aunt's thoughts or feelings. When the clip showed the cult members holding up their cups to the ocean, her aunt inadvertently snatched the phone from her.

"Who is this young boy?" Autumn demanded, pointing her finger at the scrawny teenager.

"That's the boy I was telling you about. That's Yusef," Season sighed.

"Wait, who?" Autumn asked as she held the phone closer to her eyes to see.

"Yusef. He's from around here."

"Season, I've never seen that boy around here in my life. Where does he live?"

Season thought for a moment, trying to remember exactly where Yusef told her. "He said he doesn't live too far from the ocean. A couple of yards to the nearest jetty."

"To the nearest jetty?! Season, there's no houses around that area. Just some boats and a long boathouse, which I'm pretty sure he doesn't live there with Mr. Peasant. He's an old, old man. Unless…"

"Unless what?"

"Look, this boy has lied to you. There's no "Yusef" in this town, okay," dismissed Autumn in a stern voice. "Besides, I told your narrow behind to stay away from that area, and you didn't listen."

"THERE IS TOO A BOY NAMED YUSEF, AND HE'S A LITTLE OLDER THAN I AM," Season yelled, with hurt in her eyes.

Autumn jumped up from the swing so fast, leaving Season swinging back and forth from the force. "It can't be…" she said, more likely to herself than to Season. She went down the steps to pace back and forth as if she was going psychotic. "There's no young boys around here who would even go near that place for fun. It's not your typical beach where you go to build sandcastles or play in the water. That place should not be taken for fun…it's zoning for…"

"Let me guess, the righteous ritual?" interrupted Season, rolling her eyes. "Yeah, I know everything. Even the part that I am a descendant of a crazy-ass warlock who harms children!"

Her aunt began to breathe heavily while staring Season down, "Who told you this? Where did you hear this from?"

"Doesn't matter now; I know what you've been hiding," Season growled.

"Did Mrs. DeVeau open her mouth to you about this?!"

"Why would you care? That's not the point. The point of the matter is that I know, and why would you want to live around something so vile? So evil? Why didn't you just get up and move after your parents died? Why didn't you leave like Mom did?!"

"Because I *couldn't*, Season!" she cried, melting down to the ground.

Season looked at her aunt, and for a minute, found

pity for her. She got up slowly from the swing and went to comfort her, but her aunt refused her sympathy.

"You wouldn't understand, Season," she moaned.

"Well, tell me. I'm not so hard at understanding," pleaded Season.

Autumn looked up at her and breathed slowly. She got up from the ground, walked up the steps, and sat down on the swing set once more.

"I knew this day would come once you got older. I'm still not ready to tell you this," she stated carefully.

Season sat up straight to brace herself for what her aunt had to say.

"From when I was a child up till now, it was conventional for parents to train or groom their children to enter the stages as young ladies or young gentlemen by the age of thirteen. Educating boys in academic and husbandry accounts for having a sustainable manhood to their soon to be wives and to this town. Educating girls to be overly submissive to their future suitors by cooking, sewing, gardening, and dressing like proper ladies. They followed Hollingsworth's decree. He was an old, former slave who established this town around the mid-1800s. As Hollins citizens, we must give back to this deity named Yemaja, and a witch named Akoko for the child that was taken away from them."

Season nodded, understanding the names from Hollingsworth's journal.

"In that way, we would have flourishing seasons in

crops, fertility, health, and wealth, even when living a sin-less life. The intended ritual was supposed to be for one baby to be sacrificed once a year for the sake of this town, but Pastor's Hollis' father, Levi, became greedy. He wanted more wealth from making this sacrifice, so he demanded for at least two babies to be martyrs."

Season cringed at the thought of living at the expense of a newborn's life. How could they do such a selfish act to harvest materialistic things? Before she could allow her aunt to go any further with the story, she knew she had to confess to something she was hiding.

"Um… I have to tell you something. Something that I wasn't so sure of telling you at first because I thought you were involved." Season got up from her seat and went into the house. A few minutes later, she came back holding the *HOLLINS WUDU PROCLAMATION* book in her hands to give to Autumn. Autumn, opening her mouth in fear, stepped back from the book as if it was Satan himself. She then looked at Season shockingly.

"Where did you get this, gal?" she gasped.

"I was given this by Mrs. DeVeau and Cindy to learn the truth behind this town and my family. I wanted to hear it from you, but you refused to tell me," Season pant-ed, trying to keep from crying.

Autumn rushed over to Season and put her arms around her. Season could feel her fierce heartbeat from her chest. She then realized that her aunt felt more frightened than she was.

"I was just trying to protect you. I couldn't let them do it…I just couldn't!" she whimpered, burying her head in Season's hair puffs.

"Do what?"

Quickly, Autumn lifted her head and let go of Season. She went back into the house and came back with two big flashlights and her pocketbook. The look of sadness and fear flashed across her face as she handed Season one of the flashlights.

"We're going to the truth…the falsified truth," she added.

Season didn't know what to make of that answer as Autumn rushed ahead to the back of the house. On the one hand, she wanted desperately to understand what Autumn knew, but on the other, she was afraid for her life. Where were they going in this darkness?

"C'mon gal, I ain't got all night witchu," she shouted, walking further away from Season.

Five minutes passed by, and they were now walking into the woods where Season became so familiar with, a direction that led them to the beach. They walked through the dark path with their high beamed flashlights. The moonlight helped some by encouraging the way to their unknown destination.

"By the time I was thirteen and Summer was sixteen,

Summer was to be suited for Eddie Hollis. The parents deemed it necessary to do so, considering we were a part of Omo's lineage, and Eddie was of Marion's. Of course, my sister thought differently. She and I disliked the town's ritual, and she was extremely rebellious back then. So it was only right for her to refuse her rite of passage by ruining their plans."

"What did she do?" Season inquired, whisking away some tree limbs as they waded deeper through the woods.

"Be careful where you put your feet. Snakes 'round here are the absolute worst among other things," Autumn warned before moving on with her story. "She decided to fall for Levi's second son, Xion. At first, it was just a ploy to get under the adults' skins, but then she fell in love with him. He, too, wasn't so fond of the ritual but was also afraid of his father. I guess not enough to stop seeing his brother's suitor. My parents thought Summer was beginning to accept her destiny, seeing her dressed with sophistication and interest in church, but what they didn't know was that beneath those dress frills and stockings were jeans, shorts, and skirts. She hid her sneakers in the field around the house so no one would notice once she changed into them. During the mornings and middays, she allowed Eddie to walk her to school and court her around town. Just to put on a show in front of the crowd. During the evenings, she would sneak out of the house to go see Xion. I knew all along what she had been up to, but I didn't whisper one word. We were close like that. She took care of me, and I took care of her. It was our sisterly pact."

They stopped at the edge of the woods to see the view ahead of them. The open sea looked enormously long and disturbing. The moonlight reflected its color on to the tip of the waves.

"Why are we here?" Season questioned, beginning to panic a little from the trauma she experienced.

"We're not stopping here. We have some ways to go, but we will have to walk some yards to the nearest jetty."

Season's eyes widened after hearing the word 'jetty.' "To the nearest jetty? Where are we going exactly?"

Autumn continued on walking as she gave a regretful response, "You'll see."

They went out into the open beach, making sure to keep away from the waters. They trudged through the thickness of the sand, heading north.

"What happened next?" Season questioned, hoping the story would help make their travels less demanding.

"Summer and Xion were seeing each other for months until Levi caught wind of it,"

"How did he find out?"

"That nasty Eddie. When Summer thought she was getting the best of him, he was obviously following his brother and my sister. He caught them in the action of…well, never mind. You're old enough to imply what happened."

"Oh, no!"

"After Eddie told both of our parents, they decided the best thing to do was to confine Summer to her room. I knew it hurt them to do so, but they had no choice. To them, she was impure and tainted. She needed to be shunned like a beast in heat, away from the young men in this town. During the summer, my parents had plans for her to be homeschool for the upcoming school year. She broke the 'law,' so she had to pay for it. It drove my sister crazy just sitting in the house all day, with the Bible in one hand and Hollins WUDU book in the other. She was lost and broken. The only way she thought she was going to get away from her purgatory was to rid herself from this world."

"You're telling me that my mom tried to commit suicide?"

"Yes, that's what I'm telling you," Autumn responded in a grave tone.

"What about Xion? What happened to him?"

"He was banished from this town. Levi branded him on his back, calling it 'the mark of Cain.' Because he deceived his brother, he would be known to this town as an outsider. The last I heard, he was doing quite well for himself in the outside world. He graduated from a top shot college and made a name for himself. He kept writing letters to his family, but they refused to acknowledge him. Sooner or later, the letters stopped coming, and he wasn't ever heard from again."

"Wow, poor guy. But you know, good for him. He was

too good for this place. You can't keep people from living their own dreams," Season admitted.

"That's a good way of looking at the situation, but it didn't help my sister once it came to pass that she was pregnant."

"Pregnant?!"

"Yes, the same day she was rushed to the hospital for overdosing on our mother's pills, the doctor told us that she was pregnant."

Season's mind began to work overtime as she calculated her mom's age and hers. Summer never told her she was pregnant once before. She thought that she was her mom's only child. She had Season close to the end of her freshman year in college, so how was that possible if she was only sixteen?

They were finally approaching a small low pier ahead of them. A couple of deserted boats were docked near them and a small, white desolate boathouse that looked to be decaying. They were almost near their destination, but Season knew Autumn wasn't finished with her story. They turned toward the woods again as they reached the pier, but Season couldn't keep her eyes away from the lonesome boathouse with no lights.

"Well, after the suicide attempt was unsuccessful, Summer decided not to go along with her demised plan. Killing a life inside of her would've made her worse than the townspeople, so she planned to have the baby and escape. Everyone began to ask questions about whose baby was it she was carrying, and my parents were humiliated. Levi, Eddie, and our good friend, Mrs. DeVeau, were the only souls who knew the truth. One day, Levi announced to everyone that the sacrificial offering wouldn't be set on its usual solstice weekend, but early spring, when Summer delivers her baby. No babies were sacrificed during that summer. He proclaimed that my sister's voluntary-which was far from voluntary, offering would promise them a flourishing year and a half. She wanted to die after that announcement. It prompted her to make plans to leave town before she gave birth, but she had too many eyes on her."

Season felt weak. She thought she could handle the truth but now realized she couldn't. It was coming to her all at once, like the waves grasping for her in the ocean that day. Her mother went through pure hell for most of her childhood. It was a wonder how she gained the strength to encourage children to stay inspired to reach their dreams. She wasn't a poor, defenseless person. She was a survivor of her environment and a hero.

The two were approaching a clearing with a dense patch of fog surrounding it. As they inched closer into the mist, Season saw a squared iron spiked gate. Inside of the gate stood old, mossy stones…tombstones. They were at a gravesite.

Autumn stopped at the gate and looked at Season. "This burial ground is called 'La Memoria' to remember those we lost before their time to live. After Summer gave birth to a beautiful baby boy around early March, she cried, for she knew what would become of him. My parents knew it would be a hard task for them to separate that child from Summer. The ritual was in a few days, and they had to make haste. They brought a doctor in to sedate her and stole the baby from out of his crib."

She finally opened the gate and gestured for Season to enter. Season, feeling a little apprehensive, took small steps inside of the gate. Autumn joined her and closed it. They walked down a short dirt path etched in the ground. Season stopped to observe a row of tombstones and realized the word 'baby' was attached to each name. Some read, "Baby Donnie (1967-1967); Baby Howard (1999-1999); Baby Regaine (1987-1987); Baby Netty (1900-1900); and Baby Ian (1940-1940). Each tomb reading 'baby' and their early demise made Season's heart drop, and then she wept. Autumn was on the other side, looking at one grave that was lavishly covered with flowers and small stuffed animals. Season went over to her aunt. When she got there, she looked down at a headstone that read, "Baby Maurice (2016-2016).

"This was Cindy's baby, Season. He was a sight for sore eyes," she said, clearing her voice and sniffling as she walked away.

Season stood there for a minute, taking in what Cindy must have gone through. She wanted to hug her and take back those mean things she said to her. Season walked around the back of the headstone and touched it with her hands. She said a little prayer over it and left to join Autumn.

"I don't get it. How were they able to recover the corpses from the water?"

"They didn't. Once consumed by the ocean, the little spirits belong to the water goddess, or so the devotees claimed. To restore their malicious humanity, they created these headstones to honor each family's sacrifice.

Season thought back on what she heard when she was lost in the currents. As if she was trying to be consumed by its forceful gravitation. She couldn't forget about the sounds of those cries. Is it possible that it could be the lost little souls being drowned in the sea of death? It struck out the notion that all little souls belong to the Heavenly father.

"After the ritual, Summer couldn't live with herself anymore, so after graduating from high school, she ran away. There are rules to this ritual; you have to offer up your first born. Our parents did it, Levi did it, Mother Winnie did it, and everyone else did. Five years passed when I last heard from Summer, and I was heavy down pregnant from Eddie.

"You were pregnant for Eddie?!"

"As I mentioned earlier, there are rules. I had to make atonement for my sister. She left me to fend for myself, and I was upset she left without me. I was to inherit her debt, so yes, I was engaged to Eddie. He was nasty and cruel and took advantage of me. He said he would pay for his fornicating ways once he sacrificed our first born.

After seeing my sister for the first time in years, I felt rejuvenated. She couldn't stop telling us about her free scholarship ride, which paid her way to graduating college. She majored in education to reach the students around her community and was engaged to a handsome guy who was studying to be a doctor. Her chattering ceased to a minimum once she looked down at my belly. It was a look of sadness and repentance. It's funny because I was always the quiet and smart one in the family. Summer was the one who wanted to explore the world as a Bohemian, an idea from a song she loved, *Bohemian Rhapsody*. She was always so radical. Anyway, when she figured out who was fathering the child I was carrying, she became angry at my momma and pa for letting this happen. She had never gotten over it. When I gave birth to this beautiful baby girl with a head full of curly locks, nothing else didn't matter."

Season felt terribly sorry for her aunt, so she hugged her. No one shouldn't have to give up their child for anyone or anything. Suddenly, she had the urge to ask her aunt where her daughter's tomb was so she could bless it as well.

"Where's her tomb? I would like to see it. Tell me her name, and I'll find it," she asked softly.

Autumn gave Season a remorseful look as a new fresh coat of tears streamed down her face. She was breathing fanatically as her voice gave away. "Her name is Season…"

Season cocked her head to the side and backed away, "Wait, what?"

"I named you Season… you are *my* child," she said forcefully.

All at once, Season's solicitous disposition shifted to mental confusion. The ground beneath her feet gave way, and the world she once knew with Summer became a viral hypnosis. For a moment, she couldn't hear Autumn calling out to her. She could only hear the last few seconds of her aunt quoting, *"you are my child..."*

Brace yourself, Season, you know who you are, she thought. She finally came back to the present. "No... you're not my mother. My mother's name is Summer Holidae," Season clarified as she backed away slowly.

"Season, before you were born, Summer and I plotted a day ahead. I didn't want to sacrifice you, and Summer didn't want to relive what happened to her. So we both thought it would be best for her to take you. She wanted me to come too, but it would've been too risky. The love you brought to our family changed my parents' ways, so they helped with your escape. We were ready to face the consequences of doing so."

Season broke into a hysterical cry, "Why are you lying to me?!"

"I'm not lying, baby. I would never lie about something so serious. I had to protect you. There was no way you would be a scapegoat to this town,"

"So my mom isn't my mom?" Season covered her face with both hands, pacing back and forth. "So, why aren't *you* dead?"

"We were stripped of our Pillars of Community title. We were treated horribly here, being spit on and such.

Because we were the last descendants of Omo, Levi decided to grant us mercy by not killing us."

"I refuse to believe any of this," Season declared. "I've been lied to by an aunt who posed as my mother my entire life?"

"Baby, I know you're hurt," Autumn pleaded as she tried to itch closer to Season.

"No, I'm hella hurt. I'm angry....scared....confused... I've been through all the negative emotions ever since I came to this stupid town!"

Autumn walked painfully past Season, loathing the consequences of perjury. She walked over to another grave, which stood isolated from the others, under a huge oak tree. Feverishly, Season followed her, refusing to let her off the hook.

As she reached the stone in front of Autumn, she couldn't help but read it, although it was hard to do so at first. The craftsman didn't take the time to make it as elegant as the others. Season scooped down and cast her light on the tomb. Once she was able to read the engraving, her mouth dropped!

"No! Can't be!" she shouted. She was now feeling chills creeping slowly in her body. It was enough to shock her to death, but she remained stagnant.

Autumn shined her flashlight too on the stone.

"Baby Yusef, born in 2003 and died in 2003. He was Summer's baby," Autumn stated somberly.

Chapter 13:

TROUBLE AH' BREWING

*A*fter learning the truth about Hollins, Aunt Autumn, and Yusef two nights ago, Season was overwhelmed. There was no way anybody could process something so treacherous and so mysterious. She had not heard from Yusef since the night he came to her window, so there was no way to get any verification from him. She didn't know exactly where he lived; the only area around the boathouse was the cemetery, and she couldn't talk to the dead…or could she?

On the other hand, Autumn claimed to be her biological mother, which was absolutely absurd. Not to mention, a ridiculous thought that Pastor Eddie Hollis could be her biological dad was the absolute worst. Did Autumn really expect Season to take her word for it? Because the only mother she ever knew was Summer. Despite their complexion and particular looks being a bit off, their personalities were kismet. Season got up from her vanity chair and took a picture of the two sisters off the wall. She held the image up to her face in a mirror to see if she looked more like Summer or Autumn. It did not occur to her how much she looked like a young Autumn now. Possibly, what her aunt revealed to her could've had some influence on the way she saw herself now. Only if her mother was alive. Maybe if it came from her mouth, then she could believe such a story. But her mother wasn't here to do so. Then again, there was another way to find out.

She was glad that today was her day off from the library. Her aunt, on the other hand, had to work. After that night, Autumn was treading very lightly around Season the last couple of days. She knew Season wasn't adamant about talking to her. Instead of taking the authoritarian route, Autumn decided to give Season some space. She was not even assertive in cooking breakfast or getting Season up so she could eat. She knew her niece was up when she heard her cell phone rang. So, she took the opportunity to instruct her through the door to have some cereal and milk, and then she left.

Season grabbed her phone, went outside, and sat on the porch swing. She ran through her contacts and located her father's number. Usually, she would just call him, but she decided to Facetime him in a plight like this.

Boop Boop Boop
Boop Boop Boop
Boop Boop Boop

"Hey, baby gal! How's my favorite Season of all," he joked with a massive smile on his face.

"Not good, Dad. Not good at all," Season whispered, shaking her head somberly.

"Why? What's wrong? Did something happen?" Xavier asked. His smile quickly disappeared into a more troublesome grimace.

Season could see that he was wearing his white coat and was seated in his colossal office chair. It occurred to her that what she was about to spring on him would totally ruin his day, not to mention his patients' day as well. Her father could somewhat be an emotional person when things don't go his way. One bad thing could ruin his whole mood for that day. That was one trait Season thought she inherited from him. Guess it was just a nurturing thing.

"Dad, I have something to tell you….well, to ask you."

Xavier cleared his throat as he got up from his chair to close his office door. "What's that, baby?"

"Did you know that Aunt Autumn was my biological mother?" she asked.

Xavier stretched his eyes as if feigning to hear such craziness, then cleared his throat again and sighed. Season concentrated on her father's face, reading every inch of it. She could tell when her dad was lying because he never had a good poker face.

"Did you hear me?" she cried.

"Yes, I hear you, baby girl. Look, let's talk about this…"

"No, let's talk about this right now because I'm tired of the bullshit!" she shouted.

"Season Belle Holidae! You watch your mouth when you're talking to me!" he warned.

Season simmered down after hearing her full name. Her father still had that formidable voice to silence even the birds outside. She didn't mean to talk to him in that way, but she was entitled to feel the way she felt.

He looked away from the camera, trying not to show any signs of weakness, but Season could see the tears shining from the corner of his left eye. It wasn't a pretty sight to see her dad this way, but it was one of the consequences of the action to hide something as big as this.

"I...I knew since your mom came back with you wrapped in a blanket. She told me why she had you and promised me that she would tell you when you're old enough to handle it. I didn't want her to raise you as a single parent. I love your mother, and I've grown attached to you, so I married the both of you. It wasn't in our intentions to keep you away from knowing your real mother. It killed me whenever Autumn would contact Summer, but Summer would tell her to leave you be. That you didn't need the likes of that town to taint or destroy you, whatever that meant. She only wanted to protect you from that place," Xavier explained, trying to soften his face.

"Well, if she told you the reason why she kept me away from here, why did you deem it as necessary to bring me here? That's what I don't understand!"

"Because of guilt, Season. I felt she should've told you this long after. After she left us, I didn't know how to break something so heavy to a teenage girl. I thought about it every day after your mom passed, especially when you were spiraling out of control. I didn't know what to do. Then opportunity presented itself when Autumn sent me a letter, pleading for me to bring you back. It was the right thing to do, baby."

"I want to come home. Please, Daddy. I want to come home to you. I don't care if you're not my real father. Just come get me. I'll be good; I do whatever you ask of me to do. I just don't want to stay here. I'm afraid."

"Afraid of what, baby?"

"Of these people. They're a cult! They murder babies!"

"Murder babies?" he repeated.

"Yes, some 'righteous' ritual crap where they drown an infant each year to cleanse their sins," Season explained as she wiped her nose with the back of her hands.

"Oh my God, baby, just sit tight. Let me call Autumn to see what's going on."

"She's at work, but that's not the worst part. I just need you here. I think I'm freaking out. I see things that are not there."

"What do you mean you see things?"

"A grown boy who only appears at the beach. Aunt Autumn took me to a gravesite at night to show me empty graves of babies sacrificed in the ritual. Then a grave that just happened to be the same name as this boy named

Yusef," ranted Season.

Xavier sat up in his chair as if he was struck by a sharp lightning bolt. He remained silent.

"Dad….Dad….is my camera freezing up? Are you okay?"

"She took you to a grave at night?" he finally asked.

"You didn't hear the part of Yusef? She's trying to say that I'm seeing a freakin' ghost or something," she cried.

"I'm going to call Autumn right now. Hold tight, honey. I'm extremely booked this week, but if you could hold on just a little while longer…"

"For how long?"

"Give me until next Tuesday, and I'll be sure to get you. You don't have to go back to that place ever again," he promised with a stern look.

"Next Tuesday? Dad, I need you *now!*"

"Let me call Autumn, and I'll get back in touch with you later, okay? I promise. I have to go. Love you, baby girl," he said in a hurry.

"No, Dad…don't hang up!" she yelled, but her father left the conversation.

"Did you ever get to read the last entry?" asked Cindy, popping her gum while flipping through a cosmetic magazine.

"No," Season answered as she browsed the internet at

the circulation desk.

After her morning conversation with her father, she got dressed and decided to take a cab to the library. It seemed to serve more as a safe haven than that house. At least she was around the public and, of course, Cindy. Mrs. DeVeau had some matters to handle at home and asked Cindy to hold down the place while she was gone. When Season got there, she filled Cindy in on what happened that Monday night with her aunt. Somehow, what she told her didn't come as a shock.

"You know, if you really want to know more about the article I wrote to the state and outside press, you really need to read Marion's last entry," said Cindy nonchalantly.

"Cindy, look, I know it may not be a concern for you, but I heard enough of this craziness to last my entire young adult life. In case you didn't hear me, I am a sacrificial product of some deranged cult," Season stressed.

"And yet you're here to tell the story, congrats!" Cindy praised sarcastically.

"What's really wrong with you? Huh? I understand you went through more hell than I ever had to go through, but is it right to be such a heartless bitch right now?"

Cindy slammed the magazine down and looked at Season with fury in her eyes. "Yes, I have the right! I have every right to be that heartless bitch! After that night, that's what I became! I lost a part of my soul…it drowned right in the ocean along with my baby. A part of me wished I should've ran off after college instead of returning home to my family. They didn't fight for my child being carried off to his doom. They only cared about their survival to stay alive and didn't fight for him. Sending you that video was not meant for your sympathy, Season. It was intended to show what I am fighting for. I cut off my humanity switch a long time ago, honey. I learned being dramatic and helpless in this life doesn't get you a front seat to see those assholes fry for what they have done. So, I'm sorry if I'm not reciprocating the emotions you want me to feel right now because you found out that your sad sack of a dad is a cult leader, and your precious aunt is really your biological mother. At least she cared enough about you to save you from those monsters. So just cut her some slack, and stop feeling sorry for yourself." She got up from her seat, marched her way to Mrs. DeVeau's office, and slammed the door behind her.

Season, too stunned to even say or do anything, sat there. She had to admit that Cindy put her in her place. Season prided herself on being a diligent person and argued her points when something didn't sit well with her, so why couldn't she argue her way out of this one? At that moment, she realized how much of a child she was and had a lot of learning to do. Everything wasn't just black and white, and everything wasn't about her. She wasn't ready for challenging situations and definitely wasn't prepared for the consequences of past actions that were set by her family. She wished for Summer to embrace her just once, so she could hide from all the calamity happening around her. There, she would be safe. There, she would finally tell her that she was playing a big girl's game, and she lost.

She went into her backpack and took out the book. For Cindy, she decided to read the last entry Marion wrote. As she turned to where it was, she took a deep breath and began to read:

June 19, 1866

Today, I, Marion Hollingsworth, broke ground in our new town, Hollins. After years of fighting the law to give me the land that my fellow brethren bled and died on, I was next in line to inherit the ground after my half-sisters. I would say that was the best thing that worthless devil ever had done for me, but I would be lying to say that Omo didn't have a hand in my father's wild decision-making. It wasn't until later I found out that Omo was just looking out for me before my father's "coincidental" suicide. Master Hollingsworth retracted his will to add me as his third benefactor over his property.

Sadly to say, Maryanne and Lorraine both had untimely deaths before reaching the age of thirty. I've waited drastically for their deaths, only because they were dumb Hollingsworths and they couldn't care less what happened to their father's land. Lorraine went off to marry a brute of a man who portrayed the same qualities as her father. He was a cheat and a drunk who beat her senseless day in and day out. Mostly for not minding her mannerism towards him. Sooner or later, her husband beat her into a grave. Ironically, Marianne committed suicide, drowning in the same waters that took her father.

It was quite surprising to know that my father owned most of the town where we reside. The area was literally a ghost town, right after the war in 1863 drove everyone away from here. I didn't stop at my father's property, but I managed to acquire the entire town, all thanks to Omo.

It didn't take long to get settled. Omo and the other former enslaved decided to stay to help me construct my vision. To Omo, what he considered breaking ground was to populate the reconstruction of Hollins with his seeds. He did not fancy marriage, for he thought of it as another form of bondage. Like Yemaja, he wanted to give women the gift of children. It was his acceptance of payment to see his future descendants become devotees to the town of Hollins. He also made a pact with us: we must give thanks to Akoko and Yemaja for our freedom by offering a newborn annually to the sea. Doing so will please their spirits enough to see the town prosper with good wealth and fertility. To rest assured, if an offering is not given to them, they will seek vengeance using the waves as their means of transportation, drowning everyone in this town. The devotees and I agreed to this conciliation, with the understanding that the powers invested in Omo, given by Akoko and Yemaja, we wouldn't even possess such blessings.

By my credence, the menfolk here will be gentle-men, and the womenfolk will be ladies. Although I couldn't stand my father and what he stood for, I re-spected his ideology of a grander style of sophistication and education. We, the citizens of Hollins, are not barbarians but civilized Negros who chose to partici-pate in the American Dreams in our own fashion. If there's any conflict to this credo, he or she will meet a gruesome end.

It is the week of the summer solstice, the time where the sun meets heavily upon us. Omo taught us not to wait until the winter, for we as people are not sinful occultists. We will have our first sacrifice in a couple of days, and we will thank Akoko and Yemaja properly for allowing us this opportunity to do so. Until the next entry, I will write back soon!

Season slammed the book down and looked at the cover. She instantly picked it back up and tore all the pag-es out of it, grunting and yelling at the same time. The few patrons in the library stopped what they were doing to look at the scene Season was putting on. Suddenly, Cindy came out of the office and was caught off guard by Season's performance. She tried picking up the ripped pages off the floor, but more was flying all over the place.

"Okay, just stop," Cindy demanded calmly, placing the pages in an empty bag.

"No!" Season shouted as she was continuously tearing the pages with her bare hands.

"It's okay…look, I was a little too hard on you before, and I'm sorry, but you can't just destroy a book like this," soothe Cindy as she gently took what was left of the book from Season.

Compulsively, Season began crying on Cindy's shoulder. As she embraced the poor child in her arms, she couldn't help but notice a young teenaged boy who was looking at them sternly. He quickly stormed out of the library in a huff.

"It's okay, everyone…Just a small episode. She would be okay," called out Cindy to the others. She instructed Season to go back to the office to calm down and wait for Mrs. DeVeau to come back so she could talk with her. As Season left, Cindy's attention drew back to the exit door where the young boy left.

Later on that day, Autumn received a call from Mrs. DeVeau, who told her about Season's episode earlier. She drove quickly to the library to retrieve her and bring her back home. Season went straight to her room and fell asleep. Autumn returned to work and got off around four. When she got home, Season was still sleeping, so Autumn cooked dinner. By evening, Season was awake. They both ate in silence, and Autumn cleared the dishes after that. She summoned Season to meet her in the living room, where she sat in a leather loveseat. Season took the seat right next to her with a look of shame on her face.

"What were you doing at the library in the first place? And to make a scene like that in front of everyone?" Autumn scolded.

"I didn't want to be left alone," Season spoke softly, holding her head down.

"You've could have told me, Season. And to also have your father call while I'm working? You are totally losing it!"

"How am I losing it? How am I? What sensible person would want their own child, if I'm *your* child, to come to a place like this? I don't get it. I really don't."

Autumn sighed as she placed her hand over her head. "I wasn't thinking. I just wanted you to be here with me, is all. As far as this town is concerned, I wasn't thinking about the precautions I should've taken when sending for you, and I'm sorry. That's all on me. But I wanted you back. I want you to become part of my life."

"Then move then. Get out of here!" cried Season.

"It's not that simple," Autumn answered, shaking her head.

"What's not simple? Hmm? Let's pack our bags and get in the car, and go back to Columbia. That's it! No problem," Season asserted while snapping her fingers.

"What about the debt I made? Huh? What about that?"

"You mean to tell me that you're paying for something that you don't even take part in?"

"Yes...Yes, I am!"

"WHY?!"

"Because it's the only way to ensure that they won't come looking to harm you, is what!"

"What do you mean?"

"C'mon Season, they knew I was pregnant with you. Eddie figured out that I gave you to my sister. The only reason why they are not pursuing you is because of me. I promised them I would stay to uphold the creed. No, I don't participate in the ritual, but I have to live here for an entire sentence," she cried.

"Oh no! Are you serious?" Season's body was shaking from fright.

"Those times when I came to visit you and your mother, it was only for a day or so. If I stayed any longer, they would've thought I was running away. They would have harmed you."

"You're lying," Season whispered.

"I'm telling you the absolute truth. This is not a story I just made up. I'm just as frightened as you are. And to think Xavier is coming to pick you up next week, we have to hold it together before then."

"What about the police? Why can't we just inform them?"

Autumn looked at her as if she was foolish. "The policemen in this town are just as corrupt as the citizens they serve here. They would turn us into the devotees before we could even blink."

With the loss of hope, Season closed her eyes and whimpered, "I just want to go home. Please, Aunt Autumn. I can't stay here."

Autumn embraced Season tightly, refusing to let her go. "I know, and you will leave. I promise you that. For now, let me protect you, okay? No harm will come to you if I have a say in this. I did it once before, and I'll do so again. You have my word."

Season looked up at Autumn. She wanted to believe her, but there's no way possible she could stop a whole town from getting her hands on her. She was either too optimistic or too foolish.

Ring, Ring

Ring, Ring

Ring, Ring

The house phone rang throughout the house as Autumn was calming her daughter down. She didn't want to leave this moment where she could finally hold her as a mother should hold her child. She wanted it to last forever. But she got up slowly and walked over to the cordless phone across the other side of the room.

"Hello?" Autumn answered. "Wait…Wait….slow down…what?! What did you say? Oooooh Jesus! No…. tell me you're lying. Please Lord, tell me this ain't true.

How?!" Autumn wailed, gripping the phone tightly in her grasp.

Season quickly jumped up after hearing her aunt squawking at whomever was on the other end of the phone. By the tone of her aunt's voice, she knew something tragic must have happened, but what?

"Nooooo," Autumn moaned once more, shaking her head.

"What? What is it?" Season asked, running toward her aunt.

"Okay...okay...I will. Bye!" she pressed the end call button and gently placed the phone in its cradle.

"What's happening?!" asked Season, her voice cracking.

"They...they found Cindy's body. It was washed up by the shore. It appears she drowned herself!" Autumn cried.

Season stood with her mouth opened, but no sound couldn't be heard.

Chapter 14:

THE ESCAPEES

"Hey Pooh," Suki greeted on FaceTime

"Hey Suk," Season greeted back grimly.

It was a dreary Thursday morning, with rain coming down from the skies as if it were buckets of marbles hitting the rooftop. After learning of Cindy's drowning, Autumn decided to stay home to comfort her daughter while they were both in mourning. Mrs. DeVeau thought it would be a decent and wise idea to close the library for a couple of days. It wasn't by chance that Cindy just drowned, at least in Season's mind. Maybe Autumn felt the same way, but Season didn't know for sure.

Although Season had her door closed, she could still hear her aunt's television sounding off from the other side of the wall, on the same news channel from late last night, talking about the same incident on the beach.

Newswoman: *A local Hollins Woman, Cindy Louisa Darkens, drowned last evening on Hollins Beach. Some locals passing by found the corpse near the shorelines possessing only an empty backpack located across her shoulders. The coroner placed the drowning incident around 7:00pm, and authorities are still investigating what might have occurred or caused this tragic event. Right now, it is believed to be ruled as an apparent suicide. Back to you, Kyle.*

After listening to the news, Season forgot that she was on camera with Suki and began to sob.

"What's wrong, sis? Is everything okay?" asked Suki, who was concerned by Season's unexpected distress.

"No, nothing is alright. Everything is crazy around here, and I have to leave," Season admitted sniffling.

"What's going on? Tell me. We haven't spoken for a while, but you know I'm here for you. Just please tell me what's going on with you,"

Season tried to pull herself together as she caught her friend up on the terrible current events that she discovered about herself and about this town. She told her everything…from Autumn being her real mother, Yusef being nonexistent, Cindy's "suicidal" death, sacrificial infanticides, and even the details of the Hollins' journal entries *WUDU* book. While she was doing so, Suki's angled eyes stretched to the fullest. Season didn't know if her friend believed her or not. She could not even acknowledge the stories that were coming from her mouth, but it happened.

"Girl….I….mmh," stammered Suki while shaking her head.

"I know, right? It's too far-fetched, I know."

"So, um…let me get this straight, your dad's real intentions for sending you to your mom's well aunt's hometown was to learn the truth about your real mom? It wasn't about the lipstick?"

"Yeah, if you only heard that part of my story."

"I mean, I hear you…but damn, girl, you really don't expect me to believe this, do you?"

"Suk, when have you ever know me to lie about something as serious as this?"

"True, you're far from a jokester, that's for sure. But, a real cult that kills babies by drowning them?! C'mon, this is pretty intense. What's wrong with these people? Why hasn't anyone heard about this or locked these murderers up?"

"That's what I'm saying. I know this is an isolated town and all, but is it to the extent of not being untouchable to the real world?"

"Girl….that's some Akuryō mess right there!"

"Somewhat-?

"Akuryō, evil spirit, geesh!" Suki interpreted, pitifully shaking her head.

"Suk, don't play like I'm dumb. You're doing this out of spite so you can lighten the mood, but it's not working. I'm pretty frightened,"

"Well, Shin'yū, whether you know it or not, you got

me feeling the same way after listening to you. What are you going to do?"

Season bit her bottom lip, trying to conjugate a plan. Suddenly, a light bulb came on in her head.

"Hey Suk, your cousin is still in Beaufort?"

"Last I talked to her, she was. Why? You need her to come get you?"

"Yes, and tell her I'm bringing someone with me as well."

"Who?!" asked Suki with anticipation.

"It's not a guy, Miss Hot-to-Trot," Season laughed.

Suki rolled her eyes, "Whatever. Do you want me to contact her first?"

"Good idea, but don't tell her everything I told you. It might freak her out," Season warned.

"Yeah, she's pretty scary. If she knew the reason why she was coming to get you, she probably wouldn't go through with it," Suki agreed.

"Exactly! So make something up. You're a great liar. Better than I am, by the way."

"Well, gee Seas. Thanks, I guess," Suki frowned.

"Suki, don't get your panties in a wad. I need you to do this. You remember when we were younger, and we used to play Secret Agents?"

"Oh yeah, that was fun."

"Well, this time, we're not doing this for fun. Right now, it's a real-life or death situation. We need your cousin to do her part."

"True, I got you, girl. But what would we call this mission, Agent Seas?"

Season looked solemnly at her partner in crime and replied, "Mission Escapees."

Season	*Hey Serene, are you busy? 9:32am*
Serene	*Hey girl, wassup? 9:38am*
Season	*You heard about Cindy? 9:40am*
Serene	*Omg! I couldn't even bring myself into thinking what really happened. 9:41am*
Season	*You don't have to think too hard about what happened. You know what happened to her more than I do. Let's not get beside ourselves here. 9:43am*
Season	*Hello? Serene?! 9:55am*
Season	*Are you there? 10:00am*
Serene	*I'm here. 10:05*
Serene	*I'm just afraid, Season. If I had never gone into that library that day, running my mouth… 10:06 am*
Season	*That's what you think? You think that's why they came for her? I don't think so. It's not your fault. 10:08am*
Serene	*How can you be so sure???? 10:09am*
Serene	*Season? 10:20am*
Season	*Sorry, my aunt wanted me to take the garbage out. But yeah, you know these people are crazy!!! You know Cindy, would she do such a terrible*

	thing like this? 10:22am
Serene	*Now that you say so…no, she wouldn't. At least I thought so. I don't know, but I'm scared. 10:24am*
Season	*Don't worry, I have a plan! 10:25am*
Serene	*What is it? Tell me you're not thinking of doing something crazy?! 10:26am*
Season	*No, I'm doing something that makes sense and would save our lives! We're breaking out of this town. 10:28am*
Serene	*What? Are you crazy? How? 10:30am*
Season	*No, I'm saner than the next person. WE are escaping tonight. 10:31*
Serene	*But I can't… 10:33am*
Season	*Why not? 10:34am*
Serene	*In case you forgot, I live with an insane grandmother for one, and for two, I'm carrying an extra load. I'm due pretty soon.10:37am*
Season	*So, what I'm hearing is that you rather have your child here and see your child killed right in front of your eyes? 10:40am*
Serene	*Hell no! I can't go through with that! 10:41am*
Season	*Then what are you saying? 10:43am*
Serene	*What if we get caught? Have you thought about that? What would they do to me? Or what would they even do to you? 10:45am*
Season	*Then we would have to make sure that we are careful. I would rather die for something than die for nothing at all. At least I can say we try. 10:47*

Serene	*I don't want to die, period! 10:49am*
Season	*C'mon Serene, I can't leave you here. It would weigh heavily on my conscience. We have a ride to take us out of here. 10:51am*
Serene	*A ride? 10:52am*
Season	*Yes, I can assure you that we can make it. Just trust me! 10:53am*
Season	*Serene?! 11:00am*
Serene	*Okay, I'm in. What do I need to do? 11:05am*
Season	*Pack lightly. Like you're going to sleepover at my house. I will ask for my aunt's permission. After she's asleep, I will instruct our driver to go to the place where she needs to pick us up. 11:09am*
Serene	*What will happen to your aunt? 11:12am*
Season	*She will be okay. She's been doing fine without me for 13 years, so she will be alright. 11:14am*
Serene	*What's that supposed to mean? 11:15am*
Season	*Never mind, just get your grandmother's permission first. If she doesn't agree to it, we will concoct another plan. 11:17am*
Serene	*Okay…11:18am*

"So, what do you have up your sleeve, young lady?" Autumn asked, walking into the bedroom with a sad smile on her face.

"What do you mean?" Season answered contritely, quickly placing her phone face down on the dresser.

Autumn gave her daughter an edgy look. "I just want

to know what you're up to. You can't just stay in your room all day. I know it's hard. After what happened to that poor girl, it's hard to cheer up, but…"

"Aunt Autumn…"

"Yes, love?"

"Could you answer this one question for me?"

"I could try."

"Do you really think that Cindy could have killed herself?" questioned Season, with hopes of some kind of relief that she could be overthinking things.

Autumn looked at her with doubt in her eyes, contrary to what Season thought would be a quick "yes" just to keep Season's curiosity at bay. Her expression, however, was alarming and vulnerable. There was no point in lying or protecting what had apparently gotten out of hand. Season knew too much already, and the only logical thing was to tell the truth.

"No," whispered Autumn. "I don't think she was suicidal. Even though what she went through could shape anyone into doing such a thing. Now, I wouldn't say that she got past it, but she was determined to do something with her life, or so Mrs. DeVeau explained to me."

Season looked away, refusing to let her aunt see that one tear leaving her left eye or know what she was really up to. "If you don't mind, I would like for Serene to come over…maybe for a sleepover. I think it could help me cheer up just to spend time with her."

"Mh, I don't know, Season. That may not be a good

idea, given the situation that recently occurred. Her grandmother may not want her to come over," Autumn responded while shaking her head.

"Please? I really don't want to be alone right now," Season begged.

"What am I?" asked Autumn in a shocked tone.

"You're someone who just revealed to me that I'm your daughter. I don't mean any harm, Aunt Autumn, but I'm not really ready to explore such a sensitive subject," Season feigned with a sad look of discouragement.

Autumn, hurt by what was expressed, got up slowly and walked to the door. Before she left, she turned to her and replied, "Well, if it's okay with Mrs. Winnie, then it'll be fine by me."

Season let out a massive sigh after her aunt's exit. As she was about to feel bad, her phone rang. Season picked it up and screened the anonymous call from Beaufort. She quickly answered it, hoping it was the call she was waiting on.

"Hello?" answered Season quickly.

"Hey, is this Season Holidae?" responded a raspy voice from the other end of the phone.

"Who wants to know?"

"This is Suki's cousin, Dahria. Suki told me that you needed a ride back to Columbia, and you would pay handsomely."

Of course, she would tell her such a thing.

"Uh, yeah. I need you to come to Hollins to get my

friend and me tonight," explained Season.

"Mh, okay…well, I ain't no LYFT or anything, but I'll do it. How far is that place? Is it even on the map?"

"It should be if you have a GPS," answered Season in a sarcastic tone.

"Uh-huh, okay. Well, if I'm going to take the both of you, that's double the money, honey. I'm sorry, but I am a college student, and college students are not livin' their best life without some green, ya know?"

Oh my gosh! The explanation of Suki's personality is finally revealing itself, thought Season.

"How much will it be?"

"Depends on the location. I can't have my ride going through potholes and hitting possums or Bambi's momma. With you and your passenger, that'll run you to $50, Boo."

Season screeched, "Fifty-dollars?! I thought you told me that you weren't LYFT?"

"If that's too much, then you definitely don't need my services. I'm only doing this because I owe my little cuz a favor. I really don't have to do nothing."

Season shook her head after hearing Dahria's offer and ignorance. How in the world could she get accepted to any University using such a double negative? She finally calmed herself down and decided to bite her tongue for once. Lives were at stake.

"Okay, I'll accept. Just be here by 9:00pm. Could you do that?"

"Yeah, I could do that. Why so late?"

"I have a busy day today, and that's the only time I would be able to go. Not to mention my father would be home around that time," Season lied, praying Dahria wouldn't hurt her brain to figure out an escape plan was in the mist.

"Oh, okay! Make sense," Dahria agreed crassly.

"So…I'll text you the directions if you can't find it on your phone. Please be there around 9:00pm."

"Girl, I got you! Don't worry. I'll call you as soon as I get into town.

"Sounds like a plan. See ya!"

As the day was slowly moving along, Season's patience was beginning to get shorter. She secretly packed some clothes in a big duffle bag and hid it inside of her closet. She finally received a text back from Serene reading that her grandmother will be attending Cindy's setting up at the Darkens' home around eight, so she could sneak out then. *The audacity of some people,* she thought as she threw her phone across the bed. *How dare she think about attending the bereaved home if she was a possible suspect in Cindy's death? There's no shame for the wicked.*

She went outside to check on her aunt in the garden next. Once again, the mood between them was uncomfortably tense. It was as if no one wanted to face each other. Even during disheartened times as this, it was still impossible to avoid feeling nervous. Her aunt glanced at Season walking toward her, and gave her a quick smile, and went back to wading in the soil.

"I'm sorry," Season sighed.

"Sorry about what?" Autumn asked nonchalantly, pretending to be engrossed with the dirt in her hands.

"I'm sorry that I've been a stubborn and rebellious brat for two-, no cross that, since the entire time I've been here. I didn't give you a chance, and I am genuinely sorry for my conduct.

Autumn looked up at Season sincerely. Season noticed the weariness and defeat in her dark brown eyes. Seemed as if she aged terribly since they last spoke an hour ago. She thought maybe after she escape tonight, perhaps the lights will return to her aunt's eyes again, and she wouldn't have to worry about "protecting her" against Hollins.

"You know…growing up with Summer wasn't easy," she chuckled a bit. "We never had any sister rivalries or anything, but I was awfully jealous of her."

"Why?" questioned Season with interest.

"Because she was the typical three b's: beautiful, bold, and bubbly. I, on the other hand, was brainy and quiet. She had everything, and what she didn't have, she would fight for it. I didn't want to give you up, but we both had to protect you. At that time, I was too young and too spineless to fight for you. But Summer was ready to defend you at all cost. I didn't want her to get into too much trouble than she was already in with this town. Letting you go with her was the best but hardest decision I ever had to make. Over the years, I became even more jealous of Summer because she was getting all your love and attention I craved for: your first words, your first steps, your potty training, your first missing tooth, your first day of school, your first bumps and bruises…I hated that I missed it. I hated that I gave up that right to be the first person you called 'mommy.' I felt she gained the world, and I gained nothing." she cried.

Season wiped her eyes as she quietly looked away from Autumn's heartbroken face.

"I fell back in love with you the day you first came to Hollins. After getting to know you since then, I was in awe and in shame. The very thing I was jealous of, I have come to admire about Summer. She taught you how to be a strong and mindful young lady. I realize that I don't need everything because the way you are now….that's all I need right there."

Season scooped down beside her mother and gave her a huge hug. She didn't want to let go of this woman, this woman who gave and saved her life. This woman, who she thought was negligent, was now a hero.

"Why did you bring two bags? Didn't your grandma think it would look suspicious of you to do so?" Season scolded as she let Serene in the house around 8:30pm. It was just her luck that Autumn left to go to the same destination as Mrs. Winnie. She asked Season if she wanted to tag along, but Season declined. She told her that it wouldn't help her cope with Cindy's death, and she would rather stay home. Autumn agreed and decided to leave the conversation alone and left.

"I'm sorry, but I can't just leave everything. It's hard to uproot everything to escape to someplace you haven't been," clarified Serene as she dropped her things on the floor. "Besides, my grandma didn't see these bags. She left before I got my cousin to drop me off here, so we're good."

"Okay, so Dahria should be here in about thirty minutes. I just texted her, and she texted back she was about twenty minutes away, so that's enough time to unwind. Have you eaten anything?"

"I'm good. I just don't feel right about this. My feet are swollen and heavy like cinder blocks, and I felt funny all day," Serene added, trampling to the nearest chair and heaving.

"Are you okay?" asked Season, rushing over to Serene.

"I don't think I could do this, girl,"

"C'mon Serene, we can't stay here. You can't stay here. Elevate your feet on the coffee table until Dahria gets here."

"I know I can't stay here, but I'm scared. What if what I'm feeling is a sign? Have we really thought this through?"

"I have….and we're going to be fine. Just trust me,

okay?" reassured Season, holding Serene's hands.

"Lawd, Season, I hope you're right about this."

They sat in the room for the remainder of the time, waiting for their cavalry to arrive. To past time, Season read *The Giver* to Serene, who was obviously in pain. Season knew she was in over her head by planning this escape, but she was willing to risk it. She would carry Serene over the town's line if she had to if it meant saving their lives.

Suddenly, beam lights projected on the walls, and the sound of fierce music beats trembled the whole house. Knowing Autumn was too subtle to play music this loud, she hastily went to the window to see a car driving up to the pavement. Despite turning the music down a few notches, the driver honked the horn vigorously to express his or her arrival. Season walked and opened the door to get a closer look at the car. From what she could see at night, it was a red Toyota Prius. The windows rolled down, and a young girl popped her head out instantly.

"Y'all coming or not?" the girl yelled.

Season shook her head and went back into the house. She gathered all the bags and went out to meet the car.

"Hello Dahria," greeted Season, feigning a look of politeness.

"You Season?" asked the girl.

"That will be me," answered Season.

"I popped the trunk so you could put your bags inside it. Where's the second passenger?"

"She's inside."

"She ain't coming or something?" asked Dahria with an attitude.

"She's coming. Just hold on," Season responded impatiently.

"Oh, okay…I thought I was going to be jip getting my fifty," she said, holding out her hand.

Season groaned as she placed a crisp fifty-dollar bill in Dahria's manicured hands. Her nails were as long and curly as the lead singer from *SWV*. Each nail was bedazzled in red paint and rhinestones. Season took a good look at her and noticed, like Suki, she had slanted eyes. Her skin tone was more bronze and flawless like silk. If she didn't spend time clouding up her face with makeup, she would look as if she was Suki's twin. Natural beauty is clearly overrated.

"What?! My mom loves sushi too," Dahria claimed, as if she was reading Season's mind. "So, where is the second passenger? We have to get a move on. I ain't trying to hit Bambi and her family while driving."

Season thought about correcting the senseless girl but thought otherwise. Instead, she hurried back into the house to get Serene, who laid helplessly on the couch.

"You're okay?' Season questioned, running towards her.

"I don't think so. I'm feeling pain right now, Season."

Too ambitious to see her plan fail, Season helped Serene up from the couch and put her arms around her neck. "C'mon Serene, we have to get out of here. We don't have enough time, and Dahria is very impatient."

As the two girls walked slowly out of the house, Season was bearing most of Serene's weight as they went down each step cautiously. Dahria stepped out of her vehicle to get a good look at the two girls and was in total shock.

"Hold up! Suki, nor you said anything about taking a pregnant girl. This is on a whole 'nother level here. Where's your folks?" asked Dahria with concern.

"We don't have the time, Dahria," Season yelled as they approached the car. "We need to get her as far from this place as quickly as we can."

"I…I don't understand," stammered Dahria.

"Look, what will it take? Huh? Do you need more money? Huh? Here you go," Season reached deep in her pockets to hand Dahria some crumbled bills. "Is that enough for you? I don't have the time to explain right now. We just need to leave. When we make it out of here safely, I will give you a reasonable explanation!"

Dahria looked at the pregnant girl. She looked at Season. Then she looked at the pregnant girl once more and took the money. "If we get into any trouble, I promise you…"

"We won't. Not if we hurry!" Season snapped abruptly.

Dahria opened the driver's rear door as Season ushered poor Serenity inside and buckled her into her seatbelt. Season then raced to the passenger side of the car, got in, and buckled up.

"I have a bad feeling about this," Dahria shook her head as she went back into the driver's side of her vehicle.

The car backed out of the driveway slowly until they hit the smooth pavement. Dahria turned her music off as she changed gears and drove toward town. Season couldn't help but look back at Serene, who was crying profusely with pain as they were riding. She wanted so badly to comfort her but decided to wait until they were safely out of the town's grasp.

"She doesn't look too well, Season. Maybe we should stop at a hospital," Dahria suggested, taking quick glances at Serene through her rearview mirror.

"She'll be okay. We're not stopping," groaned Season doubtfully.

"Okay…it's your call. But if I catch a kidnapping case because of you two, I'll be quick to say 'gunpoint' to the cops," Dahria rambled.

Season looked at Dahria as if she had a block of cheese for a brain. "How am I holding you gunpoint, silly? I'm not carrying any type of weapons on me whatsoever."

"I'm just saying….," panicked Dahria.

Season looked out her window to hide her worries. They drove into town quietly, as the night's blanket made the area look so desolate and eerie. They passed by the flamboyant ice cream parlor, the historic Hollins library, and some other closed businesses after five. As they stopped at a traffic light, a look of disgust and fear came across Season's face as Hollins New Deliverance Holiness church appeared on her side. She couldn't stand the looks of that place. It was an evil entity that housed wicked parishioners. The pure white-colored cornerstones were more satirical than symbolic when it came to the history of Holiness churches. It was a wolf dressed in a sheep's clothing, preparing to kill, steal, or destroy. Fortunately, the light changed to green, and the church left her view. She was relieved because the very thought of it sent shivers through her body. As if on cue, Serene's screams from the back were like sirens to proclaim its influence.

"Ooh gosh, help!" Serene hollered from the backseat.

"What's wrong?" Season quickly turned around to see a desperate Serene out of her seatbelt and slumped over..

"I...I think my water broke," she yelled.

"Oh, Hell no! Tell me she didn't say what I think she said? Oh no!!!! This is bad...this is very bad....I just made the final payments on this car, and she just messed up my seats?! It's not even leather," Dahria cried, almost driving off the side of the road.

That was the last straw. Season had enough of Suki's boujee and dimwitted cousin. The mission looked as if it was heading downhill, and she didn't know what to do. She didn't know a thing about delivering a baby, only that her father does it for a living. She wanted to call him for help but knew it would only get her into more trouble than she was already in. Undeniably so, Serene's health was more imperative than a clean escape. Season thought quickly and took out her phone and typed something into the Google Maps app.

"We have to take her to a hospital, but not here. The next hospital is fifteen minutes out of this town."

Dahria opened her mouth out of disbelief. Surprisingly, nothing came out of it. Before Season could let out a sigh of relief, of course, Dahria had to impart some words of discouragement.

"Fifteen minutes? Girl, that's too far. That girl needs a hospital now," she raged, now driving a little over the speed limit.

"You might want to slow down a bit, Dahria, or the cops could pull us over…You don't want them to see you harboring two minors, not to mention one who's about to make your backseat a delivery room!"

"Oh, no! What am I going to do?! I can't get caught. I can't get kicked out of college, for goodness sake! Why did my own little cousin involve me in this situation?!" Dahria bawled while clutching her face with both hands and her feet on the gas.

As the car jerked toward the edge once again, Season grabbed a hold of the wheel and yelled, "Girl, just drive! What's wrong with you? You're trying to kill us?"

Dahria finally gained some control and placed her hands back on the wheel but began grumbling obscenities to herself.

Hearing cries and heavy panting from the backseat and Dahria talking to herself like a crazy woman, Season knew she was way over her head. Maybe they needed to abort the mission while there was still a chance. Yes, abort mission, drive back to her aunt's and call 9-1-1 while there's always a chance for cavalry for all parties involved. They were almost close to the exit, where the town ended and the bridge appeared. The same bridge her father exchanged temporary custody to her aunt. The same bridge that marked the beginning of her troubles. The exact same bridge that welcomed the escapees with blue and red lights flashing as if they were approaching a crime scene. Dahria and Season sat up in their seats to witness the blockade at the bridge's ending with police officers standing in front of their cars.

What was even stranger was the civilians standing behind the officers holding hands as if they were the second barricade to go through. Season inched closer to the window shield, but her eyes began to hurt because of the lights. As if responding to Season's questions, the civilians marched slowly ahead of the police officers, blocking out the rays, and then began holding hands again. They continued marching until they were in plain view from Dahria's headlights. Pastor Hollis, Mama Winnie, Sis. Applegate and a few other members from the church. What was really a stab through the heart, shaking her head with tears running down her face, was her mother, Autumn.

Chapter 15:

"Take Ya Foot in Ya Hand"

*A*s the old saying goes: if you want to make God laugh, tell him your plans The cliché of it all made Season want to laugh, but not in a good way. The aftermath of it all terrified her after the police apprehended them. She literally peed her pants. She remembered Autumn looking hopelessly at her when the rambunctious group chastised them in front of the authorities. Mama Winnie was yelling obscenities more than a gambling man losing all of his winnings. Unbeknownst to her, she opened the back door viciously and was revolted by the scene. Then, she dared to call Season and Dahria "baby knappers." The EMT was already on the scene, so at least Serene was in their care until they reached the hospital. After that night, the ideal punishment for the two young ladies was wavering.

They rode in the back of a police car to the station

in silence. Once there, Dahria began spilling tears and information on why she was summoned to get the two teenagers. Surprisingly, she didn't give the male officer the crappy story about being held at gunpoint, considering she didn't have any evidence to support such a theory. The officer called her parents, and once they got there, they were enraged. Dahria got a slap on the wrist, and Mama Winnie wished for a restraining order to ban her from the town of Hollins, or she would face kidnapping and child endangerment charges. *She was lucky; at least she didn't have to come back to a place like this,* Season thought. Like Dahria, Season supposed she was privy to call her father, but she thought wrong. No phone calls were made, but Autumn followed them there, hoping they would release Season sooner than later. Once again, Season was placed in a holding cell, only this time, for the remainder of the night. Luckily, Autumn didn't leave her side. She made it her business to camp herself near the station until her child was released. By morning, Season was released in her aunt's custody. Before they could leave, she overheard the male officer warning Autumn to keep her "niece" on a tight leash, and to atone for Season's recklessness, they would have to attend the righteous ritual on Sunday since Serene just gave birth early that Friday morning.

Pondez Baron Lewis, a beautiful 5lbs 2oz bundle of joy, came into a new daylight after surviving through a horrific night. As soon as he made his opening debut, his Great-Grandma Winnie thought it would be best for

Serene not to develop an attachment to the small infant, considering how the "martyr" must be sacrificed for the greater good. It bothered Serene the whole time while recuperating in the hospital. She knew she couldn't intervene with the treacherous tradition, but she couldn't give up the nine months of commitment she shared with this small human who was inside of her—the sweet lullabies and ambitious promises she made while calming his kicks. If the little one only knew that his future would be his quick demise, he wouldn't have become so eager to see the craziness he was exposed to.

Season sat on the den floor, with her back toward Autumn. She didn't want to even look into her eyes of betrayal. She busied herself with the television in front of her, pretending to watch a marathon of the classic television show, *Gunsmoke,* which she didn't choose to watch. Knowing Season didn't care for watching old westerns, Autumn waited for her to give up her charades of interest in the show and to say something or anything to her. It turned into a long game of patience, and it seemed as if Season was winning. When the tall Matt Dillon drew his Colt revolver to shoot a duel expert antagonist and killed him, Autumn picked up the remote control from a nearby table to turn the tube off. Season stayed glued to the pictureless screen, seeing her reflection staring back at her.

"You know, I think I saw him before..." spoke Autumn quietly.

Season was silent.

Autumn continued, "It was one time last year. I was at my lowest point. So low that I thought a bottle of scotch and a walk of execution to the ocean would be the best way out of this world. Maybe I had a little bit of adrenaline before."

Season turned around slowly to take a good look at Autumn. She didn't know where the story was going, but from the look on Autumn's face and the bags under her eyes, she was exhausted. Exhausted and pitiful with no glimmer of life in her eyes. She looked at Season blandly and smiled just enough to display humility.

"At first, I remember imprinting my feet on the cold, wet sand as the water from the waves receded back to the ocean. I heard something out there...the innocence of roaring, stifling cries. Sooner or later, my maternal instincts kicked in, and for a moment, I thought I could save them. I began racing toward the sounds but found myself head deep in the water. I thought about fighting to get out of it but decided to stretch out my arms and give in. Who was I to live after 'supposedly' profiting from little lives? It just wasn't right, you know?"

Season nodded her head in agreement as she wiped her eyes.

"Suddenly, I felt I was in a hopeless fight with the current, but another force was pulling me in a different direction. I thought I died that day. I couldn't tell you how long I had been underwater. After that, I remember the sunlight shining down on my face. I didn't know if it was a dream or if I was wide awake. A young boy with a dark brown complexion blocked the sun and was staring down at me. I remembered his smile. It was the prettiest smile I had ever seen. He didn't say anything for a short while, but then he said one thing that caught my attention."

"What's that?" Season inquired.

Autumn chuckled a little, "Something Summer would always say to me as a child when I'm moving too slow or when I was trying to make up my mind. Somehow, oddly enough, this child knew what Summer would say if she saw me in that condition. He said, 'Take ya foot in ya hand.' The boy got up and left me at shore. He was gone. I never saw him again after that. All I remembered was his white linen shirt and his face.

"Yusef," Season said in almost a whisper.

"Well, whoever it was, he saved my life and gave me a purpose to keep living. After that day, I knew what I had to do to make my life right, and you were the first priority on my list, along with other things."

"What other things?"

"What you've done, Season, was reckless and dangerous. You could've gotten yourself and others killed. You didn't think things through at all. But after thinking about it last night at the station, I can understand why. I didn't give you any reason to trust me, especially after exposing you to these God-awful people. That's my fault. I don't want you to fall victim to feeling that you owe anybody your life. I didn't set a good example for you, but I'm here now to make things right."

"How?"

"By ending this evil ritual, and everything or everyone who is a part of it. Because if I don't, they would never stop until they make both of our lives miserable, including your father," she said the last part quickly while clearing her throat.

"He's not my father. He's just a donor. I know who my real father is, and he's back at home…where I should be," stated Season.

Autumn nodded her head slowly, "And I know you knew Summer your whole life as your mom, and I won't take offense if you continue calling me 'aunt.' I'd instead take that consequence than to…"

"You are my mother, Aunt Autumn. I have to honor that. I had some time to think while I was in that rotting cell. I imagined myself in Serene's place. Knowing sooner or later, after she was in labor, I knew I would have no choice but to give it up. I asked myself how I would feel about that or what would have been the alternative? Here I am, trying to escape from this place with a pregnant teenager, and I couldn't even get across the bridge. You, however, saved me by placing me in your sister's care. And for that, I'm grateful."

Autumn rushed to the floor where Season was sitting and held on to her tightly while crying her heart out, "You're one amazing gal, you know that?"

"It's an inherited trait," agreed Season while placing

her head on Autumn's shoulder.

Remembering she forgot something, Autumn quickly let go of her daughter. "Let's take our feet in our hands."

"What?" Season asked with a raised eyebrow.

"We have a plan to concoct; if they're saying you must be there for the righteous ritual this Sunday evening, we have to be ready."

"But I don't want to attend. Please don't make me go," Season pleaded.

"Don't worry, baby, everything is going to be okay. I'm asking you to trust me this time. I'm finally going to make things right."

"What do you have plans for?"

"Let's just say that it will be the last 'righteous' ritual this town will ever witness," Autumn asserted with boldness in her eyes.

Chapter 16:

SERENE'S CEREMONY

"Everything is set. It should be coming by Mr. Peasant's old place around 8:15pm, so make sure you're there by then. May God be with you," a loud female voice hollered through the phone.

Season sat at the dining table eating breakfast while Autumn was on her cell. As far away as Autumn was from her, Season could hear a great deal of the conversation she was having on the phone with the person who sounded a lot like Mrs. DeVeau. It was a Sunday morning, but something about this day was different than the last two Sundays she spent in Hollins. When the sun goes down, her attendance will be required at the Righteous Ritual. Autumn promised her that everything would be okay, but she didn't confide in Season to tell her the plan. What Season just learned from eavesdropping a few seconds ago was a plan to meet up where she assumed was Mr.

Peasant's boathouse at 8:15pm, but why?

"Sorry for interrupting your concentration, Missy," Autumn joked as she joined her at the table. "I knew you were trying to listen in on my conversation."

"Well, Ma'am, I wasn't trying to do so. I couldn't help if your phone volume was up to the extreme. Was that Mrs. DeVeau on the phone?"

Autumn replied, "Yes, that was Mrs. DeVeau on the phone."

"Mh," Season grunted and continued eating her cereal.

"You're one nosey child, aren't you?"

"What? I just asked a question."

"No, the real question is: what were you two talking about? Am I correct?"

"Well, since you mentioned it…what were you two talking about?"

Autumn chuckled a bit at her daughter's attempt to remain uninterested. She realized that Season was a trickster when it came to getting results.

"It's all a part of the plan. Don't worry. Remember, the ritual begins at 7:30 tonight, so we should be prompt and…"

Ring, Ring

Ring, Ring

The home telephone interrupted Autumn as she was about to discuss tonight's plans. She hurried to the living room to retrieve the phone from the cradle and press the button to answer it.

"Hello?" Autumn answered.

Season decided not to listen in on Autumn's conversation this time. If she was ever going to trust Autumn, she knew she had to have her best interest at heart. After finishing up her breakfast, she walked over to the sink to clean out the bowl until she heard the dynamic of her aunt's voice changed on the phone.

"What do you mean 'come to the church'? I understand it is a Sunday, but I'm not going to subject my niece to those people who were eager to incarcerate her that night…..after-service? Why?"

Season's heart began to beat faster as she dropped the bowl in the sink. There was no way she was going to that church again. Especially after knowing the pastor was, in fact, her biological father. If she looked him straight in the eyes, he could realize the truth in them.

"Eddie, please…I can't do this with you!"

Eddie? Thought Season. *Why would he want us to come over after service? Does he know?* Season walked directly to the living room to listen keenly. Autumn looked at Season as if she heard the worst news ever. Her expression couldn't hide the fear she was trying to suppress.

"Okay…" she responded slowly as she hit the off-dial on the phone. She carefully placed it back in its cradle and took in a long breath. "Around 3:00pm, Pastor Hollis would like to see us at the church."

"Why?" Season cried.

"Somehow, he knows, Season…he knows. Change of plans."

Walking up the same church steps to meet her maker seemed more frightening than walking into the sanctuary to see a rose pink coffin with her mom, Summer, sleeping peacefully in it. Unlike Summer's death, causing an incompletion of her neutral family, this evil patriarch wanted insertion in her disfigured family tree. If it was acceptance he wanted, he wasn't going to get it or anything else he coveted from her. There were no cars on the church grounds but Autumn's and a black 2019 F-450 truck parked in the pastor's parking space.

The ambiance inside of the church wasn't settling as well. It looked even darker and grimmer without the parishioners being there. The hypocrisy of solace came across Season's mind as they made their way to the church's front to the closest exit to reach Pastor Hollis's office. Season noticed Autumn was more nervous than her when she hesitantly knocked a couple of times. A deep, solemn voice called from the other side of the door, granting them permission to enter.

There he sat, in his stylish pulpit gown, with a gold cross embedded closely to his duplicitous heart, in his black leather chair. The chiseled smile on the beast's face signaled content for controlling both their fears of what he already knew. He clasped his hands on top of two books. The first one looked to be a medium-sized bible, and the second book on top was the book Season was all too familiar with, a copy of *Hollins WUDU Proclamation.*

"Well…I see my family has arrived," he gnashed.

"I…I can explain," Autumn stammered, stepping in front of Season quickly.

He halted her with one hand. "Sit. Your insolence cost you your voice to reason. Both of you, sit."

Season and Autumn exchanged glances as they placed themselves on the two seats provided in front of them.

"It took me a while to figure this treacherous act out, but I came to the conclusion that you took me for a fool. You said it was crib death, but there was never a body to confirm such a crazy story. Then thirteen years later, this child pops up out of nowhere, and I'm supposed to believe that she's here for a visit? I've done my research. While you think this child was safe with your sister, I had you tailed every time you went up to visit her. Not to mention, the sheriff in this town hired a private investigator. Come to find out, Summer never had any other children after she vanished from here," he growled.

"Eddie, I was …"

"Quiet! The only response I want from you is to answer this question. Is this the child that was to be sacrificed thirteen years ago?" he asked while veins were appearing on his forehead.

"If you're asking if this was our child that you offered up to the ritual, then yes, she is," defined Autumn in a bold tone.

Eddie chuckled a bit as he got up from his chair. He

walked over to them and sat on top of his desk. Season, too afraid to look at him, looked down at her hands.

"So, Miss Season. I take it, she finally told you the truth?" asked the pastor, dropping his voice into a more whimsical tone.

"Yes," Season whispered.

"Look at me when I'm talking to you, child," he demanded.

Season cleared her throat and looked up at the horrible man in front of her. "Yes," she spoke clearer. "But it doesn't matter. I'm not your daughter. A real father wouldn't bring harm to his own child. A real father would protect his daughter. A real father would love his daughter unconditionally. You're no father of mine!"

The pastor's face looked stunned by the words that were coming out of this preteen's mouth. At first, he was at a loss for words. It was clear that he felt a little hurt, but he didn't want her to see it on his face. As if a breakthrough was coming, showing him the errors of his ways- instead, he fought the light, and the darkness won. It was too late to turn back now. His heart was hardened, and that type of mercy was against everything Hollins stood for. He turned away from Season and looked to her mother, who was literally shaking because of what Season told him.

"I can't have what happened in the past affect what will happen tonight. Serene's ceremony will happen whether you like it or not. It's for the sake of this town that we follow our creed to the end. With that being said, Autumn, you will leave her with me until our WUDU ritual comes to pass. I have to take safety precautions when it comes to you. She needs to comprehend and respect our beliefs around here if you want her to live," he commanded as he grabbed hold of Season's arm.

"I don't want to stay with you!" Season yelled, trying to wiggle herself from his grasp.

"Season…" Autumn cried, jumping out of her seat.

"No! Are you insane? Please don't make me stay with this man! He's a killer….him and the rest of this town!"

"Is that what you're filling our child's head up with? A killer? No, I am a loyalist. A king who cares about his subjects and the success of this town. We owe all this to Omo and his lineage, which you, my dear, are a part of!"

"Your words say one thing, but your robe says another. What about your loyalty to God?" Season shouted.

"It is by his grace and mercy that he sent Omo to us. The good Lord wants us to pay homage to the Great Yemaya and Akoko so we could make atonement."

"The blasphemy! Stop it right now, Eddie," Autumn cried, walking toward him.

"You take one more step, you wrench, and I will break her arm. You have a lot of nerves claiming blasphemy. Keep it up, or the ceremony will call for two martyrs instead of one!"

Autumn shook her head, "You can't do that-it'll go against everything the proclamation stands for. The blood of an untainted nursling. She's of age to be a woman.

According to that stupid book, you would be a killer if you do so!"

The pastor gave her a wicked smile. "You don't have the authority to tell me the rules of our proclamation. You're no longer a pillar of this community. Tonight, we will need our wine for the commencement, so run along and be at the beach before 7:30, or you will never see 'our' princess ever again! Got that?"

"I…I can't leave her," Autumn said, shaking her head.

He applied more pressure to Season's arm until she squealed.

"Okay! Stop! I'll go, but if you bring harm to my child…," Autumn threatened.

"You'll what? Run away like the coward you are?"

Autumn turned to look at her daughter and said, "Honey, don't be afraid. He can't harm you. I will see you tonight. That's my word!" She reached for her daughter, but the pastor jerked her away. She walked dismally to the door.

Season cried, "Mom?"

"Yes?" Autumn's voice cracked.

"Take ya foot in ya hand," Season encouraged.

Understanding the message, Autumn nodded her head and left out the door.

Sunday night had finally arrived, and the pastor's anticipation for getting prepared for it alarmed Season. They rode in silence on the way to the beach. Dressed in a white mumu and a white turban covering his head, Pastor Eddie didn't look like the same Holiness pastor from earlier. Season reflected back on the remainder of the afternoon when he called himself trying to catch her up on Hollins' history. How Marion Hollingsworth I's brilliant depiction of WUDU saved lives and industries in town. How he made sure to keep the covenant alive, and how she could one day be his successor if she decides to live with him. Season didn't entertain this notion, for it was absurd and ruthless. If there was one thing she inherited from this man, it was her sense of doggedness when it came down to winning an argument. However, she learned quickly how to deflect his desires by planning on ways to escape tonight. When he detected her indifference, he came back with a bowl of Goldfishes and a bottle of water as a way to mock her intelligence as a toddler. He took her into a walk-in-closet located in his office and locked the door from the outside. It didn't stop her from screaming and kicking the door, but it was strong enough to hold her until he prepared himself for the ritual.

When they arrived at the beach, others were dressed in the same garments as Pastor Hollis, sitting in the sand around a white circle, all except for Mama Winnie, who was dressed in all black as if she was in mourning. She walked up to the pastor as she held a small baby wrapped in white blankets…Serene's baby! Season looked around to see if she could spot the baby's mother, and there she was, sitting in the center of the circle like she was the roasted goose in the pot as seven tall glass candles were placed around her. She looked as if she was crying all day, and her hair was disheveled. She was hardly conscious, for she looked as if she was dizzy and out of it. At that moment, Season realized that somehow she had been drugged. It was the only possible explanation to formulate, considering the state she was in and even participating in being in the center of the circle.

Season was on her way to help Serene until she spotted Autumn near the table, pouring wine in tall chalices. She, too, was wearing the same trademark with her head wrapped in a tight scarf. She gave Season a cautionary look. A look Season knew all too well and disobeyed before. For the sake of both of their lives, she decided to mind her mother's wish. Instead, she watched as Hollis took the baby from Mama Winnie as they both joined the crowded circle.

Around the circle, they were carefully grouped by gender: the male adults were on one side of the ring, and the female adults were on the other. Even the sheriff and a few of his policemen participated in the demonic festival. Strangely enough, there were no children present, only Serene and Season. Hollis, the baby, and Mama Winnie stood in the middle of the circle next to Serene. Hollis held the baby up as if he was reenacting Roots' scene when Kunta Kinte was holding up his child to the stars. Mama Winnie held out a copy of her *Hollins WUDU Proclamation* book as if it was the Bible. The ruthless pastor then began to chant some incantations in a different tongue with his eyes closed. The members surrounding him held back their heads and closed their eyes, repeating what he was chanting. Season stepped back slowly until she made her way to Autumn, who was slipping something back inside her white scarf on her head.

"What are they doing?" Season whispered, not taking her eyes away from the crowd.

"They are calling on the Orisha Yemaya and the old Bruja Akoko so they can accept their gift."

"What?! What are we going to do? We can't let this happen," Season squealed. She looked toward the ocean as the tides began to grow heavier and faster like a steam engine heading toward them. The wind picked up and slapped her face so harshly that she could have sworn it was a person's hand that touched her. And the sound…it was the same sound she heard that day inside the water, and the same sound Autumn claimed that called her into the ocean. It rang in their ears, but it didn't stop the others from chanting.

"WHAT'S GOING ON? WHY HAVEN'T THEY STOPPED? CAN'T THEY HEAR THOSE TERRIFYING CRIES?" Season hollered, covering her ears. She glanced over to Serene, and she, too, was trying to block out the sounds. When it became too overwhelming for her, she began crying out for it to stop. Young Pondez seemed to sense his mother's distress, and he cried out as well.

"HARDENED HEARTS DO NOT LISTEN TO ANYTHING THEY CHOOSE TO IGNORE, INCLUDING THEIR GUILT," Autumn explained loudly. "ONLY THE ONE WHO ACCEPTS HUMILITY CAN HEAR SUCH THINGS!"

After finishing his invocation, the calamity of it all died down. Mama Winnie pulled out a long sharp antique dagger and a small vial from her cloak. She prayed over the dagger and carved an 'X' on the baby's arms. Pondez let out a piercing scream of agony as Mama Winnie pressed the vial close to the fresh bloody wound, filling it up to the top.

"Please…no…please don't hurt my baby. Please! I can't," Serene cried feebly as she watched what was happening before her eyes.

"Season!" Hollis summoned.

Season backed away when she heard her name being called. The disturbance of it all wouldn't let her get near that circle.

"Season! Come, and collect the vial. Autumn will show you what to do next."

Season shook her head out of protest, so Autumn went in her place.

"Let me, Pastor Hollis," she replied kindly. "Let her just bear witness to this ceremony. By the following year, I will personally see to it that she's ready."

Hollis gave her a suspicious look as she flirtatiously took the vial from his hand. Then, he gave her an "if you screw me over" look as she walked away to return to her post at the long table. It didn't take Season long to realize that Autumn was playing him, and she hoped that her mom would be able to save Serene and the baby. She watched as Autumn used a small dropper to draw up the blood from the small container and released a drop in each chalice. As she was doing so, Season counted over thirty chalices, seeing how each was half-filled with red wine.

"Now, let's drink of the pureness, for we shall make atonement for our sinful actions and thoughts. Let's not forget our great forefather from my lineage, Marion Hollingsworth I, who founded this town in 1866.

Most of all, let us not forget the mystical leader that granted Marion's request to live freely and affluently at the expense of their master's riches and privileges, Omo. I've put all my needs aside and united these two families by sacrificing my firstborn," Hollis stopped talking to look at Autumn with an evil glance before continuing his lie. "If I gave up my firstborn child to something so rewarding, it shouldn't be painful for you all to do the same. So come, let us drink up, for once we are done, we shall give the baby to Yemaya after the next high tide approaches."

The cult followed Hollis to the table. They each grabbed a chalice, except for Autumn, who was not allowed to partake in the toast ceremony, considering she was banned from receiving any of the town's "blessings" that was coming soon after tonight. It was her form of punishment for the past thirteen years, and she wasn't at least a bit bothered by it. She took off her white gloves after exchanging Hollis's drink for the baby. Hollis held up his cup and toast to the ocean and consumed the entire wine. Everyone followed suit, except for Mama Winnie, who was busy eyeing Season. There was something about the child that did not rest with her.

Autumn, who noticed Mama Winnie's cupless hands and her suspenseful eyes on her daughter, was a bit uneasy. Mama Winnie then fixated her eyes on Autumn and could see a bead of sweat on her forehead with the look of desperation. Then she noticed a large trash bag with empty wine bottles. Next to it were remnants of green and white flowers and one bottle of potassium cyanide, which Autumn forgot to place in the bag.

"It's poisoned!" she yelled. "She poisoned all of ya!"

Everyone stopped their constant dialogue to listen to what Mama Winnie was trying to tell them. They didn't understand what she was saying until she pointed to the evidence under the table. As they spotted it, their eyes widened with fear. Some even tried to make themselves vomit, but it was too late. They consumed way too much to do anything about it.

Suddenly, before the adults could turn around, Serene pushed her grandmother to the sand and stole the dagger hidden in her cloak.

"What ya doin, gal? Give me that," she snarled as she tried to get up to reach for the knife, but Serene was too quick.

She bellowed out her anger as she plunged her own grandmother in the heart with the knife. Everyone was too shocked and sick to move in on her. Even the sheriff had to bend over because the pain in his stomach was too excruciating.

Serene began laughing hysterically until it changed into cries. "Season!" she called out.

Season rushed to her aid, hoping she was calling her to relieve the knife from her hand.

"Take care of my boy! Leave out this place, and don't look back. Give him the life I was unfortunate to have. You are his Jonas now!" cried Serene.

Season was startled to learn that Serene was paying attention as she read to her the Giver's last chapters. She watched as Serene turned the dagger toward her chest, and as Season shook her head violently as she tried rushing toward her, Serene stabbed herself.

"Noooo!!!" Season screamed as she broke Serene's fall. They both sank down to the sand as Season cried profusely for her dear friend. Serene looked up at her and smiled before closing her eyes and taking her last breath. She cradled her like a poor lost child who didn't receive the care and love growing up. She didn't want her life to end like this. It wasn't fair. Not fair at all.

As Season mourned for her friend, Autumn couldn't

help but notice the crowd's illness from the poison. There were a few who regurgitated so much that they were retching foam. Most were holding on to their stomach as they stumbled to the ground. Autumn, holding baby Pondez in her arms, began walking over them to reach Season, but a hand caught hold of her leg. She looked down to see the one enemy she despised—the one person who she will never give a dime of her life to ever again.

"H...help me!" he exclaimed, clutching his other hand with his heart.

"Excuse me?" asked Autumn with an attitude.

"Yo..Yo...you gon- pay fa Th-this," he wheezed.

She placed her shoes on top of his heart and leaned in with pressure. "Like I already told you, we all got to pay for our actions! Don't worry, we will be long gone before the headlines get that you pulled a Jim Jones on these people."

"Ya...WO...n't get too far. I.I.I know what you two planned for him. Too bad he couldn't face me," he gurgled until he perished.

Autumn shook her head and spit on his face. She then rushed over to Season, who was still holding on to Serene's body.

"Baby, we have to go. We're late as is. We have to get to the boathouse," Autumn panicked.

"She's dead," spoke Season softly.

Autumn stooped down to the ground while holding on to Pondez. Season thought she felt a raindrop hit her hand until she looked at Autumn, closing her wet eyes and saying a prayer over Serene's body. When she was done, she got closer to Serene and kissed the top of her head. Then she got up slowly. "I'm so sorry, baby, terribly sorry, but we have to go before somebody discovers us. C'mon."

Season looked up at Pondez in her arms, imagining him afraid and clueless at the same time. They both lost people who were dear to each of them, but she hoped that life brings him more laughter than pain, and she would tell him how valiant his mother was to see him alive and not dead.

"Let me hold him. I have enough strength to carry him," Season spoke calmly.

Autumn gave Pondez to Season, and when he reached her arms, he looked up at her with his big, oval-shaped eyes and cracked a smile before he let out a huge yawn. Season remembered the baby bag Mama Winnie was carrying and went to go get it off her shoulders. As she looked at the poor old soul, she felt a bit sorry for her and closed her eyelids out of respect.

"Let's move," she commanded Autumn as she placed the baby bag over her shoulder. "We have to leave!"

Chapter 17:

FINDING RESCUE

*T*he wind held no remorse as it rummaged through the gloomy night. It remained obscured but vocal as its screams were coming for the two renegades trying to flee with an infant in the woods. With Autumn leading the route, Season held on to the little human for dear life. Autumn gave Season her thin shawl to cover the child's head from the cool temperature and the ground debris flying around them. The trees' feisty limbs chose sides as they were batting them senseless from every direction. Not to mention the grey clouds that were dominating the dark skies, ready to deposit its fury down on them. Season knew they had to seek shelter, but to where?

"WHERE ARE WE GOING?" Season shouted.

"WE'RE HEADING OVER TO THE BOATHOUSE," Autumn hollered back, replied Autumn,

"HOW FAR ARE WE?"

"NOT THAT FAR, ABOUT FIVE MINUTES AWAY. C'MON, I NEED YOU TO HUSSLE AND BE CAREFUL WITH THE BABY!"

They continued walking while whacking tree limbs out their way. Thank God they had their phones as flashlights to help guide them. The more steps they took, the angrier the gust had gotten. It wasn't long before the rain ambushed them, so Season now held the crying baby closed to her bosoms. The more the child cried, the more she reflected on the poor wails she heard from the ocean. Finally, her spirit broke as she dropped down on her knees and began to weep.

Autumn, hearing more cries than footsteps moving behind her, turned around and rushed quickly back to them. She immediately took the baby in one arm and used the other to pick up her daughter from the ground, but Season refused to get up.

"I can't do this…I…I …thought I could, but I can't!"

"Baby, you can't give up on me now! This baby here is going to catch pneumonia if we don't hurry up."

Season covered her face with her hands and bawled more than before. It was too difficult. Too overbearing. Too painful.

"Honey, I understand how you feel. I felt the same way too. But we can't throw in the towel, especially if others are depending on us to make it," Autumn explained, hoping Season would understand that she was implying the baby.

"What if we don't make it? Huh? What if they come

for us?" Season cried.

"Baby, you don't have to worry about those people anymore. They fell on their own swords, and it's up to us to get out of here. You're just afraid to fail, is all, but don't be. Don't be like me. Don't be like your ole' mother who was afraid to leave this place because of change. You're nothing like me. You're brave, you're smart, and you're fierce. Don't forget that!" she argued.

Season looked up at Autumn to see if she was sincere. What she told her was the truth. After the first escape attempt, she gave up on hope. She got comfortable doubting herself to realize her strength. What her mother was telling her was enlightening, but was it enough? Suddenly, like a short interlude, the volume of the wind's whines was lowering. Season heard a refreshing but familiar voice from afar. Right in the direction they were trying to flee to.

"You're almost there, Season. Get up, now," echoed the voice. *"Take ya foot in ya hands!"*

"Yusef?" Season answered, recognizing the voice as she looked ahead to see if he was nearby.

"Yusef?" Autumn repeated with a sense of confusion on her face.

Season got up quickly and shone her phone as she walked ahead of a clueless Autumn.

"Season, wait!" Autumn called out as she followed her.

"YUSEF?!" exclaimed Season, wanting to hear his voice once more.

"Baby, are you okay? What's going on?"

"Don't you hear him?" asked Season, not looking back to face her mother. She continued walking the path to search for him.

"I don't hear anything. Baby, I think you need to slow down, or you'll hurt yourself," Autumn warned, trying to rock Pondez slowly while keeping up with Season.

"Follow me…this way. You got it!" replied the voice once again.

"I can't follow what I can't see," Season complained.

"Just listen to my voice…let it lead you," it instructed.

Season continued to listen to the voice as Autumn and Pondez towed behind her. They continued walking the rest of the way until they were led to the old boathouse. By that time, the wind and rain died down, but it was still a bit nippy, considering they were at another spot on the beach. She looked around, expecting to see Yusef, but instead saw another familiar face, Mrs. DeVeau!

"Head over to Mrs. DeVeau, Season," Autumn ordered, pointing toward a sizable, classy white trawler docked near the pier with Mrs. DeVeau wearing a captain hat and waving for them to come over.

"C'mon y'all, I ain't got all night! This thing is gas up and loaded. Next stop, port of Charleston!"

"Charleston?" repeated Season to Autumn.

"Yes, Charleston. I figured we hitch a boat ride with Mrs. DeVeau, and drive the rest of the way to Columbia."

"Drive? How are we to drive to Columbia? We don't have a car!"

"You let me worry about that, and hurry on!" Autumn snapped, rushing with the baby in her arms.

"Is that Serene's youngin'?" Mrs. DeVeau asked as she grabbed for the baby and helped Autumn onto the boat.

"Yes."

"Well, where's the baby's mama? Why did you leave her?" Mrs. DeVeau frowned.

"She's dead," Season stated coldly, stepping onto the boat ledge. "She stabbed herself."

"Oh my gracious, Lord," Mrs. DeVeau gasped, covering her mouth.

Autumn looked to Season with concern in her eyes. She felt heartbroken for her and long to fix whatever pieces she had left in her heart.

After a long awkward silence, Mrs. DeVeau cleared her throat and replied in a solemn voice, "Well, let's get this show on the road. I had this motor running for a while, so we should be ready to set sail! C'mon into the cabin, everyone. Autumn, where's the baby's things? Poor child, probably hungry!"

Autumn took the baby bag from around Season and told her to follow her. Too distraught, Season said to her that she would be with them in a minute. She stared out into the woods they just came out of, thinking how they had gotten out. If it wasn't for Yusef, she never would've made it out. Mrs. DeVeau came up from the cabin and noticed Season looking back.

"Waiting for someone, dear?" she asked.

"Oh, me? No…Just thinking," Season remarked absentmindedly.

"Well, help me cast off these lines, will ya? We got to get a move on!"

After Mrs. DeVeau instructed her on what to do with the lines and anchor, Mrs. DeVeau went back into the pit to move the boat directly over the anchor. Season pulled the ropes straight up. Then, the boat slowly began to move away from the dock, separating itself from the curse of this town. Season held on to the rails as Mrs. DeVeau shifted forward at an idle speed and turned the ship around to head towards their destination.

Season was about to retire to the cabin until she spotted a figure coming out from the woods, approaching the shore. It was Yusef! Season was so shocked and relieved at the same time that she wanted to tell Mrs. DeVeau to stop the boat, but it was too late. They were too far away to turn back, but not too far away for Season to see him wave a final goodbye. Then, he sat down in the sand with his knees up and arms folded on top and watched the ship sail through the now calmed night.

"He will miss you," replied a soft voice behind her.

Season turned around in time to see her mother smiling sincerely at her while placing her hands on her shoulder. She, too, looked out at the shore.

"He saved our lives…When we were in the woods, I heard his voice. That's who guided our way," Season explained.

"To be honest, baby, I couldn't hear anything, only the wind and Pondez's cries. You were the only one who could listen. You two are linked, not just biologically but spiritually. I always believe children are naturally close to their mothers, even before they are brought into this world. The satisfaction of being in a state of happiness goes both ways. I feel the same way about you, even before you came here. I know the feeling. You made Summer the proudest mother, and I do believe that Yusef is grateful for that. Just remember this, this place…this sea brought you two together, but it didn't separate you. There's a patch in all of us… that love is in here," Autumn said, pointing to her heart.

Season nodded her head in agreement as she grabbed for her mother tightly. It wasn't until then that she noticed her mother shared the same heartbeat as hers.

"Can't sleep, little gal?" Mrs. DeVeau inquired, sensing Season was behind her as she was steering restlessly through the night.

"I took a small nap earlier, but I couldn't get any good sleep. How long before we get there?"

"Oh, another twenty minutes or so. It's not that far."

"I didn't know you were a helmsman," Season joked.

Mrs. DeVeau laughed, "Gal, please! I consider the term 'captain' of the sea."

"How did you get into steering?"

"Believe it or not, my second good-for-nothing husband taught me. He was a professional fisherman. Fine as wine, but mean as a wolverine," she laughed again.

"Pardon me for saying so, but he must have been loaded."

"That he was…that he was…We were together for nineteen years until he decided to up and leave me for a Becky tramp."

"A Becky tramp?" Season questioned, giggling at Mrs. DeVeau's choice of words.

"Yea….who that gal is? The one with the 'beehives'?"

"You mean Beyoncé?"

"Yeah, her. Didn't she say something like that?"

Season smiled at what Mrs. DeVeau was alluding to and responded, "Yea…something similar to that."

"Yeah, I like listening to that gal. Excellent entertainer."

"That she is."

"Anyway, the whore, my husband's name," she said, making Season chuckle again. "Croaked and died a year later. Those young gals can't take care of no ole' men at his age. Their cooking alone will cause gas, diarrhea, indigestion, and a heart attack all at the same time."

Season shook her head admiringly at her former boss, loving every minute of her humorous spirit.

"Come to find out," she continued, "he left me pretty well off, but what surprised me was out of all his prized possessions, he left me with this boat. I guess he noticed how I took a liking to it, and he made it his business to teach me how to take care of it. Got good at it too! I thought he had gotten jealous of my skills. HA! But you want to know one fact about me that I recently discovered from that Ancestry DNA kit?"

"What's that?" Season anticipated.

"Well, to begin with, I've changed my surname back to DeVeau after my second husband passed. I learned the DeVeau's genes from my father's side dates back into the mid-eighteen hundreds, where some of my ancestors were in the business of slave importation."

Season frowned, "Oh, wow! That news must have been shameful to learn about your bloodline."

Mrs. DeVeau nodded her head, "True, we all have some past skeletons we dug up in our family that we're not proud of. I think being ashamed causes us to shield ourselves from the truth. I believe in taking what we learn from the past and use it as a rescuing tool for the future. We have to rescue our future generation by doing better and by loving everybody til' it hurts. Ya understand?"

"Yeah, I've never thought about it that way," Season mumbled, holding her head down dishonorably. Then she thought about something she wanted to ask Mrs. DeVeau for a while but never had the chance to do so.

"Why Hollins? If you knew these people were capable of committing such terrible things, why didn't you leave or report them?"

Mrs. DeVeau looked at Season and gave her a half-smile.

"When I first moved to Hollins, I wasn't aware of their history. Sure, I thought the people were a little strange, not to mention my husband was from the area. After spending some time down there, and discovering their past history, a part of me did want to leave. I even threatened my husband, but like those people, he was stuck in his ways. He figured he had to make atonement for disgracing his family by marrying me. You see, I wasn't like those people… they knew that, and they hated me for it, but I could give two cents. The only people who had ever shown any kindness to me were your grandfolks. I loved them, and they loved me. But it wasn't enough for me to stay. I was on the verge of giving up, but something happened that made me change my mind."

"What's that?"

"Your aunt and your mother. They were so young… so innocent….so afraid. That day, when they arrived in the library, I could see the difference between them and the others. They were raised right by their folks. To love and to cherish life. I guess your grandparents felt as if they were prisoners in their own hometown because of their ancestors. You see, guilt can cause humility, but it can also cause you to feel as if you are less than zero. Thinking you owe everyone in the world because of other's mistakes. To a certain degree, we do pay for our mothers and fathers' sins, but we can't let that consume our lives. I'm telling you this because I know you think your lineage dealt you a bad hand. It's only bad when you fold it and don't play smart. You're a brilliant girl. You remind me so much of Cindy," she said soberly with tears gathering in her eyes. "So ambitious, but also self-loathing. Just be humble and love yourself. YOU write your own history."

Season nodded and reflected on what Mrs. DeVeau was telling her.

After riding over an hour and a half on the boat, they finally arrived at the Charleston Port. It was late, and only a few workers on the docks were out near the cargo area. Luckily, Mrs. DeVeau knew the head of the port security exceptionally well and informed the person of her emergency arrival. With the workers' help, Mrs. DeVeau was able to secure dock lines from the boat to the dock. As the three-member crew got up from the cabin and stepped safely off the boat, they finally felt the sense of freedom. Even baby Pondez's babbles gave confirmation of satisfaction.

Ring Ring

Ring Ring

Autumn's cell phone went off like an alarm clock. She quickly reached for it in the baby's bag to answer it.

"Hello?"

Season leaned in to hear who was calling her mother, but she couldn't hear anything. If there was one lesson Autumn learned after being around Season, it was to turn her volume down on her phone.

"Yes, we made it. Uh-huh, everyone is safe. Wait! How far is that? No, you will just have to meet us," she frowned.

"I'M RIGHT HERE!" a male voice shouted from afar.

Season and Autumn looked up to see a wide grinning man walking towards them with a cell phone in his hand. Season was so overjoyed that she couldn't hide it all in.

"DAD?!" shouted back Season as she ran rapidly to Xavier and gave him the biggest hug a daughter could ever give her father. She nearly knocked him over as he returned the gesture by holding her tightly.

"My baby Season…I'm sooooo happy to see you again!" Xavier sighed, nearly suffocating her.

"Dad! I'm so sorry. Please don't send me away ever again. I'll get it right this time, I promise," Season begged, crying all over her father's cotton shirt.

"No, I'm sorry. I shouldn't have sent you there. I reacted out of impulse, and daddy's sorry. You don't have to get anything right! You're my daughter, and I love you! You're not going anywhere if I can help it," promised Xavier.

Autumn looked at the inseparable pair. She had a look of content on her face as they held each other for what seemed like an eternity.

Chapter 18:

A NEW NORMAL

Anchorperson 1   *"Good morning, South Carolina! I'm Natalie Erns…*

Anchorperson 2   *"And I'm Kyle Newman."*

Anchorperson 1   *"And you're watching channel 8 SCEARLYFLASHNEWS. The first top story on this Tuesday morning is a tragic one. As you may recall, on November 18, 1978, the world suffered a massive loss as more than 900 civilians, including children, died in what was known as the Jonestown Massacre. The calamity was one of the world's most catastrophic mass killing events in our history, and it appears that history has repeated itself again.*

In the small town of Hollins, located deep in the low country of South Carolina, a distinguished pastor by the name of Edward Hollis led a vast amount of cult members to their doom late Sunday evening due to poisoning. Rachel Maroon has more on the story, Rachel?

Anchorperson 3 (Rachel) *Thank you, Natalie. Right now, I'm at the local beach where the crime allegedly took place. From where I am standing, a little over twenty-four hours ago, about twenty-five cadavers were found all over, including the remains of the town's sheriff and deputies. One of the leading low country detectives, Detective Riley Richardson, carefully examined the crime scene and noticed two fatally stabbed victims, an African American teenage girl and an African American elderly woman. The deceased teen had the murder weapon in hand, assuming it was, of course, a murder-suicide. Detective Richardson, along with his investigation team, also found chalices near the victims, pieces of Water-Hemlocks (a hazardous plant that can be lethal if ingested), and a bottle of cyanide poison near Pastor Hollis' body. We can safely assume that the pastor was indeed, in fact, the culprit behind the foul play. Behind me is a long-time citizen of Hollins, who lives not too far from here, at a boathouse, Mr. Johnny Peasant. Mr. Peasant, were you present during the tragic incident of that night?*

Peasant *No, I can't say that I was. I tried not to associate myself with them people. They're bad news!*

Rachel   *Could you elaborate more on that, sir?*

Peasant *I've been born and raised here all my life. And this place will suck the life outta ya. Make ya feel as if ya have no chance to make something out ya self. Those people ya found on that beach, it wasn't no accident. They were evil! It took a bunch of dead bodies fa y'all ta figure out or even care that people in Hollins were witch people. They kilt many and prospered from it. What's wrong with America today? Ya only care about what goes in pockets instead of worryin' 'bout people.*

Rachel   *Sir, you seemed irate about what happened. Why hasn't this been reported? Why haven't you taken the precautionary steps to expose this sort of practice?*

Peasant *Ha! And risk them killing me and throw my body in the sea? I tink not! That's what happened to dat young gal, Cindy, a few days back. They killed her! Check the local newspaper, for God's sakes! She took the precautionary steps, and ya see what happened to her? Yes, I'm irate!*

Rachel   *You think this group was responsible for the death of a young girl?*

Peasant *Lady, I don't tink, I know dat they are responsible fa dat gal's drowning! Hell, if ya get a rescue team ta search all ova dat dere water, ya see dead babies' remains. Dats what they do, they kilt babies!*

Rachel   *Umm, Natalie, I am a bit disturbed by these allegations. There seemed to be more depth to this* *story than what meets the eye. There will be a follow-up on this investigation, and I'll keep you posted. Back to you, Natalie.*

Kyle   *Oh my, did you hear what the witness's insinuations were?*

Natalie   *Well, first of all, let me just say that it is comforting to know that the children of these victims were safe and present in their own homes. They were not allowed to attend the terrible event that took place that night. This matter should be taken seriously and carefully looked into. What has been reported to me could hold some veracity to what this witness is insinuating.*

Kyle   *Oh?*

Natalie   *Yes, two days ago, before the incident, there was a report document submitted to the Federal Bureau of Investigation, written by a Hollins victim, detailing the history and practice of this town. I can't go into full details, considering it's still an ongoing investigation, so there will be more information to follow for the next couple of days. We'll keep you posted!*

CLICK

Xavier turned the television off as he lounged back in his recliner with the look of nervousness on his face. Season was also there to witness what the news was reporting and looked back at her father to confirm it. Autumn was nursing Pondez in another room, but she heard every word coming from the den. After she finished giving Pondez his bottle, patting the smallness of his back, and rocking him to sleep, she joined the rest of them, looking at the blank screen. There was no denying that what they had been through was devastating, and how they got through it was by God's grace and mercy. It was a bit surprising how old man Peasant was still alive, more so, how he didn't discover Mrs. DeVeau's boat near his pier as they made their escape that night.

"What if someone saw us? What if Mr. Peasant saw us departing?" Season panicked as if reading everyone's thoughts in the room.

"I don't know, sweetheart," replied Autumn doubtfully. "I don't want to press my luck just yet, but if Mr. Peasant was like the same old fair-minded man I once knew, he wouldn't say anything, not assuming he saw us."

"But what if he did?" questioned Season again.

"Mr. Peasant was a voluntary outsider to the community. He didn't want any parts of what was going on in Hollins. He knew our family fairly well. Like Mrs. DeVeau, we treated the ostracized ones with respect. Like our parents taught us, be kind to others. You'll never know when you will need them," Autumn explained with conviction in her eyes.

"Let's just see how the next couple of days will unfold, sweetie," Xavier comforted as he went over to Season and sat on the floor next to her. "I won't let anything or anyone hurt you; you have my word."

Season shook her head with uncertainty, "I don't know, Dad. This may be too huge to bury. This kind of stuff isn't normal, especially a crime as big as this. I feel guilty."

"Guilty of what?" Xavier asked, raising an eyebrow.

"Half of those children in that town lost their parents. Aunt Autumn, I don't mean to sound unappreciative, but what if they found out what we did? How did you slip the poison in the drink?"

Autumn sighed as she went to sit on the other side of Season. "Well, that's a bridge I have to cross when I get there. As for you, you have no need to feel any guilt based on my actions. You're innocent, and so were those babies who were killed. Those parents knew what they were getting themselves into when they agreed to uphold this silly creed. At least I feel better knowing that Hollins or Hollis doesn't have any control over my life and that you are safe from harm."

"She's right, you know?" Xavier added sadly. "I feel guilty just sending you there in the first place. I shouldn't have ever agreed for you to go down there. The second you told me about it, I should've dropped everything and got you. I apologize, Season."

"So what now? What will happen to Aunt Autumn and Pondez?" Season asked, looking at both adults.

"Well….," Xavier answered, scratching his head. "I can safely say that they can live here until this whole thing dies down."

Autumn nodded her head in agreeance. "I'll find a place for Pondez and me as soon as it is safe."

Season looked to her mom with concern in her eyes. "Where would you go?"

"Don't worry, I won't go back. It took me through hell and high water just to depart from that place, and I won't return again. I'll find a place up here and get Pondez situated here. I'm looking forward to starting over."

"Well, I don't want you to leave just yet. I want you to stay here as long as you want. Well, as long as I want you to. This house has four bedrooms in it, so you can make yourself at home in the guest bedroom you're sleeping in now. Pondez can take the other room. Oh, we can make a nursery for him! That will be awesome, and …"

"Whoa! Whoa," Autumn chuckled nervously. "You have some bright ideas, Missy, but as I recall, your father is the legal owner of this house. I can't overextend my welcome just because you say so."

"Dad doesn't mind? Don't you, Dad?" she turned her head to face her father, detecting the familiar, reluctant countenance he made whenever Season pressures him into a corner.

"You just don't give up, do you, gal?" he asked, suddenly grinning while he playfully pulled on her bushy ponytail.

"Well, some things in life are not debatable, you know this," she smiled, tapping his hand to make him stop.

"Sure, Autumn, you and Pondez can stay as long as

you need. Whatever brings light into my baby girl's eyes or this home is always welcome!" he smiled.

"YESSS!" Season shouted.

Autumn gave him an appreciative smile, "Thank you, Xavier. I'm beyond pleased with this decision."

Knock, Knock

Knock, Knock

Ding, Dong

Xavier got up from the floor quicker than the others. "Who's that knocking and ringing my doorbell like they're the police?"

Season and Autumn exchanged a worried glance as Xavier went to look through the peephole. He laughed and told them to calm down as he opened the door. Season got up to see who was at the door and saw her friend, Suki, holding two of her favorite candy packages.

"Girl! I came as soon as I heard the news on the television. Well, I rode my bike to the store to get these for you and then rode straight here to see you. Are you okay, girl? Did they do something to your mind or something? How did you get away? What happened, girl? Girl, don't you know my cousin isn't talking to me at all because of you? What happened down there?" Suki asked, not waiting to hear Season's response.

Season laughed at her clueless friend as she pulled her in for a hug. She missed her dearly, and just being able to hold her brought comfort. She was glad that Suki was her ace.

"Sis, I know it's been some weeks since we last saw each other, but you're holding me too tightly! Could I breathe?" Suki huffed.

"I'm sorry," Season stressed, finally letting her go. "Come on in, and let me introduce you to my mom."

"Oh snap! Your real mom's here too? You mean, your Aunt Autumn, who's your real Mom, right?" Suki ranted as she crossed the threshold. "Hey, Mr. Holidae? How's it going?"

Mr. Holidae shook his head and laughed at Season's boisterous friend. "I'm doing fine, Suki. Thanks for asking. How are you?"

"I'm doing great now that my sis is home!" she beamed.

"Come on, Suk," Season asserted as they walked to the den area. "Aunt Au...I mean, Mom, meet Suki. Suki, this is my mom, Autumn."

Autumn offered her hand as she smiled. "Nice to meet one of Season's friends. She talked about you quite a lot."

"Wow, you're prettier than Season described you to be. She favors you a lot," Suki replied while ignoring Autumn's hand and grabbed her for a hug.

"Oh my, you're not a shy person at all," Autumn responded, shocked by Suki's boldness.

"No, ma'am, I'm not. If you're Season's real mom, then that makes you my family as well. If you make her happy, then I'm happy. This is a package deal you have to take, ma'am."

"She's right," Season agreed, grinning.

Autumn giggled, "Well, I think this is the best package deal I have ever received. What you youngins' would say? I'm down for that?"

Everyone giggled at Autumn's attempt to use millennials' slang terms.

"No, mom…don't," Season giggled again.

"Well, I hate to break up this family reunion, but may I borrow Season for a minute. I mean, is she allowed to go outside?" Suki asked.

"Sure, just make sure you're back in time for lunch, Season," asserted Xavier as he went straight into the kitchen.

"C'mon, let's go…" demanded Suki, pulling on Season's arm.

"Okay, girl…chill out, don't pull my arm out!"

"Nice meeting you, Mama Autumn," Suki smiled.

"Nice meeting you too, Suki. And Season, remember what your dad said," warned Autumn.

"I know, I know, I'll be back. I promised," assured Season as they rushed out the door.

As they stepped down the porch, the girls were quiet for a moment before Suki broke the silence.

"I like her. She's nice,"

"Yeah, I didn't think we would make it. I thought she was just as mean and malicious as the others, especially after finding out that she was my mom. At first, I felt it would be wrong for me to get close to her; she wasn't the mom I grew up knowing, you know? After a while, I began to realize that it was okay. It's okay to let someone in to trust again. I guess seeing Yusef for the last time, I …"

"Hey, is it true that he's really a ghost like you told me over the phone?" interrupted Suki in a shaky tone.

"He's a part of me," Season smiled.

"What's that supposed to mean? You know what, tell me the whole story, how did you manage to escape that place?" inquired Suki, picking up her bike.

"Another time, Suk…another time," Season sang.

The girls walked to the garage where Season last placed her bike. She felt secured as she hopped on it. They were about to go on a small adventure until one of the West's kids kicked a ball so hard from their yard until it almost reached Season. If she hadn't dodged the ball in time, it would've hit her directly in the head. Instead, she fell off her bike onto the ground.

"Sis! Are you okay?" Suki asked, rushing off her bike to check on her.

"Yeah, I'm okay. It didn't hit me," she replied. She got up, spotted the location of the ball, and picked it up.

"That's right, sis! Give them youngins a piece of your mind. Bad kids! Always up to no good. That woman has too many kids anyway. Doesn't make any sense," Suki fussed, clenching her hands into a fist.

Season walked to the West's yard, heading toward the children. They couldn't be more than ten years of age. Three of them were boys and one girl. They all looked regretful and frightened as Season approached them. The oldest of the four decided to defend his brothers and sister by boldly stepping ahead of them. He was ready for whatever Season was about to do to all of them.

"Is this yours?" Season inquired politely.

The boy gave her a confused look. "Yeah," he snapped.

"Then let's play a game of kickball then, boys against girls. Your sister, Suki, and me versus you and your brothers. C'mon!" Season challenged with a confident smile on her face, giving the ball back to the boy.

"All right!" the little girl shouted as the rest seemed interested in getting the game started.

Suki pulled Season away and whispered, "Girl, I know we ain't bout to play 'recess' with these little runts. I thought we were going to ride out to the country club. Maybe check to see if Micah's there?" she sang as she moved her eyebrows up and down.

Season looked back at the children as they bragged on which team will win. A few weeks ago, she would've insulted them or vigorously hit them with the ball and laughed. Now, she had a newfound respect for her neighbor's children. They deserved to play. They deserved to laugh. They deserved to live.

Epilogue:
"Thy Will Be Done"

(Three Years Later- 2022)

Summertime came once again, and life spoke in the Holidae's home. There was a clear sense of hope, a clear sense of love, and the greatest thing ever...family.

After accepting an RN position at Richland Memorial, Autumn saved up her money and moved her and Pondez, who was now a toddler, down the street into a beautiful three-bedroom home. Not that she wasn't grateful for Xavier's hospitality, but she wanted to consider her new slate something she can do independently. This new life marked a milestone of her finally living her own dreams instead of sacrificing them for others. It was clearly a further step in the right direction for her. Season understood her mother's intentions and wanted nothing but the best for her. In fact, she would visit her every day, babysitting

Pondez whenever Autumn had to work late at the hospital. Just as long as Autumn remained close to her, Season knew things would work out just fine.

After a few years of hard work, Season successfully perfected her swimming career. Thanks to Coach Vie's vast connections, Season was qualified to compete in the Summer Olympics. It was one of the highest achievements Season was fortunate to take part in, and everyone in the community was rooting for her, especially her best friend, Suki, who had sewed a picture of a pair of pink goggles on Season's swimming cap, along with the initials *SAS,* representing the bond between her and her two mothers. At first, Suki wanted to rearrange the letters around to spell out "*ASS*" as a joke but thought otherwise. Season was so touched by her best friend's gift that she promised her she would wear it for good luck during the meets.

As for Hollins, the investigation didn't take too long to close, as it was ruled to be an apparent murder-suicide. There were no claims of what really happened that night besides Mr. Peasant's, who strangely passed away shortly after his five minutes of fame on camera. His death and the "mystery" document sent to the FBI brought many concerns and press to the mysterious little town. Many journalists, freelance writers, and historians wanted to know more about this Hollins WUDU proclamation that took place under America's nose, but the civilians, especially the children, refused to speak to any outsiders who were interested in their sanctimonious livelihood. Two years ago, a real-estate mogul bought out the whole town and made it an extravagant beach resort. Hollins' living remains, along with their WUDU proclamation bibles, fled when the tourists came pouring in. The town was now extinct, but the question that remained for the newcomers was the cryptic graveyard with small tombstones that read only short lives for the dead. What was the story behind it?

Xavier was in his office reflecting on his childhood. It wasn't pleasant or innocent. At most, it was dark and depressing. Being the child of a ruthless sadist was not a life he wanted to be associated with. The happiest moment of his life was when he met someone who shared the same ambitions he shared. They ran away together and lived the American dream. Being Summer, she had a soul to give an unfortunate child a life both her and Xavier felt was cheated from them. He loved that child just the same and promised his newly found family security and happiness. It wasn't until three years ago, after Summer's death, that he received a letter from home that made his house of cards come tumbling down.

Xavier got up from his chair and went to a small safe that was placed behind his desk. He entered his secret security number, and it opened for him. There were no important documents, just a book entitled <u>HOLLINS WUDU PROCLAMATION</u> and the blue envelope. He took out the envelope and held it in his hand for a while. Soon after, he took out the letter and read it for the millionth time:

To my dearest baby brother, Xion,

The good Lord finally made a way for me as he gave me answers to your whereabouts. For years, this mouse and cat game was a challenge! You've really perfected your game of hide and seek, but in the end, I was destined to find you. Father always said that you were book smart, but I was always strategic. I knew you couldn't have gone too far from your roots. Just far enough for you to cross out of Hollins.

I'm writing because I put two and two together and realized you and that wretch cheated me and this town. I tried to get it out of her sister, but she wouldn't tell me anything, so I hired my own investigator. I had Autumn followed, hoping she would lead me to what I was thinking about all these years. The guy I hired was able to take some pictures of this secret getaway and imagine, to my surprise, what he found... You, Summer, and a full-grown preteen child.

The math didn't quite add up. Then I thought about it...thirteen years ago, you were in medical school at the time, still staying in contact, and Summer abruptly appeared out of nowhere. Shortly after, Autumn just gave birth to our baby girl. When it was the day of the ritual, my child mysteriously died; coincidently, Summer left town like a thief in the night. There was no proof of my child's remains, for Autumn informed us that she gave the little corpse to the sea. I thought it was somewhat odd for her to do so, considering how both sisters were never too fond of our traditions, so I had my suspicions all these years.

Oh brother! You've betrayed me before once you stole and impregnated my Summer! I thought you would learn after your baby boy to never go against the ritual or this town! And now you're fathering my seed I was supposed to sacrifice to this town? Damn you! You are a gruesome Cain against Yemaja! For that, you have to pay! Give my daughter back to me, or you shall reap sooner than you sow! Folks say that it's a thin line between love and hate, but you double-crossed that threshold and spat in my face! Things will never be the same between us again. You have three days by the time you receive this letter, or I will make my presence known at your doorstep.

Your Long Lost Abel,
Pastor Edward Hollis

As Xavier read his brother's threatening letter for the last time, he couldn't help but place a winning smile on his face. He knew his plan would work, despite feeling guilty of scarring Season by putting her life in danger. But the truth had to come to the light.

The same day he received the letter, he called Autumn to inform her of Eddie's intimidations and his plan to respond to it. There was a lot of coaxing he had to do to encourage his sister-in-law to step up to the plate and face his brother, but in the end, it worked out. He checked in on them almost every day through Autumn. He contacted Mrs. DeVeau, a great friend of his, to educate Season on the terrible history of Hollins, hoping she wouldn't get comfortable in such a place. Mrs. DeVeau also helped plan the escape. When the next sacrificial ritual cycle arrived, he didn't expect the ladies to bring a small infant with them, but Autumn was like Summer. She had a huge heart.

Xavier walked back over to his security box, took out the Hollins bible, and casually walked over to the fireplace that was crackling so peacefully. He tossed the letter and the book into the fire, watching it amusingly being consumed by the flames.

"Thy will be done," he stated in a strange dialect tongue.

If you enjoyed *The Patched Sea*, check out Loodie's debut novel, *Pure Innuendos* and her short story, "Jimmy Arthur."

"People in this town keep secrets hidden as if it's their birthday suit. You're digging in a place where worms are present. If you dig deep enough, you might not like what's in that steel vault!"

Like every small town in the rural south, Coppertown has its quirks and its secrets. Jessica Winslow, a young, beautiful curator at a local museum, feels it is up to her to unravel these skeletons starting with an exhibition project called "Black Widow Swamp," one of the town's most embarrassing myths. After receiving an anonymous "top secret" file on the mysterious landmark, she opens up a Pandora's Box to a seventy-year-old murder case on a drifter by the name of Tresstina Bandeau. As Jessica digs deeper into the truth, she realizes the real truth is in her backyard, and she's not safe from what is coming her way.

Emma Ann Singletary is not just an ordinary teenager; she's a caulbearer. To most of the townspeople, she's a "special child." Only Emma doesn't know why she's so special or how to embrace her gift. When an old wanderer visits her family's place of business and residence, the bizarre encounter piques Emma's curiosity as she  takes the initiative to learn more about this strange old man, Jimmy Arthur, and herself.